BRAYBROOKE

# INDEX

# BRAYBROOKE

## NICK EVERARD

The Book Guild Ltd

First published in Great Britain in 2024 by
The Book Guild Ltd
Unit E2 Airfield Business Park,
Harrison Road, Market Harborough,
Leicestershire. LE16 7UL
Tel: 0116 2792299
www.bookguild.co.uk
Email: info@bookguild.co.uk
X: @bookguild

Copyright © 2024 Nick Everard

The right of Nick Everard to be identified as the author of this
work has been asserted by them in accordance with the
Copyright, Design and Patents Act 1988.

All rights reserved. No part of this publication may be
reproduced, transmitted, or stored in a retrieval system, in any form or by any means,
without permission in writing from the publisher, nor be otherwise circulated in
any form of binding or cover other than that in which it is published and without
a similar condition being imposed on the subsequent purchaser.

This work is entirely fictitious and bears no resemblance to any persons living or dead.

Typeset in 11pt Minion Pro

Printed on FSC accredited paper
Printed and bound in Great Britain by 4edge Limited

ISBN 978 1835740 538

British Library Cataloguing in Publication Data.
A catalogue record for this book is available from the British Library.

Dedicated to the 350 or so inhabitants of Braybrooke, the friendly little north Northamptonshire village where my family and I have lived happily for twenty-five years. They will no doubt recognise some minor geographical simplifications, and I trust will indulge me in these. No resemblance is intended to anybody, living or dead: in particular to the blameless inhabitants of the two local farms which feature prominently in the story.

I am grateful once more for my dear Kiki's tolerance when I should probably have been doing something useful around the house.

The smaller of my two cocker spaniels, Rosie, not only appears in the book but also qualifies for a co-writing credit on account of being a loyal and uncomplaining laptop rest whenever I sat down.

**Nick Everard** is a former Army officer who has worked subsequently in the City, schools adventure travel and recruiting/headhunting. He became Regimental Secretary of the Royal Lancers in July 2021. Nick is married to Kiki; they live in the village of Braybrooke on the Leicestershire/Northamptonshire border close to Market Harborough and have two grown children. *Braybrooke* is his third novel; the first (*Clean Kill*) was published by The Book Guild in May 2022 and the second (*Past Unbecoming*) in May 2023.

# PREFACE

## THE MURDER OF MAJOR EDWIN COWLEY

*B*raybrooke is not a true story. However, nearly one hundred years ago, the village was indeed the scene of a murder; a well-known one at the time. At the outset of this project, I planned to write the story of that killing, *In Cold Blood*/Truman Capote style; however, though the facts were easy enough to establish, little underlying detail was available – I would have had to fictionalise much of it, and I was wary of treading upon unknown local sensitivities – so, ultimately, I decided against it. However, I did work some of the details of that murder (notably the location of the body, the weapon used and how/when it was procured) into my otherwise wholly imaginary tale.

So here's what really happened in Braybrooke all those years ago.

Just before 7pm on the evening of Tuesday, 12 July 1932, bricklayer's labourer John Brotherton, a resident of Little

Bowden, was cycling from Market Harborough towards the nearby village of Braybrooke. Shortly before reaching it, he encountered Percy Loake (forty-eight), whom he knew.

Loake lived in the village, though he worked as a handyman on Admiral Sir David Beatty's nearby Dingley estate. There was a brief exchange about the weather as Brotherton passed by, during which he later stated that Loake seemed 'in a pondering mood'.

At about 7.40pm that evening, bachelor Major Edwin Cowley (sixty-three), a well-respected local gentleman farmer and veteran of the Boer War in South Africa and the Great War, was out checking his stock as usual. Whilst in a field he owned called Top Close, about a mile south-west of Braybrooke, he was shot.

The shooting was witnessed by farm labourer Reginald Wilkinson from between four hundred and five hundred yards away, who was walking on the track between Braybrooke and Great Oxendon: after two shots from a distance of about five yards, Major Cowley fell forwards and was then shot for a third time from close range whilst on the ground. The gunman ran off towards Braybrooke. Wilkinson hastened with another man he had alerted towards the fallen major, who had been fatally shot through the head. He remained with the body until police eventually arrived from Kettering; his companion headed towards Braybrooke to raise the alarm.

Gerald Bassett, from Desborough, met Loake returning to Braybrooke a short distance outside the village. According to a subsequent local newspaper report, in response to Bassett's greeting, Loake replied calmly, 'I have had my revenge on the ****** who has been with my wife.' Bassett's reaction to this is not recorded.

Not long afterwards, Brotherton was walking in a nearby field with the young lady he had cycled over to visit when he met Loake again. He asked, 'How are you, Percy?'

Loake replied, 'If anyone asks for Ted Cowley, tell them he is up in the corner. I shot him dead.'

Brotherton did not take this seriously, despite his companion having been alarmed by three distant shots a short time before.

At around 8.30pm, Harry Coe, neighbour, saw Loake next door in a potato patch behind his house. He was holding a pistol and appeared to be agonised. Coe anticipated what was coming and went outside, telling Loake not to be a fool.

Loake said, 'Goodbye, Harry – don't come too near,' put the gun to his forehead, fired and dropped dead.

An inquest on both men was held in Braybrooke on 14 July. In addition to confirming the above facts, it ascertained that Loake had bought a .410 double-barrelled shotgun pistol and a box of twenty-five cartridges from an ironmonger in Market Harborough on the afternoon of the murder; no license was then required for such a purchase. Twenty of these cartridges were in his jacket pocket at home; three of the remainder had been fired at Major Cowley and a fourth had killed Loake himself. The fifth, unfired, was in the second, cocked barrel of the pistol.

Loake's twenty-one-year-old son, Reginald, testified that in recent months his father had frequently accused his mother of going with other men, specifically Major Cowley, for whom she had once kept house. He did not believe this to be true, and his mother emphatically denied it. Around 6pm on the evening of the murder, his father had become wild and excited; after a bitter row, he had rushed out of the house, leaving his wife weeping.

A little after 8pm, Reginald was told by a neighbour of rumours that his father had killed Major Cowley and went into that neighbour's house to learn more. Shortly afterwards, there was a shot from his parents' back garden.

Verdicts of murder and suicide were returned by the inquest jury after only fifteen minutes: it expressed sympathy towards Loake's widow and son, plus Major Cowley's unmarried sister Margaret, who lived with him.

The two funerals were held back to back at All Saints Church, Braybrooke a few days later. There must have been some interesting conversations in the churchyard.

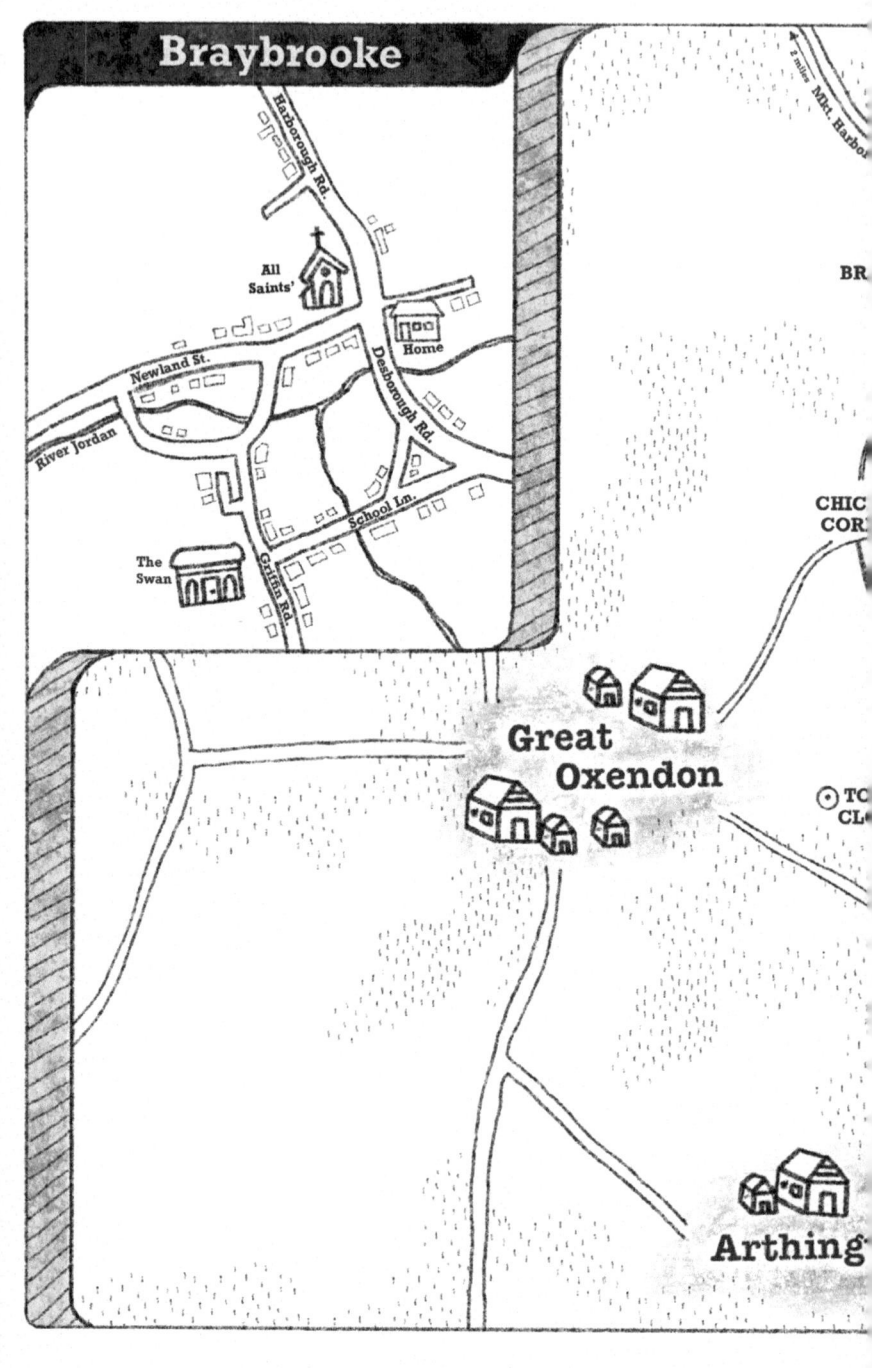

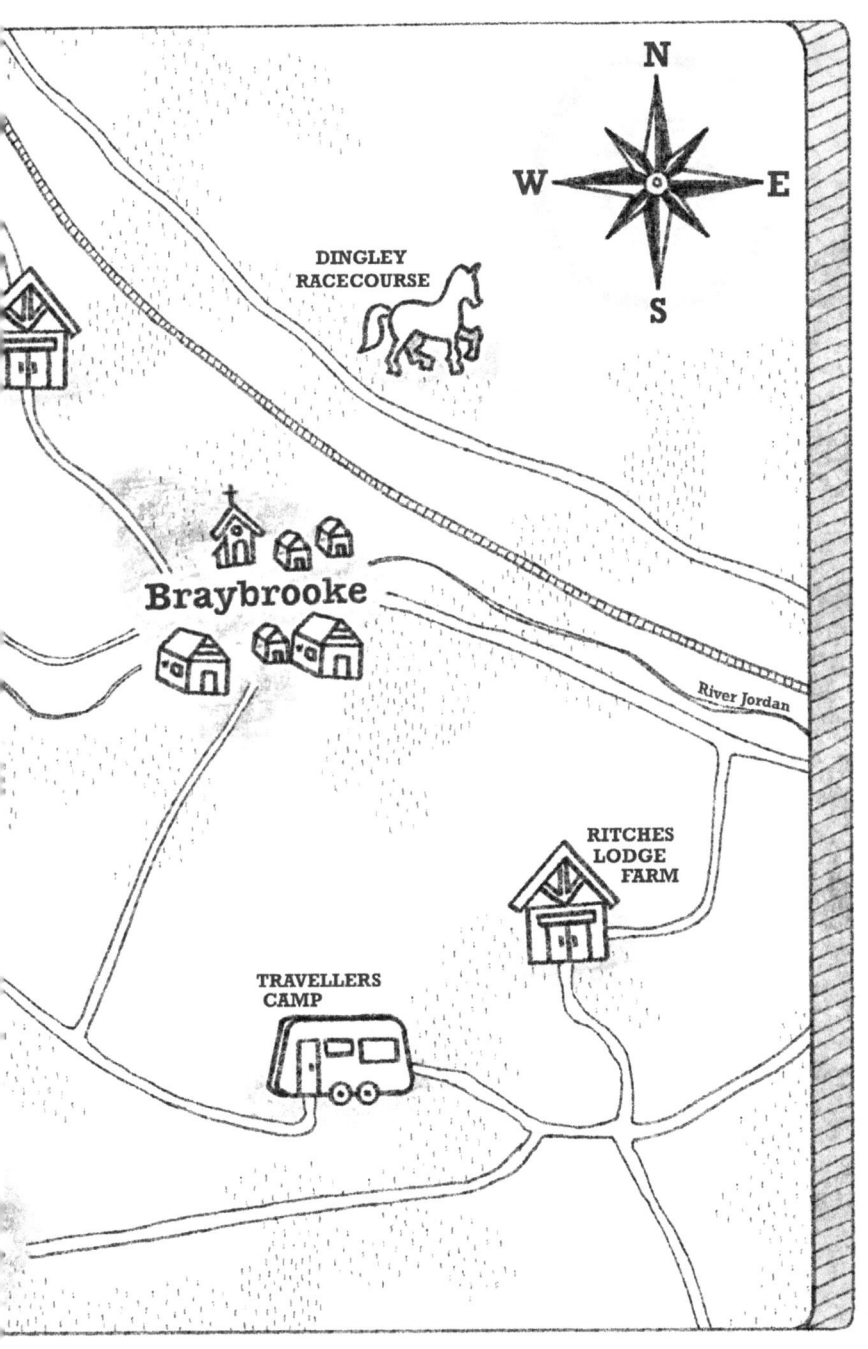

# CHAPTER ONE

You know that phrase 'the body was discovered by a man walking his dog'? It's so common in news reports that it's almost a cliché. But when you're that man, I assure you there's nothing commonplace about it. I'll never forget that day as long as I live, despite everything that followed, which you might think would eclipse it.

I've got two dogs – cocker spaniels – Theo (who's big, strong and blond, approaching two) and small blue roan Rosie, who's five. They're lucky, since we live in the small village of Braybrooke in the north Northamptonshire countryside, where there are well-recognised footpaths and also some tolerant, neighbourly farmers. So they get a good outing every day – if not with me then with my wife, Lucy, or sometimes both of us together. Or maybe the children, if one of them is home: twenty-year-old twins – they've both flown the nest to university now.

That sunny Saturday afternoon in March I was walking them by myself, and as normal, the dogs stayed on their leads till I had passed the church and headed off west along Newland Street, past the row of houses on the left, which peters out into an unpaved lane.

There are any number of routes you can take once out of Braybrooke, and since it was the weekend, I thought we'd take one of the longer ones. We went almost as far as the neighbouring village of Great Oxendon along the lane, climbing slowly all the while for about a mile and a half, before coming back in a gentle loop via a public footpath which led through a big field. That field is on a slope, with the path crossing it in a diagonal descent, and I know now that it's called Top Close. I didn't at the time, despite having lived in the village for nearly ten years.

The dogs were gambolling ahead of me without a care in the world, through pasture which was three or four inches high, and I was in high good humour in the gentle sunshine. A few sheep were standing around up by the gate onto the lane that runs along the top of the ridge, which drops down to Arthingworth on the other side: unusual, but insofar as I thought of it at all, I assumed they'd got through the hedge from the field next door, which we were fast approaching. They were a good hundred yards away, and I didn't worry about them at all: my dogs are good with livestock.

The footpath leads across a stile, and as we approached it, I saw Theo nosing curiously at what looked like some discarded clothing, some thirty yards ahead. Rosie joined him and then leapt quickly back, looking uncertainly around for me. I shouted at Theo to leave whatever it was alone and strolled blithely on.

The first thing I noticed a few seconds later looked like a

dirty white glove, stretching out from the pile. At that point I was just curious.

When I was fifteen yards away, I could see that the pile had a human form.

From five yards it was obvious that it was a body, face down. The white glove was a bare human hand.

\*\*\*

What I remember above all in those first moments was my strange calmness.

'Bloody hell,' I said quietly, which I flatter myself was pretty mild under the circumstances.

I got the two dogs on their leads and hitched them to the hand-post by the stile, then turned back to look at my unwelcome discovery.

My first thought was that someone might have had a heart attack, or a stroke, and I was beginning to think about my rusty first-aid skills, but I soon saw that there was far too much blood for that. I knew enough about forensics from novels and TV shows not to disturb a potential crime scene, though I did briefly touch the outstretched hand. Cold, as I suspected.

I could hardly believe it, but it looked very much as if I had stumbled on a murder victim.

I had my mobile on me and immediately called 999. The operator was efficient and businesslike; she didn't seem to turn a hair when I said I had discovered a body and that there were signs of violence. She took my name, spelt it back to me and made me describe carefully where I was in terms of the lane running along the top of the ridge from Great Oxendon. I assured her that I would be standing on it to meet the emergency services. She confirmed to me that the police and an ambulance were on the way. I didn't think the latter would have much to do, but no doubt there are protocols for these things.

I undid the dogs, and we made our way the hundred yards or so up the slope to the hedge that flanked the lane. As we did so, I called our landline: like most women I know, Lucy never seems to have her mobile on.

'Hi,' she said cheerfully, a faint hint of surprise in her voice given that I'd left home less than an hour earlier.

'Listen,' I said. 'This is serious. I've found a body.'

'A body?' she replied, Lady Bracknell-like.

'Yes. A dead person. And I don't like the look of it. The police are on their way.'

'But... who?' she asked. Not a question I expected, but then shock produces strange reactions in people.

'I don't know,' I said, though in truth even then I had my suspicions. 'A man. He's face down in pretty long grass.'

'How awful...'

'Yes. Now, can you bring my Range Rover up here to collect the dogs? Go out of the village up the hill to that signpost I once hit on the ice and turn right down the lane along the Arthingworth ridge towards Great Oxendon. I'll be about three quarters of the way along it.'

'Yes, but...'

'Just do it, darling, please. I'll have to stay here to talk to the police.'

'OK,' Lucy said meekly, which was unlike her. 'Five minutes.'

The gate in the hedge appeared to be closed, but once I reached it, I could see that in fact it was ajar – only inertia was keeping it shut. That in itself was unusual for a farm gate, I thought, as I hitched the dogs to the gatepost. The four sheep made off unhurriedly down the hill as we approached, giving us a wide berth; I thought the rest of the flock might have escaped whilst the gate was open and that these were just strays. I could see that at least one of them was heavily pregnant; it was, after all, the lambing season.

I'd been there only about three minutes when I saw the Range Rover coming along the lane towards me at a fair lick. We got the dogs in the back swiftly enough, and then Lucy turned to me.

'Where is it?'

I indicated down the slope. 'By the stile.'

My wife glanced briefly in that direction, but there was nothing to see in the grass from that distance. I doubt she looked too carefully anyway, knowing that it wouldn't be a pleasant sight.

'Your friends are here,' she said, indicating down the lane towards Great Oxendon, the opposite direction from which she had come. And indeed, I could see a marked police car heading swiftly towards me; there was no siren, but its blue light was flashing.

And with that, she did a neat three-point turn in the gateway, gave me a brief, worried wave and headed back the way she had come.

\*\*\*

I turned back towards the approaching BMW police car and saw that a second unmarked vehicle was following it, with another liveried police car behind that. They stopped in convoy on the lane, and two policemen stepped out of the leading vehicle, both in high-visibility jackets and looking serious.

'He's down there,' I said to the leading officer, indicating the sloping field. He was still adjusting his hat.

'Thank you, sir,' he said briefly. 'CID will want to talk to you.' He indicated over his shoulder to two individuals in plain clothes walking purposefully past his car. The first was tall, dark, lean and fit – probably about thirty-five – his blue suit looked good on him. The second was a woman with brunette hair cut in a short bob, around the same age, also well dressed in a sober grey trouser suit under a light zip-up jacket. She was handsome in a rather austere way, but then it was a pretty austere occasion.

'Mr Robert Rowland?' asked the man.

I nodded briefly.

'I am Detective Inspector Peter Yardley. This is my colleague, Detective Sergeant Fiona Challis.'

The woman inclined her head briefly; she seemed friendly enough but did not smile. I shook hands with both of them rather self-consciously.

'Well, shall I show you?' I began uncertainly. I could see the officers from the third car beginning to put out what I assumed were police *Stop* signs.

'In good time, sir,' said the detective. 'First, please tell us why you were in that field.'

'I was walking my dogs,' I replied, surprised. 'It's a public footpath. I use it often.'

'Where are the dogs now?' asked the sergeant.

'Well, my wife collected them,' I replied, feeling absurdly guilty. 'I knew I'd have to talk to you and didn't know how long that would take, so I gave her a ring and asked her to pick them up. You probably saw her turning round in my Range Rover as you arrived.'

There was a momentary pause, as if the two police officers were considering the likelihood of my wife heading off with a weapon, or an accomplice assassin, or so I imagined. But then they moved on.

'Tell us what happened,' said Yardley.

'Not much to tell,' I replied rather helplessly. 'We were heading home across the field; I live in the village you can see in the dip over there – Braybrooke. The dogs were ahead of me. When I got within about thirty yards of that hedge, I saw them sniffing at something that looked like a pile of old clothes.'

The police said nothing.

'Near the stile. It's about a hundred yards down the slope,' I continued, indicating.

'Only it wasn't a pile of old clothes, was it?' said Yardley, concluding my tale for me. 'Very well. Show us.'

\*\*\*

I opened the gate into the field, made sure it was closed again once we were through and turned back to the two detectives.

'Something you should know,' I said. 'When I first got up here after finding the body, this gate was ajar. As you can see, it opens outwards: only the gravity of the slope was keeping it shut. That's not like people around here. They know not to leave gates open.'

I saw Detective Sergeant Challis note this down.

'And also – you see those four sheep over there?' I pointed, and they both nodded. The sheep were grazing peacefully a couple of hundred yards away down the slope but some way from the stile, further back up the path I'd taken as I approached it. 'They were right here by the gate, where we're standing now. They moved off when I came up with the dogs.'

'I see,' said Yardley briefly. Challis was still writing.

'Well, follow me,' I said and headed down the slope.

After about sixty yards, the body became visible, still looking deceptively like a mound of clothes. Soon we were less than twenty-five yards from it. I turned to my companions. 'That's it,' I said.

Yardley said nothing but stayed us with his hand and ventured carefully forwards. Challis and I watched her boss as he made his preliminary assessment. He took at least five minutes, circling the body from a few feet away but touching nothing. Then he headed unhurriedly back up the slope. 'Have you touched anything here?' he asked conversationally.

'Only that outstretched hand to make sure he was dead. It was cold.'

'Cold, was it? Sure?'

'Absolutely certain. And it was only for a second; anyone could see he was dead with all that blood. I'm no expert, but it looked like he'd been shot in the head.'

The policeman looked at me briefly, as if making an appraisal. I heard the ambulance arriving up on the lane as he did so.

'I agree,' he said after a moment and turned decisively to his colleague. 'SOCO,' he said. 'Now.'

Challis turned on her heel without a word and headed back up the slope, no doubt to radio in her superior's demand.

'Scene of Crimes Officer,' explained Yardley.

I nodded politely, but I'd seen enough police procedurals on TV to know what the acronym meant.

'You were quite right to call us, sir, so thank you. Now, do you have any idea who that man is?' He indicated the body.

'Yes,' I replied.

# CHAPTER TWO

'I can't be certain till I see his face, but I think he's called Edmund Ayling. He's a local farmer. I believe he owns this field.'

'Know any more about him?' said Yardley, beginning to walk back up the slope.

'Not much I'm certain of, I'm afraid,' I replied apologetically as I fell into step beside him. 'Single I think, or possibly a widower. My wife is much more up on who's who in the village than I am; I work in London during the week.'

'Age?'

'Around fifty – maybe a little older. I could be wrong.'

'Where does he live?'

'Braybrooke Farm. You can see it from here. On the left-hand side. See it?' I turned as we reached the gate and pointed towards Braybrooke, across the stile and nestling in the low ground about a mile away, towards which the dogs and I had been gradually descending. The farm buildings half a mile or so north of the village to the left of the road to Market Harborough were obvious.

Yardley looked hard and then beckoned one of the uniformed policemen over. 'See that farm?' he said, indicating.

The policeman nodded.

'Get down there and check it out. Let me know who's there; we'll be down to question anybody who is after speaking to SOCO, so don't let them leave. If anyone who lives there is not present, I want to know who and where they are.'

The policeman nodded, turned away without a word and beckoned his colleague. Their BMW was on the move in seconds.

Yardley was deep in thought as Challis closed in. 'SOCO in thirty minutes,' she said.

Yardley stayed silent.

'Do you need me anymore, Inspector?' I ventured as the detective continued to reflect.

He seemed to start. 'We undoubtedly will, Mr Rowland,' he said after a moment. 'But not for now, can you please give DS Challis all your contact details?'

I did so in less than a minute, and Challis smiled for the first time as she snapped her notebook shut. 'That's it, Mr Rowland. You are free to go. We'll be in touch. Thank you for your assistance. Don't say any more than you have to at this stage.'

I looked at Yardley, who smiled reassuringly. 'We can run you home if you want?'

I shook my head. 'I'm happy to walk; it'll clear my head.'

\*\*\*

I called Lucy briefly to tell her I was on my way home, and she too offered me a lift, but I was happy to go on foot and reflect. It wouldn't take me more than twenty-five minutes.

Was it indeed Edmund Ayling? I was pretty confident as I crossed the stile, giving the body a wide berth. He wasn't someone I knew well, but it was his land, and almost certainly Lucy would confirm that.

A couple of hundred yards beyond the stile I met a middle-aged couple walking their black Labrador up the footpath as I descended: the Johnsons. Sam was a local builder, and rather a successful one. Annie played the organ in the church, not that Lucy and I went that frequently: Christmas, Easter; Harvest Festival, that sort of thing. They smiled in neighbourly fashion as I approached.

'Lovely afternoon,' said Sam. He was cheerful, burly and balding, about my age but undoubtedly still pretty fit. Intuition told me he'd been a rugby player in his youth.

I paused before replying.

'No dogs today?' asked Annie.

Challis's warning was still fresh in my mind, but I had to say something. 'No – no dogs. Not now anyway. Look, both of you, I don't think you should go any further.'

'Why on earth not?' asked Sam, taken aback. 'You look terrible. Are you alright?'

I grappled with what to tell them.

'Rob?' said Annie, concern writ large on her kindly face.

'Look, something has happened, just the other side of the stile. The police are there…'

'What?' asked Sam.

'Someone has died. That's all I can tell you. I discovered a body. They're still investigating.'

There was a shocked silence for a couple of seconds.

'Who is it?' asked Annie. 'Anyone local?'

I thought it best to apply a little discretion here. 'I don't know. A man. He was face down. I just called 999 once I'd established he was dead.'

Sam looked as if he thought this was a fairly feeble effort but held his tongue.

Annie, a practical woman, was more forthright. 'You're right of course, we can't go up there and disturb them. Come along, Sam. No doubt all will become clear in time.' She strode off down the slope with Sam a pace or so behind; he lingered only to glance briefly over his shoulder to confirm that their dog was following. There was no question of waiting for me.

But that was no problem; I wasn't in the mood for small talk.

\*\*\*

It was about 4.30pm when I got home, and Lucy greeted me with a large and very welcome cup of tea. She wanted to know everything of course, so once we were settled at the kitchen table, I told her.

'It couldn't be Edmund, could it?' she said when I got to that part, her eyes widening.

'All I'm saying is that it looked a strong possibility to me,' I replied, 'but I couldn't see his face, so I can't be sure. The police are checking at Braybrooke Farm.'

Lucy reflected briefly, then checked her phone and

dialled the stored number on our landline – mobile reception is never great in our low-lying village.

I raised my eyebrows and was about to query her.

'Shhh,' said my wife, waving me away whilst the phone rang on. Eventually, it kicked into an answerphone; she slammed it down impatiently without leaving a message. 'Well, he's not at home. No answer. God, surely not?' She seemed rather more than simply upset, almost distracted.

'Do you know anything that might have a bearing on this?' I asked suddenly.

She looked up in shock and indignation. 'No, of course not.'

'I'm just asking if you've heard something. Gossip. Anything at all.'

She paused to think for a second or so but then shook her shoulder-length brown hair decisively. 'No. I have no idea. Let's just wait and see who it is, shall we?'

\*\*\*

We didn't have to wait long. It wasn't much after 6pm before there was a knock on the door. It was Detective Sergeant Challis, and she looked tired.

'Good evening, sir,' she said, as I stood in the hallway. 'Would you mind if I came in for a moment?'

'Not at all; of course not, please,' I replied, opening the door to her. I sensed Lucy appear behind me as I did so, restraining an overfriendly Rosie, who loves greeting visitors. 'This is my wife, Sergeant. Lucy. And that's Rosie, one of the dogs I was walking.'

'DS Fiona Challis,' said the detective, offering her land.

Lucy hesitated for half a second before taking it as best she could with her free hand. One female sizing up another. They were only a few years apart in age.

'Lucy Rowland,' she said. 'You look as if you've had a very long day. Would you like a cup of tea?'

Challis paused for only a moment. 'That would be very welcome indeed, Mrs Rowland. Thank you. No sugar please.'

'Come on through,' I said to our unexpected guest, leading her down the corridor into the drawing room as Lucy retreated to the kitchen, the spaniel firmly gripped by her collar. 'Do take a seat,' I encouraged her.

She sank gratefully down onto the sofa, and Lucy was back with mugs of tea for all three of us moments later.

'What can we do to help you, Sergeant?' I asked.

Challis paused for thought, and the quizzical expression suited her: not classically beautiful but definitely attractive. 'The man whose body you found this afternoon is indeed Edmund Ayling, Mr Rowland,' she said.

'Oh no,' cried Lucy. 'How terrible.'

'And he was murdered?' I asked.

'No question of that, sir,' replied Challis. 'We've only got the opinion of the scene of crimes team at present, but they seem certain he was shot from the front with a shotgun, possibly twice. And then a further shot to the back of the head once he was on the ground, which was obviously fatal. The coroner has already ordered a post-mortem on Monday which should confirm all that.'

I saw Lucy puckering up with shock, though she said nothing, and I waited for Challis to continue.

'You're clearly a key witness, sir, being the man who

found him. I wonder if I could ask you a few questions – just background?'

'Does my husband need a lawyer?' Lucy intervened, rather overdefensively I thought.

'He's certainly entitled to one if he wishes, Mrs Rowland,' replied Challis calmly. 'Though I am not interviewing him under caution, and if he has nothing to hide, as I'm fairly confident is the case, then I suggest it is probably unnecessary. I repeat – I am just trying to get some background information.'

'Of course I don't have anything to hide!' I exclaimed. 'Fire away – whatever you want.'

'Very well. How long have you lived in the village?' asked Challis.

'Around ten years,' I replied. 'I'm a Londoner, though Lucy's parents come from this part of the world. We wanted to give the children a rural upbringing, whilst still being within commutable range of London for my work. It's just over an hour on the train. We've never regretted it.'

'And excuse me for asking, but you are how old now?'

'I'm forty-nine.'

'And I'm forty-six, if it makes any difference,' interjected Lucy stiffly.

Challis ignored her. 'In the time you've been here, I suppose you must have got to know Edmund Ayling fairly well?' she continued.

I shrugged rather helplessly. 'Not really. Enough to say hello to. I'm not here during the week – well, I am overnight, but I travel down to London daily. My wife knows the village much better than I do.' I looked across at Lucy for help.

'Certainly, I knew him,' said Lucy. 'A very cheerful and friendly man, surprisingly so since he lived alone.'

'Widower, I think you said up there on the hill, Mr Rowland?'

'No – his wife left him,' interjected Lucy. 'Not long before we got here.'

I hadn't been aware of this and looked across in surprise.

'How do you know about that?' asked Challis, echoing my thoughts.

'We share a daily. She cleans for me here on Monday, Wednesday and Friday mornings, and on Tuesdays and Thursdays she goes to Edmund. Or used to. So just chit-chat over coffee. That's how I know.'

'Could you please give me the name of this cleaning lady, Mrs Rowland?'

'She's called Lesley Logan,' replied my wife.

Fiona Challis wrote the name down carefully, secured a contact number from Lucy and then turned to me again. 'Can I check some timings with you now, sir?' she asked.

'Sure.'

'When did you start your dog walk?'

'Straight after lunch. So I suppose about quarter to two,' I replied.

Lucy nodded briefly in corroboration.

'And you called 999 just after 3pm, we've checked the log,' said Challis. 'About an hour and a quarter. It matches the distance you told us you walked.'

'Glad to hear it,' I replied, with mild irony, which I think was lost on the detective.

'Now, the route you took, up the track to where it meets the road near Great Oxendon, then back across the field via the public footpath. It's a loop, isn't it?'

'Yes, it is,' I replied.

'And you could see the stile from the track on your outward leg. I'm not asking you; I've been there.'

'Yes – I wasn't looking for it, but I know you can see it on the side of that hill for most of the length of the track, though it runs parallel to a stream; there's some thick vegetation that sometimes screens it. It's probably about four hundred yards away at the nearest point.'

'Nearer four hundred and fifty,' said Challis coolly.

I nodded my acceptance.

'And on that outward leg, you did not see anyone on the side of the hill?'

'Nobody. The only people I met during the whole walk were a local village couple, the Johnsons. They were coming up towards the stile with their dog from this side once you'd told me I could go, probably doing the opposite of my route. This was after I'd found the body of course. They turned round on my advice.'

Challis wrote this down too. 'And in all that walk, did you hear anything that might have been a shot, or shots?'

'I did not. Though neither was I expecting to, of course.'

The detective nodded, closed her notebook with satisfaction, drained her mug and rose to her feet. 'That figures. You told us the body was cold when you found it. We believe the killing happened quite some time before then.'

In the doorway, Challis turned to face me, her hand outstretched. I thought she was offering a handshake and began to respond awkwardly before I realised it held a police business card.

'If anything occurs to you which may assist in this case, please call me, Mr Rowland,' she said. 'Anything at all, however minor. And any time.'

# CHAPTER THREE

Despite the stresses of the day, I slept well and awoke thoroughly refreshed on Sunday morning. I languished too long in bed reading the paper on my iPad and then announced to my dozing wife that after breakfast I was going for a dog walk.

'Didn't work out too well yesterday, did it?' Lucy retorted sleepily from beneath her duvet.

'I'm going to retrace my steps,' I declared. 'See if anything jogs my memory. Come with me – I could do with another pair of eyes on the case.'

'The case? A sort of Watson to your Holmes, then?'

'Well, yes I suppose so.'

'God, these sudden enthusiasms. They never end. This is the latest, I take it?'

'It's not every day one stumbles across a murder,' I replied, rather put out. But she was right; I am indeed prone to sudden enthusiasms, always have been.

Lucy sighed, swung her improbably long legs out of bed

and headed unenthusiastically towards the bathroom. 'All right. But only if you make breakfast,' she announced mock-grumpily over her shoulder.

I'm rather a dab hand at scrambled eggs so had no reservations about accepting this condition. Since Lucy had purloined our en-suite as normal, I headed for the family bathroom off the landing and was downstairs within twenty minutes, feeding Theo and Rosie. I held off making the eggs for a bit, knowing that there'd be a delay before my dear wife put in an appearance. But as ever, it was worth the wait, and she looked very decorative when she did.

It was decidedly overcast as we headed off past the church, with a hint of rain in the air. We each led a dog.

'Anything specific we're looking for this morning, Holmes?' Lucy enquired, linking our free arms as she did so.

'I'll know it when I see it, Watson,' I replied gravely, and her blue eyes sparkled happily. She seemed completely over the shock of the previous day.

We strolled on in companionable silence till we were almost out of the village, where we let Theo and Rosie off their leads, and they scampered around cheerfully. Within a hundred yards, the road had become a track, and a further hundred yards beyond that we were out in open country, albeit with a stream on our left and trees beyond it on the far bank. They weren't sufficient to impede our view up the slope to the stile over half a mile away, set in the hedge running at ninety degrees down to our track and up to the road running along the top of the ridge.

'I see what you meant last night,' said Lucy. 'From here, you can't see beyond the stile – most of that far field where you found the body is screened by the hedge.'

'Exactly,' I replied. 'What the Army calls "dead ground" – rather appropriately in this case.'

'So you wouldn't have seen anything that happened there, would you?'

'I wouldn't, and I didn't,' I said.

'But remember what Challis said last night: it probably happened earlier.'

\*\*\*

Soon we came level with the hedge which led up to the stile, and for the first time, we could see the full extent of the field on the far side, including where the body had lain. There was of course no sign of anything connected with the events of the day before by then.

But somebody was in that field, a good six hundred yards from us. A blue Land Rover, towing a trailer with a distinctive red top. A sheep trailer. A lone figure was doing up the rear ramp. I pointed wordlessly and turned towards Lucy.

'That's Jack Diggle,' pronounced Lucy confidently. 'I recognise the vehicle.'

'Who the hell's Jack Diggle, Watson?' I asked.

'He works – or worked – for Edmund. I think he's from the traveller camp. Lesley says Edmund swore by him.'

I turned back to look at the hillside again. There was indeed a traveller camp about a mile from the village, located near the county boundary, as such things often are. People were afraid of the inhabitants, and shunned them, spreading fearful rumours, but apart from some thoughtless driving through the village, I wasn't aware that they'd ever done anything specific that affected me. I was, however, in no doubt that Edmund would have been going very much against the grain of local advice in employing anyone from that background.

Suddenly, I had an epiphany. 'He's rounding up those four sheep,' I declared, turning excitedly to Lucy. 'You know, the ones I told you about that were hanging around all yesterday.'

'I suppose he must be,' she replied calmly.

'But that's fair enough, isn't it, if he worked for Edmund?'

\*\*\*

I thought Watson might well be right, but with DS Challis's 'anything at all, any time' directive fresh in my mind, I thought it best to let her know, even on a Sunday, though Lucy told me I was wasting my time and ruining what remained of the poor woman's weekend.

My mobile has one of those nifty business card scanner apps on it which I use a lot at work, and I'd automatically scanned Challis's card in the previous evening when she gave it to me, so her number was to hand, and I called her straightaway. She picked up straightaway too.

'DS Challis.' Curt and businesslike.

'Er, Detective Sergeant,' I began awkwardly, 'it's Robert Rowland. You told me last night to call you if I came across anything relevant to the death of Edmund Ayling.'

'Yes, sir,' she said coolly. 'What is it?'

'Probably nothing, at least that's what my wife thinks,' I replied, noticing Lucy's firm nod out of the corner of my eye. 'But we're on that same dog walk again now. We're where the track meets the hedge leading up to the stile, where it becomes possible to see the full extent of the sloping field where the murder took place. Do you understand?'

'Top Close?' she replied, which was incidentally the first time I'd heard the term. 'Yes, I understand.'

'There is a blue Land Rover towing a sheep trailer in there, which has a red top. One chap, a long way off of course, but judging by the vehicle, my wife thinks he's a man called Jack Diggle, an employee of Edmund Ayling. He appears to be taking away those four sheep that were milling around yesterday. He's just moving off now.'

'More of a boy than a man,' whispered Lucy. 'And mention that he's from the traveller camp.'

'I heard that, thank you, sir,' said Challis primly. 'That may be very useful information. Thank you, absolutely the right thing to call me.'

She rang off. I looked at Lucy, and both of us shrugged. We stayed watching the Land Rover till it left the field by the gate at the top and then turned left, as would anyone who was heading for the traveller camp.

***

We continued on our walk, and some twenty minutes later I showed Lucy the exact spot I'd been when I first noticed the body because the dogs had been sniffing around it. Then we moved forward to where it had actually lain. There was no sign it had ever been there and, bar a little trampled grass, none that the police had been either.

We were just discussing this point when a marked police car drew up at the gate onto the lane – it was a small Vauxhall patrol vehicle, not a powerful pursuit car like the

BMWs of the previous day. I saw two officers getting out, both female.

'I bet they've been sent by Challis,' I told Lucy. 'They're going to wonder what we're doing here.'

She nodded, and we started making our way the hundred yards up the slope. The two officers eyed us cautiously from beyond the gate; as I got closer, I could see that neither looked over thirty, and they were tense, understandably perhaps.

'Good morning, officers,' I said cheerfully as we approached, hoping to put them at their ease.

'Morning, sir,' said one of them cautiously. 'May I ask what you are doing here?'

'You may. It's a public footpath; my wife and I are exercising our dogs.'

The police officers looked uncertainly at each other till Lucy came to their rescue. 'Forgive my husband. What he says is correct, but in fact it was him who found the body here yesterday, having discovered it whilst on exactly this walk. He was just showing me.'

There was a strained silence. 'I called Detective Sergeant Challis about half an hour ago to tell her we saw a vehicle in this field; we think it was removing sheep,' I said, attempting to break it.

'Sheep?' replied the first officer, blankly. They were an unlikely looking duo – she was a good foot taller than her silent colleague.

'Yes,' I said. 'Didn't she send you along to check?'

'Never heard of her,' came the reply. 'What body?'

# CHAPTER FOUR

Where we live, the county boundary snakes hither and thither, and technically our house is about four hundred yards inside Northamptonshire, though we have an LE postcode. This produces anomalies, because our nearest town, Market Harborough, only three miles away, is in Leicestershire. Northampton is over seventeen miles away. Because I'd automatically said I was in Northamptonshire when I made my 999 call, it was Northampton police who were alerted. It transpired that these two officers were from Leicestershire and claimed to be standing in it as we spoke, even though we were only a hundred yards from where I'd found the body.

It took us about five minutes to sort this out, and the two police officers then departed in good heart, seemingly caring little about the details of the murder case on their doorstep. Perhaps they were just glad it had dropped into someone else's lap.

'Odd, though,' said Lucy when I expressed this sentiment, as she stared after the receding Vauxhall. 'You'd have thought their neighbours would have informed them about a murder right on the county border.'

'Perhaps they did.' I shrugged. 'Those two were fairly junior. It may not have reached them.'

On we went, and as we re-entered the village, I suggested a quick drink in our dog-friendly local, The Swan. It was shortly after midday. Lucy agreed readily enough, and soon we were ensconced comfortably in a corner of the pub, me with a pint of excellent Everards Tiger bitter and my wife with a gin and tonic. The two dogs lay under our feet on their leads, warily eyeing a rather noisy Jack Russell owned by a burly man standing at the bar. He wasn't someone we knew.

Lucy and I were chatting away contentedly about this and that when suddenly I became aware of a lull in the hubbub around the bar. I glanced up and saw that most of the people there were staring at us, some more surreptitiously than others. It wasn't hostile, just curious. I was nonplussed.

Suddenly one of them broke away and headed over to our table, clutching his pint. He seemed friendly enough, and we did know him a little, because he lived in a cottage pretty close to us, but of course, being useless at such things, I couldn't recall his name.

'Hello, both,' he said, cheerfully enough, and sat himself down at our table.

'Hello, Ivor,' replied Lucy, on the ball with who was who, as ever.

'Afternoon,' I said cautiously, backing her up.

Our uninvited guest took a long sip of his pint and looked us both up and down. I could see his erstwhile companions at the bar watching closely.

'Bit surprised to see you here,' he said conversationally to me. He was probably about sixty but looked older and was beginning to run to seed, a farm labourer, as I remembered now. He was still wearing a flat cap, even though we were inside: old school. No doubt he'd led a pretty hard life.

'Why's that, Ivor?' I replied, slightly defensively. I wasn't sure what was coming.

'Understand you found Edmund?' he said.

'I did,' I said, in a neutral tone. I had little idea how much he knew, or how close he'd been to the murder victim.

'Shot, they say.'

'Who says?'

Ivor spread his hands in conciliatory fashion. 'Just people.'

'They're right,' I replied shortly. 'The police are investigating.'

Ivor took another sip of his beer and looked thoughtful. 'No chance it was suicide, I suppose?' he said eventually.

'None whatsoever,' I said.

Ivor nodded, got up ponderously and returned to his friends at the bar. Lucy and I looked at each other, returned to our drinks and were out of there in under five minutes.

\*\*\*

'I should have known better than to go in there,' I said apologetically to Lucy as we made our way the three hundred yards or so to our home. 'People were bound to be curious.'

Lucy was unfazed. 'Murders don't happen every day in places like this. I suspect they were talking about nothing else anyway even before we turned up.'

'Why do you think Ivor said he was surprised to see me there? It felt almost as if I shouldn't have been.'

My wife shrugged. 'Just clumsy phrasing, I think. He's not the most articulate of men.' After a pause, she continued, 'Odd that he asked whether it was suicide.'

I said nothing for a few seconds, then turned to her again as we reached our drive. 'Remind me – Ivor who?'

'Chubb. Ivor Chubb. Long-established village family.'

'What does he do?'

'Works for Ned Logan.'

'Who is…?'

Lucy sighed. 'You really know nothing, do you? He's the other farmer in the village, aside from Edmund I mean. Ritche's Lodge Farm. Husband of Lesley, who works for us. Or had you forgotten that too?'

\*\*\*

I seldom saw Lesley, because I was generally in London on the three mornings a week that she worked for us, but the next day, Monday, it turned out that there was a rail strike. I hadn't registered this, not having read an email from my diligent PA Clare over the weekend, so I was back home in ill-temper after a fruitless trip to Market Harborough station well before 8am, to my wife's considerable surprise.

It didn't matter greatly. I have a home office, and over the course of the pandemic, my company had kitted it out very effectively so that I could work remotely. It wasn't ideal, because in my line of business (the Lloyds insurance market), personal relationships and face-to-face meetings still matter. However, aside from a working lunch which Clare had already efficiently rearranged, there was no significant impact, and indeed a day working on a few longer-term projects I'd been meaning to get round to for a while was no bad thing. I could still access the firm's systems and electronic files.

I was doing just this at about 10.30am when my office door opened suddenly, without a knock. Lesley entered the room before she realised I was there. She pulled up with a start.

'I'm so sorry, Robert,' she said, surprised. There was a soft burr to her accent, which did not hail from the East Midlands. 'I had no idea you were in here. I was just going to give your office a quick clean.'

'Don't worry,' I said. 'I was about to break for a coffee anyway. Do you want one too?' I took in the hesitant woman in front of me whilst I waited for her reply. Good-looking, certainly. I guessed she was about my age or a little younger; a tall brunette with a full figure which somehow conjured up the word 'ripe' in my degenerate mind.

'Well, I'd better finish this,' she replied. 'I'll do it whilst you're having your coffee. It'll only take me ten minutes.'

I nodded and squeezed awkwardly past her in the doorway, too close for comfort – my home office is not a big room. On the way along the corridor to the kitchen, I reflected on how little I knew about her.

'Bumped into Lesley,' I said to Lucy over coffee in the kitchen. 'Just about literally. Caused her a bit of a shock, I think. She wasn't expecting to see me.'

'Sorry, I should have warned her,' replied Lucy. 'She's nice, isn't she?'

'I'm sure she is. To be honest, I don't think I've ever had a proper conversation with her; I'm so rarely here when she is.'

'Lesley is a good person,' stated Lucy emphatically. 'Life is not easy for her.'

'Money? Is that why she's helping us with cleaning?'

Lucy shrugged. 'That's part of it, I think. And she's damn good at it – absolutely reliable.'

I got the feeling that this line of questioning wasn't particularly welcome so moved on to other topics, drank my coffee and returned to my office.

There was no sign of Lesley.

\*\*\*

And so the morning wore on. By midday, I could see through my window that it was pouring with rain outside, and suddenly Lucy was at my office door.

'Are you busy?' she asked apologetically.

'Nothing that can't wait,' I answered. 'Why?'

'Lesley only works for us in the morning, as you know. She needs to get home. Look at the weather.'

'How did she get here?'

'She bikes over when it's fine. Misjudged it this time! It's barely a mile. I wondered if you could chuck her bike in the back of your Range Rover and run her back? I'd take her myself, but I'm waiting for that deep freezer maintenance man – any time between 11am and 2pm he said.'

I sighed and got up from my desk. 'Of course. No problem.'

Lesley was waiting in the kitchen with her blue coat already on when I reached it, looking shyly and unnecessarily apologetic. 'This is so kind of you, Robert...' she began.

'Nonsense, it's a five-minute round trip. It wouldn't be very neighbourly of us to let you ride home in this! Where's your bike?'

'In the hallway,' answered Lesley, with a rather disarming smile.

'Wait here then, and I'll bring the car to the door,' I said.

On my sprint to the garage, I reflected on how much men like rescuing damsels in distress. At least I do; something to do with a knightly chivalry complex probably.

It was the work of a moment to get Lesley's bike in the back of the Range Rover, and then I opened the passenger door for her with a flourish, doing my parfit knight impression.

She got in gratefully, buckled up her seat belt and looked around. 'Nice car,' she said, as I buckled up myself. All men like their car being complimented, especially by the fairer sex, and it was indeed less than a year old.

'Well, it probably doesn't lead as hard a life as Ned's farm vehicles,' I replied, as I nudged the car into Drive.

She smiled briefly at me in reply, looking rather strained, I thought.

'Terrible about Edmund, isn't it?' I ventured conversationally as we headed down the drive. There was no reply. I wasn't even sure Lesley had heard me; she seemed to be miles away.

Ritche's Lodge Farm is only about three minutes away: after a few hundred yards heading east towards Desborough, you turn right at the crossroads, and it's half a mile up the hill. I was about to swing right into the yard when Lesley suddenly placed her hand on my arm, an unexpected surprise. She turned quickly towards me.

'This'll be fine, Robert. Drop me here.'

'Nonsense,' I said. 'It's still pouring down. I'll get you nearer than this.'

Before she could object, I swung the car into the farmyard. I had never been there before; it looked pretty run-down, but then nowhere looks its best in a biblical downpour.

'Thank you,' she whispered urgently. We were twenty feet from the house.

I nodded, raised the rear tailgate, lifted out the bike and then opened her door. My engine was still running. 'A pleasure, my lady.'

Lesley was smiling at this feeble performance with her eyes downcast as she got out of the car when the door of the house opened. Ned Logan appeared: a tall, lanky, red-haired fellow in his mid-fifties. He had about two days' stubble.

I didn't know Ned except by sight, and he made an irritable half-gesture in my direction, accompanied by an accusatory stare. I can take a hint as well as the next man, so I began to turn my car around. But I saw in the mirror that he wasn't looking at me anymore anyway; he was focused on his wife. And he was angry.

# CHAPTER FIVE

'What's with the husband?' I asked Lucy as soon as I got home.

She looked quizzically at me. Clearly, I'd need to explain.

'Lesley didn't want me to drive into the farmyard, then when I did to save her from being drenched, Ned gave her the evil eye. He didn't seem too happy to see me either.'

'Did he say anything?' asked Lucy.

'No. But I'm pretty certain he gave her hell once he got her inside.'

My wife paused for a moment. 'Would you say that Lesley is attractive?' she asked, seemingly with no agenda beyond abstract curiosity.

The question caught me by surprise, but I answered it truthfully. 'I would. She can't be far off fifty, but she's a very good-looking woman. Great figure. The sort men can't help noticing.'

Lucy allowed herself a tolerant smile. 'Certainly not you.'

My wife knew her husband and that he had an appreciative eye. But she also knew that I was a firm disciple of Paul Newman's philosophy: 'why go out for a hamburger when you've got steak at home?'. I knew which side my bread was buttered, and Lucy had nothing to worry about.

'Ned notices that other men notice. Were you flirting with Lesley before Ned appeared?'

'I'd hardly call it flirting,' I protested. 'I made a very weak joke as she got out of the car, and she was good enough to smile at it.'

'That exchange will have done Lesley no favours if Ned saw it.'

'It was just a couple of seconds. You have to say something when you drop people off; you can't just drive away.'

'I bet he wasn't smiling.'

'No, he wasn't,' I admitted. 'I hope I haven't inadvertently caused Lesley any trouble.'

\*\*\*

I ruminated on this episode for most of the afternoon, to the extent that in terms of work I was almost completely unproductive; I just wasn't in the mood. When Lucy called me down for a cup of tea at about 4pm, I returned immediately to the events of the morning.

'How do you know all this stuff about Lesley and Ned?' I asked.

Lucy shrugged. 'She's helped me around the house for over three years. We talk. She trusts me, and she knows I won't gossip. I think it helps her to cope, so I listen. Amateur psychology.'

'What's her background? That's not a local accent.'

'No. She's from the West Country. Dorset, I think,' she replied. 'Difficult childhood; I don't know the details. But a farming family. She took herself off to agricultural college somewhere a long way from home as soon as she decently could.'

'Where she met Ned?'

'She did. They became an item and got married about twenty years ago. No children, but everything was hunky-dory for the first ten years I understand.'

'What happened?'

'Well, Lesley says he'd always been rather possessive, but over all that period it was nothing more than an irritation which she'd learnt to live with. Then Ned had an accident, a couple of years before we arrived in the village.'

I looked at my wife enquiringly.

She took a sip of her tea and carried on. 'Quad bike crash. He wasn't wearing a helmet; it rolled over on him, and he was very badly concussed, as well as having a couple of broken ribs. In hospital for over a month, Lesley says. They're bloody dangerous, those things.'

'But he survived, and he seems unharmed, so…?'

'He's never been the same since, according to Lesley. Very short tempered and irritable. Not so diligent on the farm, which apparently he always used to be – he's let things slip, which is why she goes out now to earn extra money. And the possessiveness has got completely out of hand. He demands to know where she is every minute of the day. Plus…' She hesitated. 'Well, no more sex,' she admitted finally. 'None at all since the accident.'

'Perhaps he no longer can,' I replied. 'So whenever he

sees her with another man, it reinforces his insecurity, which he was predisposed to anyway. Hence why he gave me such a glare this morning.'

'Yes,' said Lucy simply. 'Poor them. Who's the amateur psychologist now?'

I ignored this, being unconvinced that my soft-hearted wife had calibrated her sympathy entirely correctly. 'Poor her, you mean,' I replied.

\*\*\*

The next day, Tuesday, the trains deigned to work again, and so I headed for London. It was a perfectly normal day in the office and around the insurance markets, principally on the floor of Lloyds, where I've been a specialist reinsurance broker for over twenty-five years. I still enjoy it – one of the few parts of the City where one can escape from behind a screen; indeed must do if you are to be any good. I have many friends there.

I was back home just after 7pm, and as usual, Lucy and I settled down over a drink in the kitchen to compare our days. I didn't have much to tell her, but she mentioned to me that there had been quite a lot of police activity in and around the village, including a police helicopter overhead.

'Did they come and question us again?' I asked.

'No. Not at all,' she replied. 'I couldn't really work out what they were doing. Perhaps just being seen around and about the village to provide reassurance?'

I thought there might be something in this, though it seemed an expensive way to go about it, and I was just about to say so when the phone rang. Lucy answered it, gave a brief affirmative answer and then passed the handset to me, mouthing the words, '*Harborough Mail*', our local weekly.

'Hello,' I said. 'This is Robert Rowland.'

'Mr Rowland, good evening,' replied a youthful voice. 'My name is Frank Carey. I am sorry to call you so late. I'm a reporter with the *Harborough Mail*.'

'Good evening, Mr Carey,' I replied cautiously. 'What can I do for you?'

'Well, it's my understanding, sir, that it was you who discovered the body of Edmund Ayling a short distance outside Braybrooke on Saturday and that you subsequently raised the alarm. Would you care to confirm that?'

I thought feverishly. It was the truth, and it was already public knowledge, as the scene in the pub on Sunday had confirmed. No point in denying it provided I was not sucked into speculation.

'Yes. I was walking my dogs. I called 999 immediately.'

'Could you see how he met his death?'

'I understand he had been shot, or at least that was the original impression of the police. You'd have to confirm that with them of course. Their inquiries are ongoing.'

He seemed to preen with his reply, as many people do when imparting fresh information. 'Actually, I think they've pretty much wrapped it up. The only thing that is ongoing is their raid on the traveller camp. They're there now.'

\*\*\*

Well, you take these things at face value. I answered a few more questions, sufficient to give the reporter some quotes, and then turned to Lucy as soon as I had put the receiver down.

'It seems the police think the travellers were involved. He says they're raiding the camp now.'

'I wonder what evidence they've got?'

'They're up to all sorts of mischief there, so people say,' I replied.

'Allegedly. But surely not murder.'

I thought for a moment, pulled out my mobile to check the number and then dialled DS Challis on the landline.

She picked up straightaway. 'Yes, Mr Rowland?' she said. So she must have stored our number in her phone.

'Er, I don't wish to disturb you, Sergeant,' I said, 'but I am hearing rumours that the police are raiding the traveller camp. I assume this is in connection with the Ayling murder?'

'Well, I'll make no comment on the phone about that,' she replied. 'However, I have just finished interviewing some people at the pub. I'm barely three hundred yards away. I could drop by for a few minutes to update you if you wish. Your interest in the case is understandable.'

'By all means,' I replied. 'See you in a few minutes.'

I barely had time to warn Lucy before Challis was at the door, and again we offered her a cup of tea, which she accepted. We adjourned to the drawing room, as we had before.

'So please tell us the latest,' I began once the three of us were settled.

'Off the record, you're not far adrift,' began Challis. 'We followed up that lead you gave us on Jack Diggle, and officers visited the camp to talk to him. There was a lot of unease when the question of sheep arose, and not just from him. We believe that Ayling's flock was about thirty strong.'

'Sheep rustling?' asked Lucy. 'I understand there's a fair bit of it about.'

'There is, Mrs Rowland, too much. So today's raid on the camp is designed to ascertain if there is any evidence that those sheep have ever been there. Apart from the four that Mr Diggle took away, we have no idea of the rest of the flock's whereabouts.'

'So no direct link to the murder?' I asked.

'Not as yet. But the theory that Mr Ayling stumbled across the theft of his sheep certainly has to be investigated. We think it is a strong possibility.'

I told her about the call from the reporter. 'He thinks you've concluded that the travellers did it.'

'Then he's wrong – wishful thinking, like too many journalists. They all want to be the first to break a story. We have an open mind on the matter.'

# CHAPTER SIX

Once DS Challis had left, I changed swiftly from tea to whisky and mixed Lucy a gin and tonic.

'What is it?' she asked, as we settled down across the kitchen island. 'I can see you're softening me up with a gin that strength. Spit it out.'

'Ayling,' I replied. 'Tell me about him.'

'What do you mean?' asked Lucy curiously.

'Well, you said yesterday that his wife had pushed off. I never knew that. What's the story?'

'I'm not entirely certain,' my wife answered. 'But I think probably another woman. Or women.'

'Was he like that?'

Lucy paused for thought. 'He had a certain reputation, put it that way. And he was interested in women. Beyond a purely social level. You can always tell.'

'He never tried it on with you, did he?'

Lucy laughed. 'No. Nothing beyond flirty comments. But he was like that with everyone; it was just who he was. Nothing pervy. He was actually a very amusing man.'

'And Lesley worked for him? An extremely attractive woman not far off his age, alone at his house twice a week.'

Lucy frowned. 'I see what it looks like. But she's never mentioned him making a move on her; I think she would have done if he had. She liked him. He made her laugh, and there's not much laughter in her life.'

'Well, Watson,' I said in my best mock Holmes tones, 'I believe there may be more to this than meets the eye.'

'I doubt it,' laughed Lucy. She hesitated for a moment, and I wondered what was coming. Then she decided to spill the beans on something. 'I'll tell you someone he did have a fling with,' she said hesitantly. 'Marlene Filler.'

I did a double take. Marlene was German by nationality; she'd met and married her husband Steve Filler, who ran the local care home, whilst he'd been serving with the British Army of the Rhine some twenty years earlier. Though I didn't know Steve well, I'd heard the story over a pint in the pub amongst a group one Saturday morning a few years previously. He'd been a military medic of some sort, and she was a German nurse.

Inasmuch as I'd ever thought about her at all, I definitely didn't have Marlene marked down as the type to stray; she'd always seemed dowdy and dull. I didn't think I'd ever exchanged more than the blandest of greetings with her.

Lucy saw my dubious expression and shrugged. 'Still waters run deep.'

'Does Steve know?'

'No idea. You don't see them together much.'

\*\*\*

On Wednesday morning I was sitting in some interminable management meeting in the London office when Lucy texted – I had my phone on silent, but I saw it flash up.

Once I had escaped (too long later), I retired to my desk to take a look.

*Important developments, Holmes*

*Ayling's brother has turned up. Staying at Braybrooke Farm. Nobody knew he had one.*

*Police have taken in three travellers for questioning.*

*Awaiting your return to Baker St for further consultations.*
*Watson*

I smiled and pondered my reply. *Look forward to hearing your deductions.*

It seemed a long day, and although I was as busy as ever, my mind was on other things. I took a slightly earlier train home than normal, claiming it was Lucy's birthday (she has about three a year).

So I was home by about 6.30pm; Lucy and I settled ourselves down in the kitchen over a drink without further delay so she could update me on the day's developments.

'So the brother…?' I began.

'Well,' Lucy replied, with heavy emphasis, 'he just appeared apparently, arrived late last night. Seems to have a key. Someone reported movement in the house to the police this morning. They went round there sharpish, but apparently, it's all legit. Andrew, he's called.'

'Have you seen him?'

'No – this is all rumour control central, i.e. the Women's Institute. Three of them rang me up. He's a younger brother. They reckon he's around forty. Very good-looking, Joan says.'

'Joan Sims? She must be eighty if she's a day!'

'She's allowed to look,' my wife remonstrated.

'Remember, more like,' I retorted. 'OK then, has anyone spoken to this Adonis?'

'Yes, he went into the pub for lunch I'm told. Hoovered up everyone's sympathy for the loss of his brother, and a few free drinks too. He says he's here to clear the house, or at least to assess what needs to be done. He doesn't seem to have seen much of Edmund in recent years.'

'Does he own the farm now, then?'

'I have no idea,' replied Lucy. 'I suppose it depends on the will. I would have thought the former wife might have a claim.'

'Unless Edmund cut her out of his will, of course,' I said. 'Not uncommon after a divorce, is it?'

'I suppose,' replied my wife. 'Something to investigate. Now, the travellers.'

'All right, tell me about them,' I said, taking a swig of my whisky.

'It's just the WI rumour mill again. Apparently, the police went in mob-handed this morning and lifted three men. But it doesn't seem it's about the shooting. It's the sheep.'

'Probably the easier offence to get them on, Watson,' I said. 'Especially if they've got physical evidence. A holding charge, maybe? With murder to follow?'

'Maybe.' Lucy didn't sound convinced.

\*\*\*

Being late March and almost spring, it was still just about light after supper, and since there were a couple of letters to post, I told Lucy I would stroll the three hundred yards through the village with the dogs to the postbox, which was just beyond The Swan. It could perfectly well have waited, but I needed to stretch my legs after my day in the office. From this small decision, much followed.

I had just posted the letters and turned for home when a battered blue Land Rover pulled up just beyond me, parking beside the pavement, and a young fellow emerged: a farmhand by the look of him. The vehicle didn't have the red-topped sheep trailer attached, but I knew instantly who the driver was.

'Evening,' said the young man, as he passed around the front of his vehicle on the way to the pub. He looked friendly enough, so before I had even thought about it, I responded.

'Evening. Are you Jack Diggle, by any chance?'

The young man stopped and looked at me cautiously. He was slimly built and had reddish hair with a small moustache. He couldn't have been more than nineteen. 'Who wants to know?' It wasn't said threateningly, just with curiosity.

'Well, I'm Robert Rowland. I found Edmund Ayling on Saturday, after he'd been shot. I've since learnt that you worked for him.'

The young man relaxed. 'Yes. Only for a year or so. Good boss, he was.'

The words tumbled out of me before I had a chance to stop them. 'Fancy a drink?'

Jack looked surprised to be asked but not unhappy. 'All right. Don't mind if I do. Only got a few minutes, mind.'

He didn't say why, and I didn't ask. Clutching the dogs on their leads, I led him through The Swan to the back garden, where there was an unoccupied table in the corner under one of those space heaters.

'Pint?' I asked, as we took possession of it, and I tied the dogs to one of the table's sturdy legs.

'Sure. Tiger,' Jack replied, and I headed back into the bar. I had to wait a couple of minutes to be served so took the opportunity to send Lucy a quick text.

*Watson, conducting investigations: having drink with Jack D. Holmes x*

I don't think Conan Doyle's Holmes signed his notes with a kiss, but my Watson would get the idea.

I returned with our two pints of Tiger and found Jack playing with the dogs. He looked up when he saw that I'd noticed, seemingly embarrassed at his childish behaviour: a boy trying to be a man.

I sat down, and we both took a sip.

'So,' I said.

'So,' he replied warily.

\*\*\*

The pause became awkward.

'Tell me about how you came to work for Edmund,' I began.

Over Jack's shoulder, I could see looks being cast in our direction from other tables; they did not seem altogether approving. I spotted Ivor Chubb and put it down to being seen drinking with a traveller. Jack was oblivious, his back to the garden.

'Known him since I was a boy.' He shrugged. 'Saw him one day struggling with a flock of sheep. I helped, and one thing led to another.'

I nodded. 'I saw you moving those four sheep from Top

Close the day after it happened: Sunday,' I said. 'The police told me to report anything unusual, so I did. I hope it didn't get you into trouble.'

Jack shook his head resignedly and took a sip of his pint. 'When anything bad happens, it's always us in the frame,' he said. 'I can't blame you for reporting it. Of course, the police then raided the camp.'

'Were the sheep there?'

'No, of course not.' He saw that I was mystified and carried on to explain. 'They live in the sheep pens at Braybrooke Farm. That's where I took them. I'm still feeding them there.'

'So what happened to the rest of the sheep?' I asked.

A shrug. Jack didn't look at all defensive. 'There were thirty of them, so twenty-six missing. They either got out onto the lane or were taken. There's a rustling problem round here. Edmund probably tried to stop them. That's not wise.' He saw me looking at him quizzically. 'Nobody from our camp. They all knew I worked for Edmund, and he was a good neighbour.'

'But the police still arrested three people, didn't they?'

Jack looked dismissive. 'For other stuff.' I made no reply, and he continued. 'If you're determined to blame us travellers, there are plenty of others around here you know. You've heard of Justin Park?'

I was indeed aware of the much bigger traveller camp just south of Market Harborough; it was about four miles away. I nodded.

'I don't think it's them either though,' continued Jack, with a shake of his head. 'Too close for comfort, even if they wanted to. Someone further away I reckon.'

We both fell silent and took a sip of our beers.

'Where was he, exactly?' asked Jack after a moment or two. 'The police wouldn't say.'

'Just the other side of the stile, in Top Close,' I replied. 'My dogs found him.'

'Definitely shot?'

'So the police tell me. There was plenty of blood.'

Jack nodded and drained his pint. 'Got to go. Thank you for the beer. A sad loss.'

I thought he might be on the verge of tears as he left, but maybe I'm rationalising things after the event; it's easy enough to do.

# CHAPTER SEVEN

When I got home around 9.30pm, Lucy was of course agog to hear about my encounter with Jack Diggle, and how it had come about. I outlined what had happened in a couple of minutes.

'He seems a very decent lad,' I concluded. 'I'm sure he was telling the truth, especially if the four sheep are at Braybrooke Farm, which I'm sure they are. It's probably as he says – thieves, but not from around here.'

Lucy nodded, and then I could see her remembering something.

'Braybrooke Farm – there's a bit of news there I should have mentioned earlier,' she said. 'Edmund's brother, Andrew, he texted Lesley today, after she'd finished here with us. Wants to meet her tomorrow. She forwarded the text to me. She's worried.'

'Not unreasonable, surely? She'll be going there on a Thursday anyway; presumably they haven't met before, and he just wants to make sure they do.'

'It doesn't read like that. Here, take a look.'

Lucy's body twisted awkwardly on the kitchen stool so she could extract her phone from the back pocket of her jeans. She scanned it briefly and handed it over, pointing out the text Lesley had forwarded.

*Dear Mrs Logan, following my brother's sad death, we must discuss your future at Braybrooke Farm. Please meet me here at 9.30am tomorrow. Best wishes, Andrew Ayling.*

'Hmm, I see what you mean,' I replied. 'Rather abrupt, isn't it?'

'I rang Lesley back when I got it,' said Lucy. 'I told her it's pretty unlikely he's going to give her notice out of hand. If he's going to sell the place, it'll need to be kept clean. Plus, presumably he's going to be up here for a bit anyway.'

'Still, if she's pushed for cash, I can see why she's concerned,' I said.

'We might be able to give her a few extra hours here,' mused Lucy.

'Let's not get ahead of ourselves. If she doesn't tell you tomorrow, you'll find out about that meeting when Lesley comes in on Friday.'

\*\*\*

I usually have a bath when I get home from the City, and despite the rather late hour, I decided to do the same that evening whilst Lucy watched *Gogglebox*, which she loves. I've never been remotely interested in it.

Out of habit, I took my phone into the bathroom with me. It pinged just as I was dipping a toe into the rather overhot tub. With some relief, I removed my scalded foot and picked up the phone from the shelf above the sink. Stark naked, I perused the newly arrived text whilst I ran the cold tap.

*Thanks for the drink. Edmund death disaster. Keep in touch?*

Jack Diggle. I had no idea how he had obtained my mobile number but didn't ponder long on that, because having been involved from the start, I was of course intrigued by the whole situation. I may even have fancied myself to be a genuine detective; I'll admit now that was foolishly naive.

*Sure*, I replied.

I put my phone back on the shelf, tested the bath temperature again and eased myself in. It had been a long day.

\*\*\*

Lucy was in bed when I returned from my bath, and although she was holding a book, I knew her well enough to understand that she was not focused on it.

'Penny for them,' I said as I scrambled in.

'What?' she replied, turning all innocent on me.

'You're thinking. That's dangerous.'

'Well, yes. I'm concerned about Lesley's meeting tomorrow.'

'No point,' I replied. 'Not until you know the outcome anyway. And even then, not much you can do other than lend a sympathetic ear if she needs one.'

There was a reflective pause from the right-hand side of the bed (it's always been that way with us – me on the left), and then an angry sigh of frustration.

My wife had concluded I was correct but didn't like it. She turned her back decisively on me and turned out her light. 'Goodnight.'

'Goodnight,' I replied and turned out my own light too. She's not to be messed with in that mood.

\*\*\*

The next day, Thursday, I had just arrived in the office when my mobile rang. Though I didn't recognise the number, the 01858 landline code was local to us, so I picked up immediately.

'Mr Robert Rowland?' asked a man's voice. Educated, confident.

'Speaking,' I replied guardedly.

'This is Andrew Ayling,' said the voice. 'Edmund's brother. I called you at home; your wife very kindly gave me your mobile number.'

'How can I help you, Andrew?' I replied. 'I'd heard that you were in the village.'

'I understand from the police that you found my brother's body on Saturday?' he asked. Not much in the way of preliminaries; something of a sense of entitlement came across.

'I did indeed.'

'Well, a phone call is not the right medium, but I'd very much like to hear about that if you'd be kind enough to talk to me about it. Perhaps I could invite you round for a drink?'

'I work in London during the week,' I began dubiously.

'Not a problem. I'll be up here for a while yet,' replied Andrew. 'Perhaps over the weekend?'

I didn't really want our weekend to be taken up talking to a stranger. A sudden thought struck me. 'Tomorrow night maybe? I'm at a conference in Birmingham. Should be back well before 6pm.'

There was a moment of hesitation. 'Fine. Friday. Shall we say 6.30pm then? By all means bring your wife if you wish.'

It hadn't occurred to me not to, but I didn't make an issue of it. 'I will. And thank you. I look forward to meeting you then.' I rang off and looked briefly at my mobile: 9.21am. Andrew would be talking to Lesley in under ten minutes.

# CHAPTER EIGHT

When I got home that evening, Lesley's meeting was of course the first thing I wanted to hear about, as I was sure she would have told Lucy.

She had.

'He's sacked her,' Lucy said bluntly. 'Or given her notice. Still expects her to come in as normal for the short time he'll be up here. Amazing how some people behave.'

'Well, no doubt it was an informal arrangement. No contract. If it's just him and he's trying to keep costs down, it's understandable, I suppose.'

'Understandable doesn't mean right. Don't expect me to speak to him.' She tossed her head as she said it; that's a definite warning sign in our household.

'Actually, we're going to have a drink with him tomorrow,' I said and braced myself for the reaction.

'What?'

I explained, and though Lucy was still none too happy, she eventually acceded.

'I suppose it'll be interesting to see what he's like,' she grumbled. 'There might even be some scope for Holmes and Watson.'

She was trying to put things on a cheerier footing, so I played along.

'We must try to understand the family background better,' I said firmly. 'Whether they got on and if there's a Mrs Andrew Ayling. That sort of thing must be the focus of our investigation.'

No sooner had we agreed on this than my phone pinged as a text came in. I picked it up curiously and started in surprise.

'What?' asked Lucy.

'Jack Diggle. He's been sacked too.' I held the phone out to her.

*Dismissed from Braybrooke Farm. He'll regret it.*

'Hmm. Is that a statement of fact or a threat, do you think?' asked Lucy, handing it back to me.

I hadn't thought of the alternative and more sinister explanation but could see that it was equally valid. 'A very sound observation, Watson,' I said. 'I am impressed.'

She gave me a playful preen in return, but I could see that she was genuinely pleased. Compliments paid to wives are seldom wasted.

\*\*\*

'By the way,' said Lucy later, whilst we were reading our books in bed, 'the funeral's next week.'

'What?'

'Wednesday, 2pm, in the church here. That's one thing Lesley did learn before she got fired.'

'But they haven't caught the killer yet. Bit soon, surely?'

'Police have released the body, Lesley says. They've told Andrew they've got everything they need from it. He wants it done before he has to head home. Which is reasonable enough, I suppose.'

'Inquest?'

'I don't know about that. But the funeral's definitely happening next week.'

I paused to think for a moment. In my experience there are 'funerals' and 'Funerals'. At a 'funeral', death is routine or expected, generally because of old age – there's a fair turnout, but nothing spectacular. At a 'Funeral', life has been cut short prematurely – by a car crash, say, or a heart attack. Or indeed a murder. There'll be many more people at the service, with a range of motives, ranging from the benevolent (a genuine desire to support the family) to the ghoulish (a wish to be part of something sensational, or tragic).

Edmund's would definitely be a 'Funeral'.

'I'll take the day off,' I announced. 'There'll be a big turnout.'

'No need to, surely?' asked Lucy. 'I can represent both of us.'

This was entirely true. The thing was, I realised that I wanted to be there.

'Do you think Holmes would allow himself to miss such a key event?' I asked her, with mock incredulity. 'He is pursuing this case with vigour.'

Lucy looked at me with a lazy smile and then laid her book very deliberately aside. 'Vigorous, is he?' she said, turning slowly back towards me. 'Suppose he proves it, then?'

***

The next day, I headed off early down the A14 towards Birmingham for the conference, which was due to start at 9am. Accordingly, lots of industry people I knew were overnighting in the city, particularly those who lived in London. I was well aware of what that generally led to: a few sore heads in the morning, and even some 'no-shows' at the conference. In my younger days, perhaps I'd have been amongst them, but now I preferred domesticity, and after all, it was only an hour's drive.

Nobody can pretend a hotel-based conference on insurance broking is going to set the pulse racing, but as a director of my firm, I was expected to be there, so I tried to make the best of it. This turned out to be no great hardship: there were one or two very good speakers on my specialist market, whose cards I took, plus there were enough chums around to make lunch quite a convivial affair, particularly for those not driving, which unfortunately did not include me.

It was all over by 4pm, and though there was then a general move to the bar to round things off, I broke away as soon as I decently could, mindful of my evening invitation from Andrew Ayling.

I was home shortly after 5pm, which gave me enough time for a relaxed bath before I headed out again. Lucy had no particular updates for me, though plainly she was not greatly looking forward to what the evening held; I can always tell when that's the case, as she takes even longer than normal to get ready, though I must admit the end result is always worth it. And so indeed it was on this occasion.

It's less than half a mile west on the Market Harborough road to Braybrooke Farm, the opposite side of the village to the Logans' Ritche's Lodge Farm, and it was a damp evening, so we took the car. As we turned into the hundred-yard drive, I noticed immediately how much tidier and more prosperous the Ayling establishment was to that of the Logans'; I'd never had cause to compare them before. Outside the large 1930s house were two expensive cars – a black Porsche Cayenne SUV and a white, sporty Audi S3 hatchback.

'Neither of those are Edmund's, are they?' I mumbled as we drew up alongside the two cars. I noticed as I opened my car door that the Porsche had a slight dent at the back and a personalised plate; it was probably a bit older than I'd first thought.

'No. Edmund had some sort of Mercedes – I saw him driving through the village in it fairly often. Grey. Don't ask me what type,' replied Lucy as she extracted herself the other side.

'So his car will be one, probably the Porsche. Whose is the other, Watson?' I said, as I closed the door of my Range Rover.

'We're about to find out,' replied Lucy, nodding at the front door. And indeed, it was opening.

By the time we reached it up the short path, it was open, and there stood a tall, elegant, middle-aged woman with shoulder-length, ash-blonde hair, dressed in a blue trouser suit. 'Hello,' she said, extending a friendly hand to me. 'It is very good of you both to come. Please do come in. I'm Amelia Ayling.'

\*\*\*

When a woman with the same surname as a man opens the door to a house and he is under the same roof, then the logical assumption is that they are man and wife. I still think it was mischievous of Amelia not to dispel that misconception at the outset.

Andrew was waiting for us in the drawing room and had just opened a bottle of champagne – I heard the cork pop as we walked down the corridor behind Amelia. He was in his early forties, wearing a black roll-neck sweater under a green smoking jacket: *typical Porsche driver's attire*, I found myself thinking uncharitably. He had brown, curly hair, tinted, I thought, to avoid any hint of grey, and was of medium height, rather more of a cosmopolitan character than I could ever remember Edmund being, who was a true countryman and always very casually (indeed scruffily) dressed.

Nonetheless, he had a friendly, open smile: as we entered the room, he put down the bottle and extended his hand to each of us with confident charm. 'Andrew. I am so glad to meet you both, and thank you for coming.'

We exchanged pleasantries, and as he poured the drinks, I found myself looking around the room, which was well decorated in Laura Ashley style, if that's your thing. I'd never been inside the house before, but clearly Edmund had not been short of money.

Andrew didn't invite us to take a seat, so we all stood there rather awkwardly once we had our drinks.

'Well, I suppose we should cut to the chase,' said Andrew, breaking the ice. 'The police have explained broadly what happened. But you were there – the first on the scene. Would you mind telling us about it?'

I shrugged and took a sip. 'Not at all. It's quite a simple story. I was walking my two dogs along the public footpath. We were descending across the field called Top Close, towards the stile, if you know where that is?'

Andrew nodded. 'The police showed me earlier today.'

'I arrived later,' said Amelia. 'But I know it.'

This should have been a warning to me, but I ploughed on, oblivious. 'The dogs were ahead of me and started sniffing around something. I thought it was a pile of rags, and of course once I got closer, I saw that it wasn't. So then I went up towards the road, where there's a gate. I called the police, and then Lucy too, since I knew I'd be there for some time.'

'To come and collect the dogs, you see,' explained Lucy.

'You couldn't see it was Edmund – the body?' asked Amelia.

'No,' I replied. 'Not definitely; he was face down. But I knew we were on his land; I was pretty confident it was him. That's what I told the police, anyway. They were on the scene very fast.'

'Something about some sheep?' asked Andrew.

I took another sip of the excellent champagne. 'Yes. There were four of them milling about, near the gate, which was unlatched. The remnant of a flock of thirty, I now understand. The police seem to be of the view that this was a case of sheep rustling, and Edmund had disturbed the thieves. Or maybe he was trying to catch them.'

'You aren't of that view?' asked Andrew sharply.

'No. At least not the local travellers. Too close, and

Edmund's farmhand Jack Diggle came from there. Maybe a gang from further afield.'

'You know Jack, do you?' asked Andrew.

'Not well, but I've talked to him; I think he's a decent fellow,' I replied.

'I believe you've dismissed him, isn't that so?' asked Lucy coolly.

Andrew gave her his best attempt at a winning smile. 'Well, I've given him notice. Not quite the same thing. There are no sheep to look after.'

'What about the four who are left?' my wife replied.

'Oh, those have gone,' Andrew said, waving a hand airily. I didn't like to ask where.

'And Lesley Logan has gone too?' Lucy was like a dog with a bone.

'Yes. A housekeeper is no longer necessary. Nobody will be living here in a few days' time once the funeral is over.'

There was a lengthy pause.

'So what is going to happen to the farm?' I asked.

'That will depend on Edmund's will,' said Andrew. 'We're still looking for it.'

The resulting pause became rather difficult, and as a result, I fell into the trap which had been brewing ever since we'd arrived. 'I suppose he cut his former wife out of it?' I asked. 'She pushed off years ago, I believe.'

I sensed Lucy stiffen and saw the expression freeze on Andrew's face.

'Yes,' said Amelia quietly. 'I did.'

# CHAPTER NINE

Amelia was very good about it, but there was a certain froideur in the air after that, and we beat a retreat as soon as we decently could, gulping down our second glasses of champagne to finish the bottle quickly.

'Honestly...' began a vexed Lucy, once we were back in the car. 'What on earth...?'

'Well, how was I supposed to bloody know?' I countered, before she could get into her stride. 'She left the village before we ever arrived. She opened the door and said she was Amelia Ayling. I naturally assumed she was Andrew's wife.'

'Andrew is gay,' said Lucy firmly.

'How do you know?'

'Trust me, women know these things,' she replied, in a tone which brooked no argument. 'Plus, I've actually seen her before.'

'Well, that will have helped no doubt; certainly better than your gaydar. When?'

'Not physically. The Women's Institute, you know? They

have photo albums. I've been shown them. She appears. I recognised her straightaway.'

'You could have told me,' I said as I pulled out savagely into the road. 'You must have known that in the circumstances I'd jump to the wrong conclusion.'

There was no reply, and I looked across. My wife was struggling to contain herself and finally couldn't. 'It was so funny,' she burst out eventually. 'I'll dine out on that for years.'

'What?'

'Holmes' deductive powers at their zenith. And your face when you realised.'

There was no answer to that, or at least I couldn't think of a witty retort quickly enough, and anyway, we were already home. I got out of the car without a word, taking what was left of my injured pride with me.

\*\*\*

The next day was of course a Saturday, and after a suitably lazy start, I decided to take Theo and Rosie for their normal walk at just after 11am. Lucy declined to accompany me since it was rather overcast. There are any number of routes I could have taken, but for some reason I decided upon the reverse of the walk I had done on the day I discovered the body. Thus, I soon found myself gradually ascending the hill where I had met the Johnsons, with the stile looming in front of us.

I find that one of Sod's many laws is that if you don't particularly want to meet someone, you invariably will, and so it was on this occasion. I lifted the two dogs over the stile without a thought, and it was only after I had clambered over into Top Close myself that I realised I was not alone.

There stood Amelia Ayling, upon the spot where her husband had died. She turned around in surprise as she heard me, and I could see that she had been weeping. Feebly, she tried to wipe her tears away with the back of her sleeve.

'Amelia,' I began hesitantly, 'I am sorry to have surprised you.'

There was a momentary pause, then she shook her head vigorously. 'No need. It's a public footpath. You have every right to be here.'

We both felt awkward, so it was pretty much a matter of saying whatever first came into my head. 'Look, I'm sorry about last night. Not having met you before, I simply jumped to the incorrect conclusion.'

She smiled. 'Again, no need. My fault. I began to sort of wonder if you'd got the wrong end of the stick after a few minutes, but it was too late to bring it up then. It was quite funny actually.'

'That's what Lucy thought,' I admitted, relieved at how she was taking it.

There was another awkward pause, and this time, Amelia broke it. 'How far are you going?' she said, pushing down a muddy and overfriendly Rosie.

'I'm doing the reverse of what I did on the day, actually,' I replied. 'It's a circuit. Back along the track down there to the village.' I pointed.

'I know it well,' said Amelia. 'Mind if I come with you?' She looked at me anxiously.

I was surprised but not displeased. I liked her, and she was certainly an attractive woman: a Barbour, jeans and wellies is never the most flattering of attire, but she was the type who could carry it off with aplomb.

'Not at all,' I replied and meant it. 'Glad of the company.'

We started making our way across Top Close to the corner where we would meet the track in companionable silence. Eventually, I felt a need to say something. 'How long since you left here?' I asked.

She looked at me curiously with big grey eyes. 'Just over eleven years.'

I nodded. 'We've been here ten. Lucy did recognise you though; she'd seen your picture in some WI album.'

'Yes – I was a bit of a stalwart.'

Silence returned, until I broke it once more after a minute or so. 'Why did you leave, if that's not too personal a question?' I could sense her scrutinising me carefully. 'No need to answer if you don't want to.'

She smiled. 'It is indeed a personal question. But I don't mind, especially now Edmund's dead. He had a woman problem. Or more accurately a women problem, plural.'

A reply was obviously expected. 'I see,' I said carefully. 'Understandable then.'

Amelia shrugged. 'It happened several times. Mostly it was purely physical, and he agreed to change. But then he got seriously involved with someone. So I decided to go.'

I said nothing, and she continued.

'I thought it would shock him, and indeed it did: the affair ended there and then. He begged me to stay. But I was over the mental leap by then and had made plans. He brought it on himself.'

'No children?'

'No,' she said simply. 'What about you?'

'Yes – two,' I replied. 'Will and Ginny. First- and second-year students; they're both in London.'

We ambled on in silence for a bit.

'And have you remarried?' I asked eventually.

'Ha!' she said, with a harsh laugh. 'Edmund and I never even divorced!'

'Hence why you are up here, I suppose?'

'Well, he was of course my husband, and I did still care about him, as you saw when you caught me unawares by the stile,' Amelia replied. 'And there's a funeral to plan. But beyond that, as far as I can see, Edmund never changed his will from the one I have. Meaning that…'

'Unless he specified otherwise, as his wife you'll inherit the farm,' I concluded on her behalf.

'Yes – that's about the size of it,' Amelia confirmed. 'However, Andrew apparently thinks there is another will, which cut me out and left the farm to Edmund's family, meaning him; there are no other siblings. He's looking for it, though there's nothing lodged with Edmund's solicitor.'

'Awkward,' I said. 'Being under the same roof I mean.'

'You could say that,' said Amelia with an ironic smile. 'I'm here to protect my interests.'

\*\*\*

Once back in the village, we were soon approaching the junction of Newland Street and Griffin Road, where it would be time for us to part, with me heading straight on past the church till I reached home. Amelia had told me she was going to meet Andrew in The Swan, so she would need to turn right, winding her way through the village till she reached the pub after about two hundred yards.

We paused just before the junction whilst I put the dogs

on their leads, as I'd need to cross the main road before I reached home. Amelia waited whilst I did so and then turned abruptly towards me. 'Thanks for letting me accompany you,' she said brightly. 'I was feeling rather down, as you saw. You've cheered me up.' She still seemed a little fragile I thought, waiting anxiously for my reply.

'It was a pleasure, really,' I said. 'And I'm glad we cleared up that little misunderstanding of last night.'

Amelia laughed, very naturally, and suddenly leant forward to give me a peck on the cheek. It was completely unexpected, and I was at a loss. Before I had thought of anything to say, she turned smartly on her heel and began striding off down Griffin Road, past the little Methodist chapel, seldom used these days. She looked over her left shoulder to give me a little farewell wave.

I half-reciprocated, but she had already turned away, so I started towards home, which was no more than two hundred yards away.

I'd taken only a few steps before I perceived a figure standing in the gateway to the churchyard on the left; I hadn't seen him before because of the gatepost, but he would certainly have witnessed my parting from Amelia. Ivor Chubb.

'Morning,' I said, as I came abreast of him.

'Good morning indeed,' he said cheerily. 'It was for you, anyway.' It wasn't said in any nudge-nudge or malicious way; just an observation, and I wasn't sure of the intended implication.

'What do you mean, Ivor?' I asked curiously, pulling up.

'Oh, nothing – don't mind me,' he said with a chuckle and indicated the receding figure of Amelia. 'Mrs Ayling. Fine-looking woman. Always was.'

'Just a dog walk together, and an accidental one at that; I bumped into her outside the village. I wouldn't read too much into what you just saw.' I smiled.

'I won't,' replied Ivor. 'But seriously, people can get the wrong idea.'

'What on earth are you saying?'

'Not her,' responded Ivor, jerking his thumb. 'I know she hasn't been around for a decade or more.'

I was still mystified and said nothing.

Ivor sighed. 'Look,' he said, in a long-suffering tone. 'You know I work for Ned Logan at Ritche's Lodge Farm?'

'Sure.' I nodded.

'Well, he's got it into his head that you have eyes for his wife. And he's a man who cares.'

'That is absurd,' I snorted. 'Granted that Lesley works for us three mornings a week, but I'm very seldom there when she does. I did give her a lift home the other day in the pouring rain when I couldn't get to London because of a rail strike, and Ned saw us. But you know how far that is – I doubt we were in the car together for more than a couple of minutes.'

'Flirting, Ned says,' said Ivor, stoutly.

I felt exasperated and, what is more, guilty, even though I had nothing to reproach myself for. 'Ridiculous,' I replied. 'I made some feeble joke when Lesley got out of the car, which she was good enough to smile at. That's all that happened.'

Ivor shook his head resignedly. 'I believe you, really I do. I've been there: Ned once found me having a cup of tea with Lesley in the kitchen. But that's all in the past now. Be careful. He's watching you. He gets sudden obsessions about people, and you're the latest.'

\*\*\*

'Developments, Watson,' I shouted into the kitchen as I was changing out of my boots a couple of minutes later.

'Come and tell me over a coffee,' came the reply.

Which I proceeded to do. I explained my chance meeting with Amelia; her tears; my apology to her for the previous night; our walk together; her unterminated marriage to Edmund; and, finally, the will issue.

'You've been busy, Holmes,' said Lucy, with mock solemnity. 'I'm impressed. Genuinely.' She paused for a moment, and I could sense the cogs grinding. 'She couldn't have done it, could she?' mused my wife eventually.

I was startled. 'Why on earth do you say that?'

'Well, think about it. What if she'd learnt that Edmund was about to change his will?'

I did think about it, for about a second. 'Pretty far-fetched,' I replied, in best Holmesian fashion. 'I'm sure she's got some alibi. She'd have to get up here undetected; not be seen around here before or afterwards; obtain a weapon; dispose of it; get notified of the death somewhere well away... I think we can discount her. And those tears I saw this morning were genuine.'

I thought this had nailed Lucy's surprising theory convincingly, but she's more stubborn than that.

'Accomplice?'

I raised an eyebrow. 'Who?'

This was met by a rather deflated silence, so I thought we'd move on. 'And in another development,' I continued jovially, 'Ned Logan thinks I've got designs on his wife.'

I expected Lucy to be amused by this patently ridiculous

scenario, but instead she was horrified. 'On Lesley? Who on earth told you that?'

Seeing this reaction, I clicked into serious mode myself. 'Ivor Chubb; I bumped into him by the church – he was just giving me a friendly warning. Apparently, it all stems from when I gave her a lift home in the rain the other day. I told you about Ned's reaction, remember?'

Lucy pursed her lips. 'Believe me, you need to take this seriously. If Ned is suspicious of you, it is bad news.'

# CHAPTER TEN

'Surely it can't be that bad?' I retorted. 'The man's known to be unreasonable in that respect. It'll soon blow over.'

'Unreasonable, that's the point,' replied Lucy. 'Unreasonable people do irrational things.' She looked more fearful than thoughtful, which was unlike her, so I thought I'd better probe further.

'As in, has he acted on these suspicions before? To a dangerous extent?' I asked.

She looked at me pensively.

'There is something, isn't there?' I asked. 'Go on, spit it out.'

'He was never charged with anything,' replied Lucy defensively. 'But yes, there's been talk.'

'Who?'

'Oh, it doesn't matter.' She shrugged. 'It was about six months ago. Ned was apparently suspicious of someone, and next thing you know, that chap's got slashed tyres, a keyed car and poison pen letters.'

'That's not funny. Who was it?'

Though she was clearly reluctant to tell me, Lucy seemed to decide that she had no choice, given that her husband was possibly facing a similar threat. 'Sam Johnson. It was all nonsense of course, but he was convinced it was Ned. Big strong guy, as you know. He confronted Ned, who denied everything, but it all stopped after that.'

I paused to visualise the burly builder I'd met on the way down the hill after discovering the body. He certainly wasn't a man I would mess with. 'How do you know about all this?'

'Annie, his wife. The WI. It was pretty common knowledge there. There's quite a lot that goes on in the village you men don't know about,' Lucy said coyly.

I ignored this feminine provocation, though not without an uncomfortable feeling that it was probably true. 'What about Lesley, what did she say?'

Lucy looked mildly deflated, even shamefaced. 'I don't know. Never asked her. Not my business.'

I thought for a moment. 'I still think it'll all blow over, assuming there's anything in it at all. But I'll put the car away in the garage tonight to be on the safe side.'

\*\*\*

That evening it was fine and sunny, and I was sitting out in the garden reading my weekly *Spectator* over a glass of excellent rosé when I became aware of a disturbance. There's always a bit of traffic passing on the road between Market Harborough and Desborough across the fifteenth-century bridge over the River Jordan (it's more of a stream really) just beyond the bottom of our garden, some thirty yards away, but I was used to that and had long ago learnt to tune it out.

This was different: it was voices. Raised voices. Female voices.

It was too far away for me to hear much, but one voice was shouting much more loudly than the other, which was replying in a controlled, barely audible fashion. I'm not a nosey person, you understand, but somehow, I found myself at the wattle fence atop our garden wall, which you can see through without being seen if you care to. It brought me within twenty yards of whatever was going on.

The woman making all the noise was Marlene Filler, whom I knew by sight but not much more. She was standing right in the middle of the road opposite our house which leads past the church and shouting (or more accurately screaming) at the other woman, who I could see was Amelia. My dog walk companion of the morning had turned to face this verbal assault beside the home of our friends, the doctor and his wife. Amelia did not appear to be intimidated in any way and was calmly giving simple, one-word answers to a barrage of abuse which included the words 'bitch', 'harlot', 'gold digger' and much else besides, together with invitations to perform the physically impossible upon herself as far away as possible.

And I'd always thought Marlene to be dull as ditch water.

Before I could understand what was going on, I'd been joined by Rosie, barking loudly at the unfamiliar noise; it was enough to provoke a glance in my direction from Amelia, if not Marlene, so I retreated gently from behind the wall back into our garden, but not before I had noticed both Andrew Ayling and Marlene's husband Steve standing sheepishly on the sidelines of the argument either side of the road. Steve was trying to coax Marlene away down the road past the church; Andrew was feebly trying to entice Amelia away to my left across the bridge, in a different direction.

When I got back to the table, I found Lucy sitting there, having poured herself a glass from the bottle of rosé. 'What was all that about?' she asked curiously. 'Someone didn't sound too pleased.'

'Marlene. I don't know what about, though I can tell you one thing: she has no time at all for Amelia.'

'Sounded a bit stronger than that.'

'Well, as you know, I'm an understated sort of chap. No doubt she has her reasons.'

\*\*\*

You know how sometimes you can miss an important piece of news just because you're away, and everybody assumes you know once you reappear since it's presumed to be common knowledge?

Monday was rather like that for Lucy and I. Off to London I went as normal, and Lucy (usually my eyes and ears in the village) departed for the christening of her former flatmate's latest progeny in deepest Norfolk, to whom she was Godmother. Odd day for a christening, but there you go.

So we were oblivious to what happened and only learnt about it on Wednesday morning, which was one of the times Lesley worked for us. It was also of course the day of the funeral, which was scheduled for 2pm, so I'd taken the day off.

I thought about mentioning Ivor's warning about Ned's fixation on me, which I presumed Lesley would instantly declare absurd, but some sixth sense warned me against that, so I didn't. The gap in our knowledge only emerged when Lucy and I were sitting down with Lesley for a mid-morning coffee in the kitchen.

Lucy started the ball rolling with a general, conversation-making query.

'So how are things at Braybrooke Farm?'

Lesley looked at her askance. 'Well, not so great after Monday I imagine.'

Lucy and I looked at each other in bafflement.

'You mean you don't know?' said Lesley in disbelief.

'No. Neither of us was here that day,' I replied.

Lucy and I waited for an explanation.

Lesley sighed before replying. 'Jack Diggle went to pick up some machinery from the farm, which he said was his. You know, after Andrew sacked him. But Andrew thought Jack was stealing it. There was a row, very nearly a fight. Amelia broke it up.'

'Turn your back for a minute here…' said Lucy, shaking her head. 'Was it all sorted out?'

'I don't think so,' replied Lesley. 'Jack was uninvited to Edmund's funeral tomorrow but said he'd be going anyway to say goodbye to his friend, and what was Andrew going to do about it?'

'You were there, were you?' asked Lucy curiously. 'Heard all this first hand?'

Lesley looked a little embarrassed. 'Yes, I'm working there till Andrew leaves, which won't be long, and I went there on Monday after finishing here since you were away. So I heard.'

'I'm surprised you were there at all given the way he's treated you,' I said.

'Well, cash is cash,' she said, casting her eyes down and beginning to blush. 'And beggars can't be choosers.'

There was a pause; I was embarrassed at my thoughtlessness and received a gentle kick under the table from my wife, together with a reproachful look.

'Well, plenty to be getting on with still,' declared Lesley decisively after a few moments. 'I'll need to leave a few minutes early today if you don't mind. To change.'

'Change?' I asked.

'For the funeral, Holmes,' said Watson sweetly.

\*\*\*

Once Lesley had left, we toddled off to get changed ourselves, and as ever, it took me a fraction of the time my dear wife required. I was downstairs with half an hour to spare before we needed to cross the road and walk the fifty yards to the church, so I made myself a coffee and sat down in the kitchen to have a think.

It wasn't quite as structured as it may appear below, but what I broadly concluded over fifteen minutes or so, and needed Holmes and Watson to investigate, was:

Marlene hated Amelia. Why?

Ned was paranoid about his wife and other men (specifically at the moment, me). Did he have reason to be, and did he constitute a genuine threat?

Who had Edmund left the farm to, and what were the implications of that in terms of a motive for anyone?

Were the police still focused on the sheep rustling theory, and if so, did Jack have a place in that?

Lots of second-order questions fell out of this of course, but I was pleased with my little analysis, to the extent of jotting down a quick summary in my phone. I was on the point of making another deduction when Lucy appeared, and of course I had to declare that she looked a vision, which indeed she did.

'Ready?' she asked briskly.

'Ready,' I confirmed, rising to my feet. 'And keep your eyes open, Watson.'

# CHAPTER ELEVEN

All Saints Church in Braybrooke is rather fine, parts of it dating from the thirteenth century, and as we approached, I contemplated the magnificent steeple, wondering for the umpteenth time at the immense time and effort its construction would have required; even today the village numbers barely 350 souls. Our forebears certainly had sticking power.

Lucy and I arrived promptly, and deliberately so, because we wanted to ensure a good view of proceedings given that they seemed likely to be pivotal to the case. We weren't family of course, but we secured seats next to the aisle about a third of the way back on the left-hand side and, having done so, nodded at each other in satisfaction before turning to examine our service sheets in time-honoured fashion.

They were expensively produced and featured a colour photo of Edmund on the rear, as is now increasingly common: he was in his prime, perhaps thirty-five, and sitting proudly on what appeared to be a brand-new tractor. I skimmed briefly through the order of service itself and noted that Andrew Ayling would be giving the oration – that might be revealing.

Trying not to be too obvious, I began discreetly scanning other members of the congregation, some already present and others still arriving of course. One row ahead of us on the other side of the aisle were the Johnsons, in quiet conversation with someone in the pew ahead of them whom I didn't recognise. Well to the rear in a pew adjoining the wall on the opposite side of the church was Ned Logan, scrubbed up but looking awkward; he'd cut himself shaving. Beside him was Lesley, who looked splendid. She caught my eye and gave me a discreet little smile. Ned twitched impatiently as she did so, and I wondered if he'd noticed, an unwelcome reinforcement of his delusions about me if he had.

I shifted my gaze swiftly and alighted on Jack as he entered the church, together with another young chap. It didn't look as if it was a familiar environment for either of them. They settled inconspicuously in a pew at the back, close to the entrance. Nearby was Ivor, with a couple of his drinking buddies, whispering together cheerfully. Their suits had all been bought when they were much younger and slimmer men, many thousands of pints ago.

Lucy turned to talk to a middle-aged couple arriving in the pew behind us. Again, people I didn't know, but no doubt the wife was a fellow member of the village's WI. I looked beyond them, and right at the back of the church, my eye fell upon Detective Inspector Peter Yardley and Detective Sergeant Fiona Challis, sitting silently together like any established couple easy in each other's company. That was probably what they wanted people to think, I surmised. Interesting.

It was a funeral of course, not a memorial service, and that meant a coffin. Suddenly, the gentle whispering of the congregation began to hush, starting by the entrance and rippling out from there, and almost simultaneously, the processional music began, played by the village's estimable organist, Annie Johnson. Seconds later, the pall-bearers appeared, led by the funeral director, clutching his black hat. There were six of them, all well used to the job, judging by the adept way they negotiated the right-hand turn onto the aisle. The burliest of them brushed against me as the procession went past, and within seconds, they had placed the coffin on the trestles set up for the purpose in the nave, another practised drill well carried out.

Behind the procession came the vicar. These days, they are spread pretty thin, and I'm never quite sure who that's going to be on the rare occasions we attend church. Some are undoubtedly better than others, but I was relieved to see in his cassock an elderly white-haired priest I knew only as Mark; he was almost certainly retired, but I had always admired his quiet humility and his simple homespun sermons. It would be a dignified service.

Then came the family.

\*\*\*

Andrew and Amelia were leading, side by side, which must have been somewhat awkward given the existence between them of the issue of Edmund's will, but they looked impressively unified. Amelia's dark suit was navy rather than black, as I recall, and she was hatless. Looking back as they approached, I caught her eye and gave her a brief nod. She nodded back solemnly in response, looking gaunt and sad but rather beautiful, and then they swept by, followed by two other middle-aged couples, presumably relatives of some sort. I was aware that Amelia and Edmund had no children, so the absence of anyone obviously of the next generation came as no surprise.

The procession settled themselves into the front pew on the opposite side from Lucy and I, with Andrew and Amelia on the outside. Then we were into the bidding prayer. As the vicar cleared his throat, I glanced at the service sheet. The Reverend Mark Hickson. The prayer itself passed me by, but it was brief.

And so to the first hymn – rather unusually, it was 'We Plough the Fields and Scatter', which I assume was a homage to Edmund's life as a farmer. The church was full, which meant over two hundred voices, and they did the old hymn full justice.

The service sheet didn't say who was going to make the first reading, and as people settled back into their pews, I was surprised to see Andrew Ayling stand aside to let out Amelia.

'The first reading will be given by Mrs Amelia Ayling,' intoned the vicar, as she reached the lectern and turned to face the congregation. Amelia looked up suddenly and waited until there was absolute silence in the church. Her eyes did not drop. It was very short but beautifully delivered – a recital from memory, not a reading at all.

*If I should go before the rest of you*
*Break not a flower nor inscribe a stone,*
*Nor when I've gone speak in a Sunday voice,*

*But be the usual selves that I have known.*
*Weep if you must,*
*Parting is hell,*
*But life must go on,*
*So sing as well.*

She kept looking straight ahead with what seemed like defiance at the end, daring someone to stand and declare that she and Edmund were separated. But of course, nobody did. I glanced down at my service sheet. Joyce Grenfell.

Amelia did not drop her powerful gaze for several seconds, and the congregation seemed collectively to exhale once she did.

There was another prayer. And then another hymn: 'Lead us, Heavenly Father, Lead Us'. And then we were settling into our pews again for the main event: Andrew Ayling.

\*\*\*

Andrew was in public relations, I'd learnt during our drinks at Braybrooke Farm, and people from that background are usually pretty adept on their feet. That said, Andrew did not appear as self-confident as his sister-in-law as he made his way rather diffidently to the pulpit, but neither was he overtly nervous. His address was pre-prepared in a slim red A4-sized folder, which he laid deliberately on the lectern and opened. Then he looked up and took stock for a moment of the many attentive faces waiting on him. I had no idea what to expect but found myself willing him to succeed.

'Edmund was my brother,' he began, 'and yet we were not at all alike, the eight-year age gap notwithstanding. I'm a city person, and he was a man of the soil, as all residents of this village will know, he lived here for thirty years.'

There was a pause; rather longer than seemed natural. Andrew seemed to be gathering himself.

'Just as you will all know how he died.'

He paused again. There was dead silence in the church, indeed a high degree of tension.

'His was a violent death, but I do not want my brother remembered simply as a murder victim. He was a generous, well-loved person who went out of his way to help people. His life had its ups and downs, and its complications, as does everyone's – indeed he and his wife Amelia, here today, were separated, something else that most of you will be well aware of.'

I glanced across at Amelia, several rows to my front and the opposite side of the aisle. I couldn't see her expression, but her head was bowed.

'What you may not know, however,' continued Andrew calmly, 'is that they were very close to reconciling.'

Again, he paused for dramatic effect and achieved that: the congregation was rapt.

'Who can tell,' he continued, 'whether that circumstance had a role in what befell him. Certainly, I cannot, and I know that the police, who I see are also here today, are still pursuing their inquiries.'

There was another long pause.

'Personally, I think it most improbable that this tragedy came about because of a few stolen sheep.'

I saw him glance up briefly, looking for someone.

'I welcome here today especially Jack Diggle, who was my brother's employee, and furthermore his friend. It pains me that I cannot keep him on, but the farm is to be sold. Also, Lesley Logan: a great support to my brother in his later years.'

No mention of the disputed farm ownership of course – it was neither the time nor the place.

'Let me finish on a note that is perhaps controversial, but nonetheless I believe it to be true. As we commend Edmund's soul to eternal rest, let us also extend our Christian forgiveness to his killer. For I believe that person to be in this church today.'

\*\*\*

There was an audible gasp from someone and a brief ripple of conversation. I cannot for the life of me now recall much about the remainder of the service, other than the shock on the vicar's face, together with Lucy's look of wide-eyed amazement as she turned towards me, mouthing, 'Wow.' Everyone else was doing something similar; only Andrew seemed oblivious of the furore he had caused as he returned quietly to his pew.

As subtly as I could, I glanced around the church as we turned to our service sheets for the next hymn, 'The Lord's My Shepherd' – possibly another less-than-subtle reference to Edmund's farming background. But I couldn't be too blatant about it, and even if there was a murderer amongst us, a guilty reaction to Andrew's denunciation was hardly to be expected. I did notice, however, that I was far from the only one looking furtively around, and the singing seemed to be distinctly more ragged than it had been for the first hymn.

A palpable sense of shock permeated around the church and completely overshadowed the rest of the proceedings. I found myself wondering what Andrew had hoped to achieve by his action, which he must have known would have a sensational effect.

And all too soon, it was over. Mark, the vicar, notified all present that there would be a short private interment in the churchyard immediately after the service and that thereafter the family would join the others in The Swan. Everyone present was invited to attend should they so wish. Then he led the coffin back up the aisle, his lips pursed in what seemed to be a thin line of disapproval. Leading those behind were Andrew and Amelia, side by side, his expression neutral, hers decidedly grieving, indeed she looked close to tears. Again, I gave her a little nod but received no reaction this time. She probably didn't even notice.

It was as we all started clumsily exiting our pews and making our way out of the church that I got my first decent look at others. Mostly they were pretty non-committal, though Sam Johnson caught my eye and grimaced with a little shake of his head when we turned into the aisle from opposite sides.

As Lucy and I shuffled up the aisle before turning left towards the entrance, we found ourselves face to face with Peter Yardley and Fiona Challis, approaching from the opposite direction.

The inspector looked phlegmatic and raised his eyebrows. His female sergeant simply looked angry.

# CHAPTER TWELVE

The Swan is about three hundred yards from the church: you turn right out of the gate where I had spoken to Ivor Chubb after my walk with Amelia and follow the winding Griffin Road through the heart of the village till you come across the old thatched pub on the right-hand side. All the way there, couples and close friends drew naturally together; there was none of the superficial chat with strangers that is so commonplace on such occasions. Lucy and I were no different. And of course there was only one topic of conversation.

'Do you think he's right?' enquired my rather subdued wife sotto voce, after looking around to ensure nobody else was within earshot.

I'd been pondering this ever since the accusation had been so publicly made. 'If it's not sheep rustlers – and I'm increasingly inclined to believe it's not – then...' I spread my hands expressively.

'You think he is!' stated Lucy firmly. 'You do, don't you?'

I nodded briefly.

'So do I. Who?'

'I really don't know.' I shrugged. 'There's a lot we don't understand. If I was to speculate, then I'd say it's wrapped up with Edmund's women issues. Maybe jealousy of him and Lesley – unmerited no doubt, but we know Ned's prone to it. So that's one possibility.'

'Who else?'

'Whoever wouldn't like him getting back together with Amelia.'

'Well, Marlene clearly doesn't like her, full stop – hence that row in the street the other day. And she had an affair with Edmund.'

'So you say,' I replied. We were passing the village hall now, and it was only another hundred yards or so to the pub. 'But I agree they're clearly not bosom buddies. Wonder what the story is there?'

'Well, I wouldn't be bosom buddies with anyone who was having an affair with you,' retorted Lucy primly. 'And I'd expect that to be reciprocated. There's probably not much more to it than that.'

'Perhaps,' I said non-committally. 'Of course, then there's the whole question of the will.'

Lucy raised her eyes enigmatically as we turned into the car park and seemed about to say something, but by then we were closing up on others at the entrance to the pub.

It would have to wait.

\*\*\*

The family were still at the interment of course when we arrived, so there was no receiving line and hence no focal point. Like everyone else, Lucy and I were therefore somewhat at a loss once we had been issued a glass of wine apiece by the waitresses at the pub's entrance. We moved through the main part of the bar, old and heavily beamed, and into the airy new annex, usually decked out as a restaurant but cleared that day to cope with a sizeable reception. There we took stock.

The first thing I noticed was Ned Logan, and he was staring at me. He looked away hastily as I met his gaze, and my eyes shifted immediately to Lesley, standing alongside her husband. Unlike her husband, she returned my stare steadily and then gave the briefest of shrugs, almost an apology it seemed. Then she turned to talk to some woman who was fast approaching her.

Lucy noticed this little pantomime and gave me a quick grimace. Then we were face to face with the two police officers. The meeting seemed deliberately contrived, though not obviously so.

Yardley made his opening gambit with bonhomie, but I sensed a measure of professional reserve as he did so. 'Mr Rowland, good afternoon. Mrs Rowland,' he said, nodding at Lucy. They hadn't yet met.

'Good afternoon, Inspector,' my wife replied, holding out her hand. 'Lucy Rowland.'

There was an awkward pause after Yardley had shaken her hand. I was about to fill it with some trite remark when Lucy beat me to it with something far more meaningful. 'Do you think Andrew Ayling is correct in asserting that there is a murderer amongst those of us in the church?' she said.

Peter Yardley was a pretty phlegmatic character, but I

could tell that he was surprised by such a direct question. He sized Lucy up silently.

'It is certainly a possibility, Mrs Rowland,' stated Fiona Challis. 'It may even be a probability. But it was not helpful to have the potential killer alerted in such fashion, even assuming his presence.'

'Or hers,' added Yardley. He paused for a moment. 'Even if not present, word will reach the killer of that outburst.'

'So I take it you've discounted the sheep rustling theory?' I asked him.

Yardley looked up sharply. 'I have discounted nothing,' he said firmly and moved on past us.

I thought Fiona Challis was going to blank me too, but she gave me a tiny smile with a little wink as she followed in her boss's wake.

\*\*\*

'That's you told,' said Lucy sympathetically, taking in my forlorn expression. 'Sorry if my question dropped you in it.'

'And here's someone else intent on telling me something, if I'm not mistaken,' I murmured quietly, looking over her shoulder.

Lucy turned swiftly around.

Marlene Filler clearly wanted to speak to me and was approaching with some determination. I took the sight in at a glance: a short brunette, probably nearer fifty-five than fifty, greying, tightly cut hair, slim figure just beginning to bulk out a bit. She had made an effort for the service and was smartly dressed in purple, albeit in dated fashion. It seemed she had been pretty once, but the harsh line of her mouth and her brusque manner put paid to that. *Rather you than me, Edmund*, I thought rather ungallantly. I braced myself, for what I did not know.

'Mr Rowland,' she began forcefully in her slight German accent as she halted in front of me. 'I am Marlene Filler. I don't believe we have ever spoken. Though of course I know Lucy from the WI.' She nodded at my wife, who seemed lost for words.

'Well...' I began warily.

The harsh mouth softened into a rictus which took in both of us. 'May I call you Robert?' she asked in the sort of coquettish little voice that generally has me running for the hills.

'Of course.' I nodded dumbly, still unsighted to what this was all about.

'I should very much like a private word, if I may, Robert,' she said in a proprietorial tone, taking me by the sleeve and steering me out of the annex's French windows into the garden, which was populated only by a few unreconstructed smokers. I barely had time to register Lucy looking worriedly after us.

Marlene turned to face me and seemed to expect me to start the conversation. Instead, I simply raised my eyebrows.

She shrugged resignedly. 'I wish to apologise,' she said after a second or so and paused to look me firmly in the eye.

'What on earth for?' I replied, utterly baffled. 'You have done nothing whatsoever to offend me.'

She scrunched up her face and shrugged again with every appearance of helplessness. 'You English, always so polite.'

There was a pause, as if she was weighing something up, then she clearly came to a decision. 'There was a fracas outside your house the other evening. Saturday. I think you may have heard it?'

'I certainly heard something. But it was indistinct; I understood nothing meaningful. None of my business,' I mumbled. 'There is certainly no need to apologise; it was all over in seconds.'

Marlene shook her head regretfully. 'Nonetheless, I lost my temper. Unforgivable.'

'If that is what this is about, then if it makes you feel any better, then of course I forgive you. We have all allowed ourselves to become riled occasionally,' I replied, in the most reassuring tone I could muster.

Marlene smiled briefly and nodded in gratitude, but her expression faded quickly into a suspicious stare. 'Do you have any idea what that argument was about?'

'None at all,' I answered truthfully. 'And even if I did, as I say – none of my business.'

Marlene looked searchingly into my eyes, gauging my sincerity. After a couple of seconds, she stepped back, seemingly satisfied. 'Good,' she said decisively. 'Had you done so, I had steeled myself to appeal to your discretion as a gentleman. But it seems that will not be necessary. Good day to you on this very sad occasion.' And with that, she was gone, strangely dignified, leaving me none the wiser as Lucy appeared at my side.

***

'What on earth was all that about?' she enquired, once Marlene had returned inside.

'Search me,' I replied. 'She seemed worried that I'd

overheard something I shouldn't have during that squabble she was involved in the other day, you know, when she was shouting at Amelia outside the house.'

'But you didn't hear anything, did you, Holmes?'

'Sadly not, Watson.'

'Careless. A potential clue lost.'

She took my arm, and we were about to venture back inside when I noticed one of the smokers eyeing me up from the opposite end of the garden. Jack Diggle.

I gave him a brief nod; he uncoiled himself unhurriedly from the benched table he was sitting at with his earlier companion from the church and extinguished his cigarette.

'Who's that?' hissed Lucy as the lanky figure made his way towards us, clutching a pint of beer.

'The sheep guy – Jack,' I replied out of the side of my mouth. 'I had a drink here with him, remember?'

Lucy nodded briefly, and I made the introductions as Jack appeared in front of us. He seemed in a friendly mood. 'Interesting service, Mr Rowland,' Jack began, in a neutral tone.

'Indeed,' I replied. 'Andrew was very complimentary of you.'

'Which you must have thought surprising, given that he sacked me,' replied Jack. 'But he's back-pedalling now, even admitted he might have been a bit hasty. Rang specially this morning to say that I'd be welcome today after all. I respect him for that, though I'd have come anyway.'

'Yes, that is a change of tack,' I said. 'What do you make of it?'

Jack shrugged. 'Reckon he's decided I had nothing to do with Edmund's death. Which I didn't. Plus, I think Amelia Ayling stuck up for me too.'

I paused to digest this. It made sense, all the more so if Andrew's right to sack anyone from the farm was potentially questionable, as I knew from my conversation with Amelia that it might be.

'What did you think of Andrew's bombshell at the service, Jack?' asked Lucy, changing the subject once the pause had become uncomfortable.

Jack looked at her seriously for a moment and took a sip of his beer. 'Reckon he's right,' he replied after a second or so. 'Someone local did it. Definitely.'

# CHAPTER THIRTEEN

We gravitated back inside and saw that the family group had now arrived following the interment. I wanted to have a quick word with both Andrew and Amelia, but of course everyone else thought likewise, and it was twenty minutes or so before the crowd around them had thinned sufficiently for us to join the diminished, impromptu receiving line. Amelia had just seen off some gushing old boy and looked momentarily frazzled as she turned to see who was next. Gratifyingly, she smiled when she saw it was us.

'We're so sorry, Amelia,' said Lucy, opening her arms to give the new widow a hug. 'Edmund was a nice man. He didn't deserve what happened to him.'

Amelia stood back after the hug and smiled ironically. 'Nice? Well, not always, but often. And you're right. Edmund didn't deserve to die like that.'

'Quite a line from Andrew,' I said quietly as I kissed her on the cheek, her brother-in-law being only a few feet away. 'There's been talk of nothing else since.'

'Yes, we discussed it this morning. He wasn't sure whether to say it or not – said he'd make up his mind on the spot. Do you think it was a terrible thing to say?'

'Not if it's true,' I replied, watching her carefully. She noticed but didn't seem to mind.

'We both think it is,' she said firmly and turned to meet her next sympathiser, leaving us facing Andrew.

I wasn't sure whether he'd heard my exchange with Amelia. Certainly, he gave no sign of it. Indeed, he looked quite invigorated, a phenomenon I've noticed quite often at funerals: individuals are buoyed by the unexpected strength of support they suddenly feel.

'Thank you both for coming,' he said before we had a chance to say anything. Lucy said nothing but smiled and leant in for a kiss; I fancied I saw a tear in her eye.

'We are so sorry, Andrew,' I said. 'And well spoken. It was brave of you.'

He smiled gratefully. 'Not the word the police used just now,' he replied. 'But thank you; I don't regret what I said.'

We moved on swiftly, as one does on such occasions: it was no time for a protracted conversation; indeed, it was probably time to start heading home now we had paid our respects. Nothing was said between Lucy and I, but long-married couples evolve a mutual empathy at such moments, and so we left the annex and headed back into the pub proper.

There's only one exit from The Swan, and Lucy suddenly pulled up in front of me. Picking my way through the throng behind her, I glanced up to see why she had halted.

The reason was obvious: she'd seen who we'd have to pass to reach it.

***

Right by the door were Ned and Lesley Logan, with Ivor Chubb not far away, clutching his pint and laughing with one of his mates. Lucy grabbed the bull by the horns and strode cheerfully up to Lesley, ignoring her husband.

'Well, what a service, eh?' she began.

Lesley smiled cautiously and began to respond.

The intended distraction didn't work. Ned was fixated on me, and before I knew it, he was tugging at my sleeve, pulling me away from the ladies. 'Mr Rowland, I want a word with you,' he said. It didn't sound like a request.

'This is probably not the time—' I began stiffly.

'Bugger that,' said Ned angrily, raising his voice sufficiently for people to hear. Ivor looked round and began to monitor the situation keenly. 'Now.' Ned realised he was attracting attention and dropped his voice again. 'Please.'

It was much more of a plea than an order this time; I had little option to accede if I was to avoid a scene. We were in the little alcove to the right of the door by now, with others instinctively giving us space, though I saw Lucy giving me a worried glance as she spoke with Ned's wife.

'If you must then. Please be quick; my wife is waiting.'

Ned looked round and picked out Lucy, still in dialogue with Lesley. Then he twisted back to me. 'Won't take long. Rumour is you're talking to my wife.'

The strange thing about that sentence is that when you read it on the page it sounds aggressive, almost a challenge. But it wasn't like that at all – there was an air of quiet desperation about it. I felt sorry for the man rather than defensive.

'Look, Ned,' I began. It probably came over as rather condescending, though that wasn't my intention. 'If you're talking about that time I brought her home in the rain to save her a soaking then please don't worry. We were in the car together for no more than a couple of minutes. That's all it was.'

'Girl's a flirt. Saw her trying it on with you.'

'No. I made a feeble joke as she got out of the car, and she was polite enough to smile at it. That's all.'

Ned looked anguished. Then he was back in pleading mode. 'Please don't get involved with her. For your own sake.'

I don't like being threatened, and as a result my response was abrupt. 'I am not involved with your wife, Ned, and have no intention of becoming so. I have a wife of my own, whom I love very much. Now please put this absurdity out of your head.' I swung away from him before he could respond. 'Come on, Lucy. We're going.'

\*\*\*

We strode home in silence, Lucy recognising my anger at being so publicly confronted. Even the cheerful welcome of the dogs didn't lighten my mood. The kettle went on immediately we arrived, precursor to many a marital confab in our household.

'What's on your mind?' Lucy said quietly once we were settled at the kitchen table.

'You know what's on my mind. You saw it.'

Lucy shrugged elegantly. 'Rise above it. People know what he's like; there'll be ten minutes of gossip before people return to the main topic around here, which is of course the murder. Don't react.'

'Easier said than done.' I paused for a moment, hesitating to raise the topic that had occurred to me on the walk back from the pub. 'Look...' I began.

'Spit it out,' responded my wife patiently, reaching out across the table to take my hand.

'Well, I don't see that she can possibly remain working here. Lesley.' There, I'd said it.

Lucy sat bolt upright. 'Why on earth not?'

'Because it'll just fuel Ned's paranoia.'

'Nonsense – you're hardly ever here when Lesley is. Easy enough to make sure Ned knows that. I'm sure she could tell him herself if it would help defuse things.'

'I don't take kindly to being threatened. So let's just remove the root cause of that threat.'

Lucy paused for a moment, and I could see her cogitating. Then she blew out her cheeks decisively. 'We simply can't do it. Impossible.'

'Why not?'

'Consider Lesley's position in all this,' Lucy replied calmly. 'One – she has money worries. Two – Andrew's just sacked her from two fifths of her employment. And three—'

'OK – I get it,' I said, as the realisation hit me. I raised my palms in surrender. 'We'd be sacking her from the other three fifths.'

'Yes. You do understand then, darling?' Lucy was still holding my hand across the table.

I nodded regretfully. As ever, she was right.

\*\*\*

We moved on to review the whole service and its aftermath.

'Coppers not pleased,' said Lucy.

'Oh, I don't know,' I replied. 'Didn't you see that light-hearted wink Challis gave me? I don't think Andrew will have done much harm. Nobody believes that sheep rustling theory, so chances are he was right. It was someone in the church.'

'I did not see that female detective wink at you, and I'm sure she took good care that I didn't,' said Lucy frostily. Then she paused. 'But it seems we have a proper whodunnit here, Holmes.'

'Yes. What does Watson think?'

Lucy drained her tea, reflected and poured herself another cup. I helped myself to one too.

'There are quite a few mysteries,' she opined after a further moment.

'Such as?'

'Well, what's the situation with the will? I'm not sure it has any bearing on the case, but it might do.'

'Yes,' I agreed. 'Do the police even know about that? Or the Amelia/Marlene spat?'

'She's probably worried that the affair with Edmund will come out. But we know about that. Everybody does.'

'I didn't till you told me a few days ago.'

Lucy raised her eyes to the heavens. No comment necessary. 'Should we tell them about those things? The police?'

I paused to consider. In truth, we had precious little to go on, and I was loath to trouble Yardley and his team with unsubstantiated gossip, nor to cause blameless neighbours unnecessary trouble. 'Let's do a bit more digging first, shall we? See if we can find out anything more tangible.'

Lucy nodded her assent. 'Something else,' she said. I waited expectantly. 'Jack. Why's he now back in Andrew's good books?'

I frowned. 'Yes, that was strange. I can understand him ringing up to reinvite Jack to the service if he thought he'd overreacted earlier, but surely that tribute in front of everyone was a bit over the top?'

We sank into a reflective silence.

'And as for Logan…' I began.

Lucy raised her hand. 'Don't. We've been there.'

# CHAPTER FOURTEEN

The next day I went to London, worked a normal day and then returned to St Pancras to find that my evening train had been cancelled or 'delayed', as the operating franchises seem to call it these days, probably on legal advice. So I had an hour to kill before the next train.

I texted Lucy to tell her I'd be late and then cast around moodily for something to while away the time. There were lots of other disgruntled passengers doing likewise on a warm evening; the first that spring. I decided to visit the station bookshop, a branch of Hatchards, which is always a standby of mine, slightly to Lucy's despair as I never leave empty-handed.

Having made the inevitable purchase, I was on my way out when I bumped into Sam Johnson, the builder, intent, presumably, on the same time-killing mission. Now, it's pretty common to meet local acquaintances who work in London on the platform at St Pancras, for obvious reasons, but I'd never seen Sam there before, whose business was all based in the Midlands.

Sam had a preoccupied look about him and was startled

when I called his name. 'Hello, mate,' he said, looking surprised. 'Bloody hell. Is it always like this?' He gestured around the crowded concourse helplessly.

'Only when the trains don't run on time. But, sadly, that's all too often these days.'

'Rather you than me, that's all I can say,' retorted Sam. He looked at his watch. 'Forty-five minutes yet. Fancy a pint?'

It was hot, and there wasn't much else to do. A pint of ice-cold lager sounded like an excellent idea.

'Definitely. Follow me,' I said, knowing that Sam wasn't familiar with the station. 'What brings you down here, Sam?' I called over my shoulder as I led him through the throng.

'Oh, office politics,' he replied morosely. 'It's a necessity I could do without. I have to come maybe twice a year.'

Within half a minute or so we'd reached The Booking Office, which, contrary to its name, these days is a swanky and upmarket restaurant/bar on the lower floor of the old original Victorian station. It's rather impressive, and Sam craned his neck as we entered like an out-of-town tourist. I found us a small table with two of those tall stools you have to perch on and parked him there whilst I went off to find some drinks. Sam made no offer to pay.

I was back in about ten minutes, which still gave us another twenty before we'd have to head off towards the train. Neither of us said a word until we'd taken a long, welcome pull at our beers.

Sam sighed contentedly and looked across at me. There was only one topic du jour of course. 'Yesterday,' he said. 'What do you reckon?'

'Provocative statement by Andrew,' I replied. 'Though, if you ask me, he's probably right.'

Sam shook his head, seemingly in disagreement, and then looked up. 'Saw your little exchange with Ned Logan on the way out,' he said suddenly.

I paused for a moment, rather embarrassed. 'Yes,' I replied. 'Unfortunate. Though I think you once had some similar issues with him?' Sam gave me a hard look, so I added hastily, 'Correct me if I'm wrong.'

'Who told you that?' he said eventually.

'Lucy,' I replied. 'She picked it up at the Women's Institute I think.'

'Women's Institute? More like Women's Inquisition,' Sam said irritably. 'They gossip too much, that lot.'

I said nothing whilst Sam took another sip of his beer. He put the glass down, having seemingly come to a decision. 'Look,' he said, 'there was a bit of an issue, but it's not what it sounds like.'

'I'd be grateful if you'd tell me, since I seem to be heading down a similar path,' I replied.

Sam took a deep breath. 'OK. It's pretty simple really. We'd done a job there – at Ritche's Lodge Farm; the Logan place. Not a very expensive one, but a good job. There was a bit of snagging to do, and my boys were onto the next project by then, so I decided to sort those issues out myself. Couple of days' work, I thought.'

'And?'

'And nothing, to start with. I knew Ned was a bit odd, but there were no dramas the first day, when he was there alone, nor the second, when Lesley was. She was friendly enough, and fed me cups of tea, but distant. Then the job slipped into a third day, when they were both there.'

He paused for another sip of his beer.

'It was like someone had flicked a switch. She was flirty, almost coming on to me, which you don't get much when you're my age, though I had my moments in my youth. I was embarrassed. I didn't want to be rude, and it would have been too blunt to tell her to lay off.' He looked up at me. 'She was doing it to wind Ned up. Certain of it.'

'How extraordinary,' I replied. 'So then you had your car scratched, I understand…?'

'I did, and I had no doubt who was responsible. I marched round there and read Ned the riot act.'

'Was Lesley there?'

'Not that I could see. If she was, she didn't show herself. Embarrassed, probably.'

I recounted my own tale to Sam.

'Pretty much the same then.' He drained his pint. 'Well, you've told him, just like I did, and I heard no more about it. It'll probably be the same for you. Come on, or we won't get seats.'

\*\*\*

When I belatedly got home, I mixed a drink for Lucy, poured a well-earned one for myself and then recounted the tale of my pint with Sam whilst we sat out in the garden. My wife raised her eyebrows archly.

'Interesting. Doesn't sound much like the Lesley I know. But at least you know what happened.' She paused. 'Would you like to know who I've been talking to today?' She sounded almost shy.

'Sure,' I replied. 'Has Watson uncovered anything?'

'Watson isn't sure,' Lucy responded thoughtfully. 'Amelia came round. She was looking for you.'

'Odd – she knows I work full-time in London. I'm hardly likely to be here on a Thursday.'

Lucy shrugged nonchalantly. 'That's what I thought. And she said she had your mobile number, so why not just call? But when I said you were out, she hung around sufficiently that I had no option but to ask her in for a coffee.'

'And what transpired?'

'Initially not much. She wanted to know what we thought of the service and whether it was out of order for Andrew to say what he did. I was pretty complimentary about the funeral and neutral about Andrew. Then she seemed to reflect for a moment before coming out with something fairly intriguing.'

I was all ears as Lucy gathered her thoughts.

'First, she asked if you – or we – knew anything more about Jack.'

'Anything more? What sort of thing? We know he's from the traveller community, that he worked for Edmund and that Andrew fired him. That's about it – other than the apparent change of attitude towards him at the service.'

Lucy nodded. 'That's it. That's what Amelia doesn't understand. She did put in a word for Jack, because she thought it was premature for Andrew to stop any assistance on the farm at this stage and shouldn't have done so anyway without consulting her. But she doesn't understand why he was so positive about Jack during the service. She wondered whether you might have any idea.'

I paused to reflect and took a sip of my drink. It did seem to be a minor mystery, but I doubted it was a meaningful one. 'Possibly Andrew was just making amends for their earlier falling-out. You know, being overcomplimentary?'

'I suggested that to her. She thinks there's more to it than that.'

'And you've seen nothing more of Lesley, I suppose? He was pretty complimentary about her too.'

'No. Mondays, Wednesdays and Fridays are our days, as you know. She'll be in tomorrow.'

\*\*\*

I set off to London the next day rather reluctantly, keen to witness what the morning with Lesley might bring. But as Lucy told me, it was probably no bad thing that I wouldn't be around at the same time as her, given Ned's sensitivities. She did not want to lose an excellent daily should Lesley decide that the domestic angst was becoming too much. Personally, I didn't consider this likely, given that we were now her only employment, but then it wasn't me who would suffer the consequences if she left.

Nonetheless, curiosity got the better of me, and I called home at lunchtime on some pretext, knowing that Lesley would be gone by midday. Lucy saw straight through that of course.

'So how was she?' I asked, once my rationale for calling had been speedily disposed of.

'Well, there were a couple of things,' began Lucy. I waited for her to continue, as I knew she would. 'First – the service. What did I think etc. She was pretty blunt about her own view.'

'Which was?'

'She thought it was inappropriate – that's the term she used. Mind you, she's got a downer on Andrew, because he's given her notice. Though she thinks that might be changing; he's beginning to realise he needs help, whether he's there or not, at least until the farm is sold.'

'But did she think he was right? About the murderer being among us?'

Lucy paused. 'I'm not sure I asked her in such specific terms. She just thought the inference was in bad taste and distracted the focus from Edmund, where it should have been. She actually seemed pretty cross about it.'

'You said there was a second thing.'

'Yes,' Lucy replied. 'After my conversation with Amelia, I thought I'd probe Lesley about Jack, in case she could throw any light on why Andrew had suddenly become so positive about him.'

'And?'

'She clammed up completely. I could see she was irritated, maybe even shocked. Changed the subject straightaway. It was odd, unnaturally so. There's definitely more to that situation than meets the eye.'

'Holmes and Watson had better get on the case then,' I said lightly.

'Yes, they had. I think they've been rather slow out of the blocks.' She sounded serious.

'OK. They must do better. See you tonight.'

\*\*\*

The next day was of course Saturday. When the children were growing up, I often used to head down to nearby Market Harborough on Saturday mornings to do a few chores with my daughter Ginny, which she loved, as indeed did : a bit of valuable bonding time. She had long since left home for university of course, but I still head rather forlornly down to town most Saturday mornings if there is nothing else on; there always seems to be something that needs doing. And so it was that day – nothing significant, but Lucy had a few errands for me to run, and I was happy to do so.

The chores didn't take long, but as I was heading back across the market square towards my car up beyond Tesco, the heavens opened – a real biblical downpour. There's a Caffè Nero on that square – it was ten yards away, and I was inside in a flash.

So were a lot of others of course, so once I had got my cappuccino, I looked around pessimistically for somewhere to sit; it wasn't a big area, and it was fugging up fast with all the damp body heat. I was resigned to standing when a woman alone at a table for two across the room caught my eye. She was looking at me, so I looked back, somewhat surprised. Then I recognised her under the hood. Fiona Challis. She smiled at me as our eyes met, so I made my way through the other tables towards her.

'Detective Sergeant,' I said, without much originality. 'Mind if I join you?'

'Not at all,' she said, dropping her hood. 'Good Leicestershire weather.'

'I thought you worked for Northamptonshire Police?' I said as I sat down.

'I do,' she said. 'But I live in Maidwell. Though the village is in Northamptonshire, Market Harborough is nearer than Northampton. So I tend to do my shopping across the county boundary unless I pick things up on the way back from work.'

It wasn't clear if there was a significant other in Fiona

Challis's life, though I knew from previous observation that she wore no ring. There was a slightly awkward pause.

'So how's it all going?' I said eventually. She looked at me with a glint of humour in her eyes. There was no need to ask what I was referring to.

'Confidential, Mr Rowland.'

'Well, you can't blame me for trying,' I said, taking a sip. 'Unusual funeral. I think he was right, don't you? Andrew Ayling?'

'Maybe.' She seemed determine to stonewall me.

'What if I had some information for you?' I said. Surely that would break her down.

'I'm listening.'

'Several things. I don't have the answers, but...'

'Go on,' she said.

'Jack. He was sacked by Andrew a few days ago. Now not only is he back, he's flavour of the month. Seems odd. Even Amelia Ayling thinks so.'

Challis looked at me sceptically over the rim of her cup. 'I'd be very surprised if Mr Diggle was directly involved.'

'You thought he was initially.'

'Preconceptions. I admit it.'

'Secondly, there's an issue with Ned Logan.'

Detective Sergeant Challis said nothing but was clearly waiting to hear more. I quickly outlined the Lesley saga and the words Ned and I had exchanged in The Swan, together with Sam Johnson's earlier experience.

'You must feel flattered,' she said lightly.

'No. I feel concerned. He's unpredictable.'

Challis accepted the rebuke with a graceful nod. 'If it escalates at all, let me know.'

'I will,' I replied. And then I continued, which I probably shouldn't have done. 'You know, I'm convinced that the root of all this is Edmund's women problems. Amelia, the possible reconciliation, Marlene Filler—'

'Who?' interrupted Challis.

'Villager. She and Edmund apparently had a thing once. She hates Amelia,' I said and recounted the row outside our house.

'Interesting. Thank you for that information, Mr Rowland,' she said.

Outside, the storm had dissipated as quickly as it had arrived, and the sun was breaking through.

'I must be going,' said the off-duty detective, standing and draining her cup. 'No doubt we will see more of each other in the coming days, sir.'

# CHAPTER FIFTEEN

My phone pinged as I was dodging the puddles on the way back to the car, but until I had made my way the three miles home from Market Harborough, I delayed looking at it.

The email was from Andrew Ayling: concise and to the point, as one might expect. It simply told me that he was leaving that day, didn't expect to return to Braybrooke in the foreseeable future and was grateful 'for everything'.

I showed it to Lucy without comment. She immediately voiced my own thoughts. 'What about Amelia?'

It was indeed slightly odd that Andrew hadn't mentioned his sister-in-law, but without really thinking about it too much, I surmised that relations between them might be slightly frosty on account of the farm ownership issue.

I concerned myself no more with this minor mystery until mid-afternoon, when I took the dogs for their normal walk. Lucy declined to accompany me for some reason I now can't recall. Heading west out of the village as I normally did, some instinct made me turn north-west after around six hundred yards at what in our family we term 'chicken corner' – a small stables complex with a public footpath off to the right, in the direction of Market Harborough. The main track made a sharp turn to the left, south-west up a slope, beyond which in a few hundred yards it would meet the hedge running down from the stile where the killing had taken place. In our early Braybrooke days, there had been a flock of free-range chickens which milled around at the corner, now long gone. Theo and Rosie were off their leads by then and ambled around happily as we followed the line of the stream after a short dog-leg back the way we'd come, with a big wheat field off to our left.

After a few hundred yards along that route, one passes a small spinney on the right, and a couple of hundred yards more brings you to the end of that field. Here you face a choice: either turn left and then left again along an unplanted path back through the middle of the crop, or pass through a large gap in the hedge and thence into the next field. It was a fine afternoon after the earlier storm, so I chose that route, which would mean a longer walk. A short right/left dog-leg, and you are climbing the gentle slope that eventually transitions to a descent towards the disused railway line, and that was what I was planning to do. However, directly ahead of me as I turned right was the rear of Braybrooke Farm, some three hundred yards away. I could see along the side of the house, and there was a car in front of it. I recognised the white Audi.

On impulse, I abandoned my intended left turn and headed instead straight ahead towards the farm. I had no idea what I would do when I got there, but then I've always believed in improvisation.

\*\*\*

Within a couple of minutes, I was approaching the house, feeling increasingly foolish as I did so, but suddenly the need to make a decision was taken out of my hands. I saw Amelia making her way to the car; she opened its door, took something out (it turned out to be her mobile, which she'd left there) and then turned back towards the house.

Immediately, she spotted me, not more than a hundred yards away by then. I saw her pull up in surprise, squinting into the sun to identify the stranger. Tentatively, I raised my hand. I think it was the dogs she recognised first, but within a few seconds, she was striding confidently down the side of the house towards me.

'Hello, Robert,' she said cheerfully, looking rather pleased I thought. 'What on earth brings you here?'

'I'm sorry,' I replied. 'I thought this path was a circuit. I'm always trying to identify new routes for our walks.' Which was true, and indeed I'd never ventured down the path I was currently on, so I wasn't going to get caught out in a lie. 'I can see now that it's a dead end. I apologise.'

'Nonsense, no need for that,' she scoffed and then hesitated for a moment. 'Tea?'

I indicated the two dogs rather hesitatingly, who had rushed up to her. They weren't wet; the rain from the earlier squall had long since dried off in the afternoon sun.

'They'll be fine,' said Amelia decisively, pushing an unruly Theo down. 'We'll only be in the kitchen. Come on.'

She turned on her heel and strode away along the side passage towards the front of the house without a backward glance, leaving me little option but to follow her inside.

I hadn't gone into the kitchen during my earlier ill-fated visit, when I'd mistaken Amelia for Andrew's wife, but it was much as I expected: all mod cons. Edmund clearly hadn't stinted himself. Amelia bustled around making a pot of tea, produced milk and sugar and then settled herself decorously on the opposite side of the island from me. She poured us both a cup, offered me some milk, took some herself, had a sip and then looked thoughtfully at me, with something like amusement. It occurred to me slightly uncomfortably that she might think I had deliberately arranged my route to get her alone. She didn't say anything, so I soon felt obliged to do so.

'Where's Andrew?' I asked. For some instinctive reason, I didn't mention the email I'd recently received from him.

'Oh,' she said, shrugging her slim shoulders. 'He's left.'

'Bit sudden?'

'Well, we had a little tiff. About you know what; I told you on our walk the other day. He flounced out. He's rather good at flouncing.' She gave me a challenging look. I understood the implication.

'Tiff or no tiff, you looked impressively united in the church.'

'Thank you,' she said, nodding gratefully to acknowledge the compliment. 'It wasn't altogether easy, but I think we carried it off.'

I took a sip of my tea to cover up another obvious pause.

'He spoke well, didn't he?' Amelia asked eventually, treating me to another disconcerting stare.

'Yes. Provocative. But I know you told Lucy that you'd discussed that.'

'We had,' she replied.

It seemed to be left to me to lead the conversation. 'One thing though,' I said in slight desperation.

'Yes?'

'Jack.'

'What about Jack?'

From the disparaging tone in which she spoke his name, I got the distinct impression that Jack was not flavour of the month with Amelia, which seemed odd, given that I knew she'd put in a good word for him.

'Well, Andrew sacked him and banned him from the funeral. Then he got reinstated at the farm and reinvited. Finally, he got all sorts of compliments from Andrew during the service.' I paused and shrugged. 'It just seemed a bit over the top.'

'And what do you make of all that?' Amelia asked pointedly. She was clearly angry – not, I hoped, with me, but certainly about something.

I stayed silent.

Amelia leant forward and then spoke with quiet steel. 'Andrew is being very good to Jack because Jack seems to have witnessed a fresh version of Edmund's will.'

I was dumbstruck. 'Doesn't a will need two witnesses?' I responded eventually. Lucy and I had redone ours about a year before once the children had outgrown adolescence, so I knew this.

'Indeed,' Amelia replied cynically. 'A friend of Jack's is the second witness. How about that for a coincidence?'

'Let me guess who the principal beneficiary of this new will is,' I ventured.

'Not me, put it like that,' said Amelia grimly. 'Hence the tiff.'

\*\*\*

Holmes had certainly uncovered something new. For a second, he thought gleefully of Watson's reaction once she learnt of it, then became an adult again and returned solemnly to the matter at hand.

'Don't solicitors need to draw up wills?' I asked. Certainly, Lucy and I had never considered any other course of action when revising our own.

'No,' replied Amelia, with a decisive shake of her head. 'Common misconception. I've looked into this, as you might imagine. It has to be signed by the testator – Edmund – and witnessed at the time by two people over eighteen who aren't beneficiaries. That's it.'

I paused for a moment to reflect. 'And did Edmund actually sign it? Are you sure?'

'Is it a forgery, do you mean?'

'Yes, I suppose I do.'

I sensed Amelia's frustration in her reply, coupled with a hint of doubt. 'Well, it certainly looked like Edmund's signature.'

'So you've seen it?'

'Not all of it. Just the signature page.'

'Well, that's damned strange, for a start. Why wouldn't Andrew show you the whole thing? The farm might not have been left to him at all; you've only got his word for it.'

Amelia gave a frustrated shrug and then leant forward. 'There'll have to be a legal determination of the validity of this will eventually, assuming it exists. If it doesn't, or it's not in his favour, then Andrew's bluff is going to be called, isn't it? So what on earth would be the point?'

This was a pretty fair question. I mulled it over for a few seconds before responding. 'And have you spoken to Jack yet or this friend of his?'

'No,' Amelia responded morosely. 'But Andrew says they'll confirm that they witnessed Edmund sign the will if need be.'

I took another sip of my tea, which gave me a few seconds to reflect. 'You know,' I said eventually, 'this is all very odd. I thought you told me on our walk that Andrew had been searching high and low for this will, which you were confident didn't exist?'

Amelia nodded unenthusiastically. 'Edmund was a bit sheepish about it, but that's what I understood he was telling me when we were thinking of getting back together. That his original will was still valid.'

'So when did this new will come to light?'

Amelia hesitated. 'Well, I'm not quite sure. Andrew confronted me with it the morning after the funeral. Where and when exactly he came across it, I don't know.'

'And when was it drafted, if it exists? When was it signed? Those are the other questions.'

Amelia seemed suddenly much calmer. 'You know, it's been very helpful to talk this through,' she said thoughtfully. 'I've been fretting and not thinking logically. Thank you, Robert. There are a lot of loose ends, aren't there?' She glanced up appealingly; if I was being cynical, I would say that it was a well-practised look. Like all attractive women, Amelia well knew how best to exercise her wiles.

'Plenty.' I nodded, momentarily distracted. Then, after a few seconds, my inner good Samaritan made one of his all-too-frequent appearances. He can be trouble, that fellow, especially when damsels are in distress.

'Tell you what,' I said, 'you concentrate on getting some answers out of Andrew. I'm going to speak to Jack. Don't give up hope.'

\*\*\*

I left Braybrooke Farm feeling pleasingly noble, having basked in Amelia's gratitude for a second cup of tea and then made my way home with the dogs the way we'd come; it took about half an hour. All the way, I was trying to make sense of what I had just learnt, but like an incomplete jigsaw, the pieces just didn't seem to fit together.

Lucy was outside doing some gardening when I arrived back and would clearly have preferred to continue, but she humoured me by coming inside for a cup of tea when I informed her that Holmes had uncovered important information in the case.

Once we were settled, I quickly outlined the developments I had discovered, having first had to explain to my somewhat sceptical wife how I ended up alone at Braybrooke Farm with the fragrant Amelia in the first place. But we got over that, and there were a pleasing number of exhalations and gasps as I outlined Andrew's recent departure, his sudden announcement of the discovery of a new will by Edmund, apparently witnessed by Jack and his friend, and Amelia's inability at the time to verify the contents of said will.

Gardening was now forgotten as Lucy morphed before my eyes into Watson. 'There are a lot of clues for us to follow here,' she said, eyes gleaming.

'I know,' I replied. 'Amelia is going to push to see the

contents of that will; she can't just accept Andrew's assertion of what it says at face value. And I'm going to speak to Jack.'

'It certainly explains why Andrew was so polite about him at the service,' Lucy said. 'He needed Jack onside.'

'You're implying that Andrew has prevailed upon Jack and his mate to support a falsehood,' I replied. 'Maybe it's simply true though: Edmund rewrote his will.'

'Where's it been all this time then?' asked Lucy. 'And presumably Andrew must benefit from it, or why bring it to light at all?'

I paused to reflect. 'Jack's a young chap, and not a particularly well-educated one,' I said eventually. 'He may not have thought through the implications of lying about something as legally significant as this. I'll explain to him in words of one syllable when I see him. It shouldn't be too difficult for someone like me to work out if he's not telling the truth.' It felt pompous even as I said it, and I knew Lucy wouldn't be taken in by my sophisticated 'man of the world' act for a moment; she's been married to me for a long time.

'He'll be much better attuned to legal matters than you think,' she said firmly. 'His community are very far from naive in that respect.'

Though I tried not to show it, I was suitably chastened, because I recognised that she was right. 'Well, I'll jump that fence when I get to it,' I said. 'But you agree that I need to see Jack?'

'Yes,' said Lucy. 'You certainly do. With me.'

# CHAPTER SIXTEEN

I didn't hang around and called Jack straightaway to see if we could fix a time to meet. It went to voicemail, so I left a brief message and then followed up with a text as backup.

Lucy and I got on with our normal Saturday routine thereafter and thought no more about our alter egos Holmes and Watson until I received a text around 6pm.

*Abroad next seven days – will call when back*, it said.

'That is distinctly odd,' said Lucy when I showed it to her. 'Those people don't generally travel abroad.'

'You can't possibly say that!' I protested. 'What a generalisation! He's as much entitled to a holiday as the next man.'

'He is,' agreed Lucy. 'I'm just saying that it would be out of character, that's all. Can you see Jack sitting on a beach somewhere?'

This was admittedly not a vision that came easily to mind, so I simply shrugged.

'I think he's trying to avoid you,' declared Lucy firmly.

'He's worried. And as we know, he may have good cause to be.'

'Possible I suppose,' I replied, having weighed this theory up. 'But things are going to be pretty difficult for him if he's not actually abroad.'

'What do you mean?'

'Well, consider this,' I replied. 'Jack's whole life seems to based around the village of Braybrooke. He lives just outside. He's supposedly still got a job at Braybrooke Farm; I don't think Amelia will be that pleased to see him in the circumstances, but she'll certainly be able to tell me if he turns up.'

'Or she could speak to him herself,' added Lucy primly. 'After all, it's not our problem.'

But I was already thinking further ahead and ignored this. 'In fact,' I said confidently, 'having told me he's away, he'd hardly dare show his face for the next week for fear of bumping into me or someone who might tell me he was about.'

'So on balance…' began Lucy.

'On balance, I think Jack genuinely is abroad,' I replied. 'I can try calling of course, but we may as well face the facts: it may be a week or so before we can talk to him.'

'Should the police know about all this?' asked Lucy.

I waved my wife away airily. 'I'll speak to Challis the next time I bump into her; I can't go running to her with every thought that enters my head. And as you say, at the end of the day, it's really not our problem.'

\*\*\*

Sunday came. I sent another text to Jack that morning with little hope of a response and, sure enough, failed to receive one. But Lucy did receive a text, just before lunch. It was from Lesley.

*Can I please come round this afternoon about 3.30pm? 15 minutes only.*

Lucy and I looked at each other in mystification once she had showed me the screen.

'Must be urgent,' I said. 'She's working here anyway tomorrow. Why can't whatever it is wait till then?'

My wife shrugged in frustration. 'I can hardly say "no", can I?' she said, after a few seconds' pause. Then she sent a brief reply.

*Of course.*

'Hmm,' I said dubiously, once she had done so. 'Do you think I should be around when she turns up? Ned's sensitivity and all that?'

Lucy's response was instant and unambiguous. 'Yes. This is our house. You are not going to be driven out of it at the whim of Ned Logan's imaginary psychodrama.'

I nodded my reluctant concurrence and returned to my *Sunday Times*. But I couldn't really focus. What on earth could Lesley want? There was no way of knowing, so I tried not to speculate, and anyway, we'd find out soon enough.

She was dead on time. Lucy answered the door, and I heard her graciously dismissing Lesley's halting apologies for intruding on a Sunday. Lesley was still gushing her grateful thanks as Lucy led her through into the kitchen, but she stopped dead when she saw me. It was obvious that she had expected to be speaking to Lucy alone.

A sudden cloud of uncertainty crossed her face.

Lucy picked up on it of course. 'Well, it's a weekend,' she said, with a hint of defensiveness. 'Why wouldn't Robert be at home?'

I suppose I could have made my excuses and left once I saw Lesley's reaction to my presence, but I was mindful of Lucy's view that I had every right to be there, and also, I am naturally stubborn. I rose from my stool as Lesley entered but pointedly made no effort to leave the room.

'Anything you want to say to me you can say to Robert too,' said Lucy, moving to my side. She still sounded defensive.

Lesley hesitated. 'It's a bit personal. It concerns Robert.'

'Look, Lesley,' I said, as patiently as I could. 'Whatever suspicions your husband may have, you and I both know that there is nothing whatsoever going on between us: it's all nonsense. So let's all three of us sit down, have a cup of tea and you can explain why you are so concerned.'

She hesitated, looking miserable, and then nodded. 'Alright,' she said quietly.

I pulled out a stool for her whilst Lucy made the tea, and Lesley sat there in downcast silence. Once we were all settled with mugs in front of us, Lucy and I waited for her to begin.

'Ned's absolutely convinced there's something going on – you and I,' she said suddenly, looking up at me.

I shrugged my shoulders and gestured helplessly. 'How can he possibly think that?' I asked in an exasperated tone. It was more frustration than anger, but either way it wasn't helpful in terms of building empathy, which was what we needed.

Lucy waded in. 'Since he drove you home in the rain that time on the day of the rail strike, Robert has seen you only at the funeral and afterwards. Correct?'

Lesley stayed silent, looking down at the table.

Lucy turned sharply to me. 'Correct?'

I nodded, somewhat surprised at the directness of her tone. 'Yes, correct.'

'So why on earth has Ned got this absurd bee in his bonnet?' asked Lucy. She was calm, but I knew her well enough to know that she was irritated.

Lesley sighed. 'He's not always logical. Not since his accident. Gets fixations.'

I wasn't immediately sure how to respond to this, and neither was Lucy.

'Look, I came to ask if you could possibly give me this week off? Given the circumstances,' pleaded Lesley. 'I thought I'd better come and explain rather than text or say I was ill or something.'

'Why yes, of course,' replied Lucy. 'If you think it'll help.' My wife sounded pretty doubtful that it would, and I can't say I blamed her.

However, Lesley had moved on: she was building up to something else. We both sensed it and gave her time.

'There have been other fixations,' she said hesitantly after a while.

'Yes, Sam Johnson, for one,' I said confidently.

It wasn't clever. I was showing off the span of my knowledge, whereas in fact what I knew was minimal, incomplete and one-sided. Lesley pursed her lips tightly.

'Yes, Sam Johnson,' she replied, obviously surprised. I saw her hesitate for a moment, and then she seemed to come to a decision. 'And Edmund Ayling.'

\*\*\*

After Lucy had shown Lesley out, she returned straight to the kitchen, as I knew she would. She didn't say anything, but I recognised her 'Watson' face, and her expression was serious. She raised a quizzical eyebrow. I was being interrogated.

'The question is, has Ned got an alibi?' I said in response. 'If his fixation on Edmund was as illogical as the one on me, then God knows what he might have done.'

'And beyond that, Holmes…?' said Lucy, apparently vexed.

I gaped at her, mystified.

'God knows what he might do again,' explained Lucy, as if to a five-year-old.

This was an angle on the matter I had not considered hitherto, and I was taken aback at the implications.

'Right,' said Lucy, grasping the initiative once she saw that I was lost for a sensible reaction. 'First thing tomorrow, you are going to call that policewoman friend of yours. You know, the detective.'

'I am?'

'You are,' she replied decisively. 'And you are going to ask her if the police have investigated Ned's whereabouts around the time of the murder.'

'Challis probably won't tell me…' I began dubiously.

'Then you tell her why you want to know!' said Lucy, in an exasperated tone. 'Either the police can rule Ned out because he has an alibi, or they can't, in which case they need to start looking at him very closely. You could be next in the firing line!'

'Unlikely…' I began.

'Don't be so bloody complacent,' shouted Lucy angrily. 'It's irresponsible. You're my husband! Edmund was shot. If you don't call her, I will. I'm scared, Robert.'

I don't like being shouted at by my wife, or worrying her. I sensed I was in the wrong so tried to claw a little ground back by sharing the blame around. 'Pity we didn't ask Lesley where Ned was at the time,' I said regretfully, implying we were somehow both at fault. It didn't work.

'Well, we didn't. Silly us. And nobody knows the exact time Edmund was shot anyway,' she snapped. 'Now, you are going to call Challis first thing tomorrow. Not the next bloody time you bump into her. Agreed?'

'Agreed,' I said humbly.

'And you are not going outside this house again at all before then, are you?' She saw the query forming in my mind. 'Why do you think?' she said, suddenly icy calm. Then she turned smartly on her heel and left me gaping.

\*\*\*

I had only just resignedly turned to the sideboard to pour myself a restorative whisky after this little contretemps when the phone rang. I thought about leaving it to Lucy upstairs, but that would only have irritated her further, so I picked up.

It was Ginny – always rather more communicative than her twin brother, but then girls generally are. 'Easter!' she announced. 'Will and I are coming home for the weekend, as you know.' She paused expectantly.

I didn't know for certain, but we were only five days short of Good Friday, so a positive reply seemed appropriate. 'Yes, I think Mum told me.'

'Can you pick us up on Good Friday? Will and me?'

'Suppose I'll have to,' I replied with mock grumpiness. 'What time?'

'I'll text you. Evening. Oh, and Dad...'

'Yes?'

'We are going to Dingley, aren't we?'

Around our neck of the woods, the standard entertainment on Easter Saturday is the local point-to-point, which is held at Dingley racecourse, three or four miles away. I'm not a great horse racing man, but Dingley is different: you park your car on the side of a hill, and the whole course is laid out in front of you in a natural amphitheatre. Everyone brings a picnic; children in their teens and twenties such as ours are home for Easter; and in fine weather, it's the biggest drinks party in the world. Lucy and I usually team up with some local chums, but this year the couple in question were on a trip to the Seychelles to mark a significant anniversary, so rather feebly, we hadn't made any alternative plans. Or at least I didn't think we had; Lucy probably had it all under control.

'Of course, as long as the weather's OK,' I replied, seeing the way the wind was blowing. The children had been going since they were toddlers, and I always enjoyed it myself anyway. I once made as much as £15.

'Great – see you on Friday!' giggled Ginny and promptly rang off before I had time to remind her to text the time she and her brother would be getting into Market Harborough.

# CHAPTER SEVENTEEN

I had a breakfast meeting – terrible things – in London the next day, which meant an earlier train than normal, and thus an earlier departure from home. Normally I would resent this, but since Lucy's froideur had not eased much overnight, I was frankly glad to get out of the house, her umpteenth 'don't forget to call Challis' reminder ringing in my ears.

And of course it meant that in literal terms I couldn't keep my promise to call the policewoman before leaving the house, but Lucy had grudgingly accepted that. However, our conversation the previous day had definitely affected me: on the three-mile drive to the station I found myself abnormally alert. I didn't realistically expect Ned to attempt anything on the public highway, particularly at a time of day when he wouldn't expect me to be about, but in his irrational state, anything might be possible.

I got on the train at Market Harborough with some relief and mulled over the whole saga since Edmund's death for the hour-long journey to London when I should have been reading the background papers for my meeting. By the time I got to St Pancras, I had reached one inescapable conclusion: Lucy was right. Though the whole Logan thing might be a wild goose chase, the police needed to know. After all, Challis had asked me to tell her if the situation escalated.

I can normally play the ebullient host well at breakfast meetings, but I was both underprepared and distracted on that occasion. My people noticed, and I sensed it, which made me feel guilty. So did the guests we had invited (fellow brokers), which made me feel rude. Nonetheless, the up-and-coming Seth Savage stepped smoothly up to the plate, and we broke up after an hour or so having agreed a reasonably satisfactory way ahead in terms of our projected strategic alliance. I couldn't wait to get back to the office and stayed my loyal PA Clare with my hand as I closed the door on her surprised face, provoking yet more feelings of guilt.

It was shortly after 9am when I called Challis. She picked up instantly.

'Yes, Mr Rowland?' she said, sounding calm and efficient.

'Erm, I think there's something you need to know, Detective Sergeant. Possibly nothing in it, but there have been developments,' I replied. 'You know, regarding what we talked about in the coffee shop. You asked me to let you know if that happened.'

'Serious developments?' asked Challis. She sounded interested.

I told her the tale in rather garbled fashion over a couple of minutes.

'So let me get this right,' said Challis. 'Ned Logan seems to have a fixation that there is something going on between his wife and you, which you told me about the other day. There isn't. Now Lesley Logan has told you and your wife that he had an earlier fixation about Edmund Ayling. And Edmund Ayling was shot dead.'

'Yes, that's about the strength of it. My wife fears that he might be coming for me next.' I said this with a manly half-laugh, but Challis put me straight back in my box.

'This is no laughing matter, Mr Rowland,' she said sharply. 'Your wife is absolutely right to be concerned.' There was a pause, and I sensed her thinking. 'Can I call you back in a couple of minutes, sir?' she asked after a few seconds.

'Of course.'

I sensed that she wanted to consult someone, and that was almost certainly right. The call back came quickly, and she was short and to the point. There were no preliminaries.

'Mr Rowland, would you and your wife be available to meet with Detective Inspector Yardley and me tomorrow morning?'

'Well, it's hardly ideal. I work in London—' I began replying.

'Yes, a murder inquiry can be inconvenient,' she interrupted tightly. 'Particularly as you apparently fear being the next victim. That is surely more important than the interruption of your normal routine.'

Put like that, there was no choice of course, and I gave a sigh of surrender. 'Where and when?'

'Would you be happy to come to Northampton police station? Say 10am?'

Seventeen miles from home. No point in prevaricating. 'Yes. We'll be there.'

'Thank you. I look forward to seeing you both tomorrow,' she said crisply and rang off.

I sighed and sent Lucy a quick text confirming our new diary engagement. At least she'd know that I'd kept my promise.

There was a timid knock at the door, and before I could reply, there was Clare with a coffee and some biscuits; slim, blonde and worried.

'Everything alright, Robert?' she asked pointedly. Having worked for me for nine years, she had earned the right to ask, being as much a friend as a colleague.

'Yes. I mean no,' I replied. 'Look, something at home. It'll all blow over soon enough, but I need to give it some focus. I'll have to take tomorrow off. Can you cancel whatever's in my diary and rearrange? Just say it's a family matter. Which it isn't, by the way,' I added hastily, as I saw her look of horror. I knew how much she admired Lucy, even though my wife was not altogether pleased at how close we were, particularly as Clare was an attractive single woman.

'Just a local matter,' I added, by way of vague clarification. 'But I have to meet some people tomorrow. Unavoidable. Sorry to muck you about.'

Clare nodded gracefully and withdrew. I knew her well enough to sense that she felt hurt I didn't trust her with the full story, and felt a heel, but frankly, the fewer people at work who knew that I was being interviewed by the police the better, even her. Rumours abound in the City, and I had seen two plus two equalling five more often than I cared to remember. So best not to let one start.

\*\*\*

We could have taken the shortcut to the A508 Northampton Road, south out of the village and then through Logan farmland via the lane to Arthingworth, joining it at Kelmarsh. Nothing was said, but by mutual consent we headed east instead, hitting the A6 and eventually joining the A508 at Lamport, a couple of miles nearer Northampton.

'Just because you're paranoid, doesn't mean they aren't out to get you,' I muttered as we turned onto the main road, trying to break the still-present ice by recycling the hoary old *Catch 22* quote as a joke.

Lucy looked far from amused.

As we entered the outskirts of Northampton, she turned suddenly towards me. 'What are you going to tell them?' she demanded.

I looked across at her in surprise. 'What I've already told them,' I replied. 'When I spoke to Challis yesterday. That's why we're having this wretched meeting.'

Lucy considered this for a couple of seconds and then responded urgently. 'Look, don't underplay it,' she said, and for a moment I thought she was about to cry. 'I mean it. You always make a joke of things. This isn't a bloody joke. Take it seriously. And anyway, it's not a wretched meeting. It might just save your life.'

I could sense her wobbling and tried to be reassuring. 'I will take it seriously, I promise,' I said, giving her thigh a squeeze. 'And Challis told me much the same yesterday. Let's just tell the story and let them know the issues that are worrying us. There's so much we don't know. The whereabouts of Jack. Where Ned was when the shooting happened. The truth about the will. Lots of stuff. If they're remotely competent, I'm sure they can put our minds at rest about some of that.'

It sounded a bit patronising, even to me, and Lucy smiled uncertainly.

'They are competent, aren't they?' she asked.

'They are – definitely.'

My wife still looked unconvinced.

'Look,' I urged her. 'You're going to be there too. If you think I'm underplaying anything, then just speak up. I'm not going to argue. Say anything you like.'

She looked rather more reassured after this and even gave my thigh a little return squeeze. Then we lapsed into silence, both lost in thought.

Before we knew it, the big glass façade of the new Northampton Police headquarters loomed into view. I hadn't seen it before and didn't much like the look of it. But I don't suppose anyone much likes visiting police stations.

\*\*\*

We parked up and made our way reluctantly inside at about 9.50am. I was half expecting to be met by a blank stare as I told the impossibly young but smartly groomed and uniformed policewoman behind the protective glass on the reception desk that we had an appointment with Yardley and Challis at 10am, but she consulted her computer screen and cheerfully confirmed in seconds that indeed we did. We didn't even have to wait – she pressed a button, and a moment later, an equally young colleague (male this time) was guiding us through some double doors along a passage.

After twenty yards or so he stopped, turned to the left and showed us into an interview room. It was pleasant and airy, albeit with rather bland abstract prints on the pale grey walls – not like those dingy, windowless places where suspects are interviewed in TV dramas. But I was confident we weren't suspects.

'Help yourself to coffee or tea. Or water if you prefer,' said the young PC. 'Detective Inspector Yardley and Detective Sergeant Challis will be along very shortly.'

After he had withdrawn, I looked dubiously at the coffee machine – one of those where you press a button and receive something warm, dark and unrecognisable in a white plastic cup a few seconds later.

'Any preference?' I asked. 'Cappuccino? Latte?'

My wife shrugged forlornly. 'Anything. They'll all taste the same.'

I got us two cappuccinos and then sat down next to Lucy on the same side of the table. Neither of us said anything. I'm not sure how Lucy was feeling, but I was both uneasy and rather intimidated.

We hadn't been waiting for more than a couple of minutes before the door opened suddenly, and Challis came in, followed by Yardley. Both were smartly dressed in navy suits.

'Mr and Mrs Rowland,' began Challis, extending her hand. 'Welcome, and thank you both so much for coming in at such short notice.' She turned to her boss, who was nodding his agreement to this sentiment. 'Coffee?'

'Yes, thank you.'

Challis kept her gaze on him. 'Which?'

'Don't mind,' said Yardley, pulling out a chair to sit opposite Lucy. 'Identical, aren't they?'

I smiled briefly. 'That's what my wife said.'

A hint of a rueful grin from Yardley. Within a minute, the four of us were settled, and there was a pregnant pause.

'Now, Mr Rowland,' began Yardley, in avuncular fashion. 'Detective Sergeant Challis here tells me that you are concerned about the behaviour of Ned Logan. Indeed, she believes you may have cause to be.'

'I am. We both are,' I replied, looking to Lucy for confirmation. She nodded her agreement.

Yardley paused and looked keenly at us both in succession. 'I know you have already explained this to DS Challis. However, for my sake, would you please explain in your own words precisely why that is?'

\*\*\*

Challis raised her eyes briefly from her notebook to meet the glance I gave her. Her expression was subtly encouraging. Lucy touched my knee with hers under the table.

I sighed and took a deep breath. 'From the top then. First, Lesley Logan works for us three mornings a week – housework. Mondays, Wednesdays and Fridays. The other two mornings she used to work for Edmund Ayling until his death.'

'Understood,' said Yardley. He was clearly waiting for me to continue.

I changed tack slightly. 'Have you met Lesley Logan, Detective Inspector?' I enquired.

'Seen her. At the church and afterwards. Not met or spoken to her,' he replied and indicated to his right. 'Detective Sergeant Challis has.'

'She is an attractive woman. Wouldn't you agree, Detective Sergeant?' I said, turning to Challis.

She looked momentarily nonplussed, and there was a brief pause. 'I would.' She nodded hesitantly.

I turned back to Yardley. 'Now, Ned Logan is very aware of that. Apparently, he always has been, but since injuring his head in that quad bike accident, it's all got rather out of control.'

'Explain.'

'Well, he can be prone to obsessions about particular men and his wife, if you get my drift. He got one with Sam Johnson, the local builder, when he did some work on their farm. You can ask him. It fizzled out after Sam confronted him. There may have been others.'

'And now he's got an obsession about you, I understand?' said Yardley in a phlegmatic tone. 'How did that come about?'

'It's quite ridiculous,' butted in Lucy, unable to contain her frustration. 'One day it was raining, so Robert gave Lesley a lift back to Ritche's Lodge Farm after her morning's work. It's barely more than a mile. He made a joke when he dropped her off; Ned saw it, and…' She raised her hands helplessly.

Yardley looked across at me for corroboration.

'It's not even as if I'm generally around when Lesley is,' I added. 'I work in London all week, as you know. The only reason I was at home that day is because there was a train strike.'

'So beyond that short time in the car, you've never been alone with Mrs Logan?'

'No. Well, a few seconds when she entered my office that day to clean it. She wasn't expecting me to be there, and I wasn't expecting her. We were both surprised.'

Yardley stayed silent for a few moments, thinking. Then he looked up sharply. 'How did you first know about Mr Logan's reaction?' he asked.

'I could see he wasn't pleased when I dropped Lesley off. But I thought no more about it.'

'Lesley hinted at it,' interjected Lucy. 'A couple of days later, when she was next in. Then she told us both unequivocally on Sunday...'

Yardley raised his hand. 'We'll come to that. How did you first find out, Mr Rowland?'

'Ivor Chubb told me,' I replied. 'He works for Ned. I met him when I was out walking my dogs.'

'With Mrs Ayling, isn't that so?' said Challis, quietly.

I was rather disconcerted by this unexpected demonstration of police knowledge. 'Yes. I met Amelia on a dog walk. It was a complete fluke. She was visiting the place where Edmund was shot.'

'As were you, I suppose?' said Yardley.

'Well, my route went that way. It was the opposite of the loop I did on the day of the killing, so obviously I passed that spot. I climbed the stile and there she was in front of me. She was crying.'

Yardley weighed this up and then nodded. 'So why did Chubb tell you?'

I paused awkwardly for a moment. 'This is going to sound odd. He was by the church gate. He saw me part from Amelia at the junction of Newland Street and Griffin Road. She kissed me on the cheek. It was completely spontaneous – I wasn't expecting it – perhaps because I'd lent her a sympathetic ear on the walk. But Chubb saw it. He made a joke of it at first but then warned me about Ned having taken against me.'

'Female entanglements, Mr Rowland,' said Yardley and looked up at me. There was challenge in his stare. I met it.

'I take exception to that,' I replied evenly. 'I gave Lesley a lift in my car because it was raining. I walked a mile or so with Amelia because I met her whilst out with my dogs. Hardly "entanglements", surely?'

Yardley said nothing but lowered his gaze.

Challis stepped in. 'He hasn't actually done anything, though, has he?' she said. 'Logan?'

'Well, he confronted me in the pub after the funeral,' I replied. 'I told you about that. Warned me off.'

'Saying what, exactly?'

I couldn't recall Ned's precise words and shrugged helplessly.

Lucy came to my rescue. 'Believe me, Detective Inspector, that was undoubtedly the implication,' she said firmly. 'I was there too, remember. He was a mix of pleading and threatening. More the former I think.'

I nodded my agreement and waited for the policeman's reaction.

'Alright,' said Yardley, after a momentary pause. 'I accept that. Now, what has changed? Why do you suddenly consider yourself under threat?'

'Because, as I explained to Detective Sergeant Challis the other day, and my wife was trying to tell you earlier, Lesley came round on Sunday to explain about Ned's obsession.'

'Which you already knew about.'

'Yes, but then she said he'd also had one about Edmund. We didn't know about that.'

'And look what happened to him,' said Lucy quietly.

# CHAPTER EIGHTEEN

Detective Inspector Yardley gave a long-suffering sigh and turned to look at Challis. 'Anything in it?' he asked.

His sergeant looked as if she hadn't expected to be put on the spot. 'I've spoken to Mr Johnson since my call with Mr Rowland yesterday,' she replied uncomfortably. 'He confirms he had an altercation with Mr Logan, whom he blamed for damaging his car.'

'Because of the wife issue?'

Challis nodded but remained silent.

'After which there were no similar incidents?'

'Not in his case, no,' replied Challis.

There was a long, reflective pause before Yardley turned back to me. 'What is the evidence that Ned Logan had a similar fixation on Edmund Ayling?' he asked, his gaze transferring smoothly to my wife once I shrugged.

'Only what Lesley told us,' ventured Lucy. 'She has no reason to lie about it.'

'And she did work there twice a week. Edmund had an eye for the ladies. Maybe Ned had cause?' I mused.

'We know about that,' said Challis shortly. 'And also about Mr Ayling's possible reconciliation with his wife. I've spoken to Mrs Ayling. But she certainly didn't mention any sort of relationship between Edmund and Lesley.'

'Doesn't mean Ned didn't think there was one,' I retorted. 'Just as he seems to think there is with me.' I left the implication hanging.

Yardley stroked his chin thoughtfully.

'There are some other issues…' I began hesitantly.

He nodded his encouragement.

'Do you know about the will?' I asked.

Yardley raised an interrogative eyebrow at Challis, who kept her eyes firmly lowered on her notebook.

'Go on,' said Yardley.

I gathered my thoughts for a moment first. 'During that walk with Amelia, she told me that she and Edmund had never divorced and that she believed the will he had made during their marriage was still extant. So the farm would come to her.' I looked up to see the detective's reaction. He inclined his head briefly but said nothing. 'However, Andrew Ayling believed there was another will and was searching high and low for it.'

'I presume he thought it favoured him, or at least disinherited her,' replied the detective. 'Did it ever turn up?'

'Apparently yes – not with Edmund's solicitor but signed, dated and duly witnessed. I had a cup of tea with Amelia the other day and she told me about it.'

'Where was it found?'

'Presumably somewhere in the house,' I replied. 'She didn't say.'

'And it says what, this supposed will?' asked Yardley, sounding pretty sceptical.

'Well, that's the odd thing. Andrew wouldn't show it to Amelia. Just the signature page. Dated about three months ago.'

Yardley raised his eyebrows again in surprise. They were very expressive, his eyebrows. 'And the witnessing signatories were…?' he enquired.

'Jack Diggle and a friend of his,' I replied. 'I can't remember the other chap's name.'

Yardley and Challis looked at each other, the latter apparently astonished, but the detective inspector was too canny a professional to give vent to that. 'Well well well,' he said.

\*\*\*

We waited for him to elaborate. He didn't.

'I've been trying to contact Jack for a couple of days, you know, to ask for corroboration,' I continued once the silence had become uncomfortable. 'Apparently, he's abroad till next week.'

'What makes you think that?' said Challis sharply. It was her first comment in a while.

'Text,' I explained. 'I called him, but it went to voicemail, so I sent a text as backup. That's what his reply said. Here, look…'

I fished my mobile out of my pocket, found the relevant text exchange and handed the phone eagerly over to Yardley. He took it without much enthusiasm, looked at it for a few seconds and then showed it to Challis before passing it back to me.

'Diggle is not abroad,' the detective inspector said bluntly. 'He was questioned by police in Brandon last week.'

'Where's that?' I said, disconcerted. 'Never heard of it.'

'Suffolk. Close to the Norfolk border. He was released without charge.'

'And what were they questioning him about?' interjected Lucy.

Yardley looked frustrated. 'Ayling's wretched sheep. A14 to Cambridge; A11 – it's a pretty quick journey to Brandon, dual carriageway all the way a couple of miles from Braybrooke. That's what sheep rustlers like, to get away from the scene of the crime. The local police are onto something there. But...'

'What?' I asked.

'They don't think that Diggle's involved.'

'Why were they questioning him then?'

The detective shrugged his shoulders. 'Suffolk police think he was doing a little freelance investigation of his own. He'd obviously heard something. Might even have been trying to help. Some local police informant told them he was asking questions about Ayling's sheep, so they hauled him in for a chat.'

'Did they find anything out?'

'Only that he doesn't know any more than me about what happened to those sheep, beyond someone from that area being involved. I'm only interested to the extent that the disappearance of the sheep had any bearing on the murder. Increasingly, I don't think it did.'

He saw my querying expression and elaborated. 'Look, the sheep were clearly taken. But they were out on the road, and our working hypothesis now is that this was a result of

Mr Ayling's killer leaving the gate onto the Great Oxendon lane open. So probably an opportunistic crime, committed locally but with the perpetrators swiftly moving the sheep on elsewhere.'

'And if that is so...' I began.

'If that is so, Mr Rowland – and we are still treating it as a theory rather than established fact – then Mr Ayling's killer is much closer to home. As his brother said in the church.'

'Have you questioned Ned Logan on his whereabouts at the presumed time of the murder?'

'We have. He says he was at home. His wife confirms it.'

\*\*\*

We left the police station shortly afterwards with a firm assurance that the enhanced police presence in Braybrooke would continue, which was comforting, but also having received a clear warning to be careful about our personal security, which wasn't.

'I think they've been slow out of the blocks,' I grumbled to Lucy as we belted up in the car. 'They've been too focused on that sheep-rustling/traveller theory and haven't paid nearly enough attention to other possibilities. Now they're playing catch-up.'

'We've found out more than they have,' concurred Lucy.

'Well, we are Holmes and Watson, after all,' I replied modestly.

Lucy's response was a rather strained smile.

We travelled on in silence for a mile or two and then pulled up at a traffic light. On impulse, I told my car to call Jack via its voice-activated hands-free system. The phone rang several times, and I thought it was just about to kick through to voicemail when Jack picked up, just as the lights were turning green.

'Hello, Mr Rowland,' said Jack's voice, amplified through the car's speakers. He sounded reluctant, but he had clearly stored my number in his phone, which was a small positive.

'Hello, Jack,' I replied, pulling away from the lights. 'Good to hear your voice. I've been trying to contact you for a couple of days.'

'Yeah, sorry,' replied Jack, sounding vaguely apologetic. 'Been away.'

'Abroad, your message said.'

There was an indeterminate noise on the other end. I decided to let it pass, no point in catching him out in an obvious lie; it would only antagonise him.

'Are you back now?' I asked.

'Will be in an hour or so. Just stopped for a break,' Jack replied. This rang true; I could hear the bustle of a motorway service station in the background.

'Look, I wonder if I could possibly meet you for a chat?' I asked. There was an urgent elbow jab to my left arm, and I looked across at an indignant wife. 'That is, if we could. My wife and I. It's about Edmund's death.'

'What about it?' replied Jack suspiciously. 'I don't know any more than you do. Or are you set on pinning it on the traveller community, like the police seem to be?'

'No, nothing like that,' I reassured him. 'We just have a couple of questions to which we think you might have the answers, having been an employee of Edmund's. You may not even be aware of the importance of what you know.'

There was a pause. 'When?'

'Well, no time like the present – plus, I'll be back at work in London tomorrow. If you're only an hour from Braybrooke, why not pop round for a cup of tea when you get back? You know where we live.'

Again, there was hesitation. 'How long would it take?'

Lucy butted in. 'Just one cup of tea, Jack. You'll be away in fifteen minutes.'

'Unless you want to stay longer,' I added.

I could sense Jack's brain whirring.

'And this might help solve Edmund's murder, might it?' he asked doubtfully after a few seconds.

Lucy and I looked at each other. 'It might,' we said in unison and exchanged self-satisfied glances.

'Alright then,' said Jack, still sounding fairly dubious. 'In an hour or so. See you then.'

\*\*\*

We had about a half-hour trip ahead of us, so there wasn't much time to spare, even without the hindrance of Northampton's notorious traffic. But, finally, we were out of town on the A508, heading north back towards Market Harborough. Lucy had been quiet all the while since the call with Jack, and I could see that she was thinking.

Just as we were turning right at Lamport with about seven miles to go till we reached Braybrooke, she came to life. 'How are you going to play it with him?' she demanded suddenly.

I paused for a moment. 'Well, firstly I'm not going to talk about him supposedly being abroad, or in Brandon, or the sheep, or anything like that,' I replied. 'Let's just focus on what we actually need to know.'

'Which is?'

'The will. He certainly witnessed it, but when and why did he do that and, rather more importantly, what does it say?'

'Do you think he'll know?' said Lucy doubtfully. 'I've often witnessed things for people without the slightest idea what they say.'

'There must have been some explanation when Edmund asked him to sign,' I reflected. 'What was it?'

Lucy nodded her agreement. 'And if he can't remember – or pretends he can't – then you can tell him what Amelia told you: he signed a document that apparently disinherits her. Did he do that knowingly?'

'We know that Andrew Ayling changed his tune significantly about Jack,' I responded. 'Is this will anything to do with that?'

We didn't know and slumped into silence for the remaining few minutes. But hopefully, we were about to find out.

Jack's blue Land Rover was sitting outside our house as we drew up.

# CHAPTER NINETEEN

Jack got slowly out of the vehicle as we pulled up alongside to the right and raised a hand feebly in reluctant greeting. Even without talking to him, I could tell at once that he was ill at ease.

'Thank you for coming, Jack,' I said enthusiastically, advancing round the back of my Range Rover with my hand outstretched in greeting. Lucy, nearer, got out of the car rather more slowly. She'd barely exchanged a word before with our visitor.

'Hello again. Lucy,' she said, all cool reserve, as she extended her hand once Jack had released mine. 'We met after the funeral.'

Jack nodded and touched her hand briefly. It didn't seem as if handshakes were commonplace in his world.

'Jack,' he replied uncertainly and stood there at a loss.

'Well, let's go in, shall we?' I said, breaking the uneasy silence decisively and heading for our front door. 'I think we promised you a cuppa, Jack?'

He gave a forced smile and waited till both Lucy and I had entered and calmed the excited dogs before joining us inside. 'Look, I haven't got long,' he said unhappily.

'Won't take long,' said Lucy breezily, as she headed for the kitchen.

I led Jack through to the drawing room and sat him down. He looked around curiously at the unfamiliar decor, accepted a mug of tea when Lucy brought it through and then turned to me shyly. 'What's this about then...'

He didn't seem certain what to call me, so I thought I'd clear that destabilising issue up straightaway. 'Robert. Robert's my name.'

He nodded, seemingly almost grateful. 'OK, Robert. Same question.'

I pondered how to proceed and decided upon a direct approach. 'Tell me, did Edmund ever ask you to witness any documentation?' I asked.

'What, sign it like?' replied Jack. He was beginning to relax. 'Yes.'

'Often?'

Jack shrugged. 'No, not really. Just occasionally.'

'Do you remember witnessing a will, Jack?' interjected Lucy, rather earlier than I would have mentioned this topic.

Jack looked alarmed again. 'Maybe,' he said cautiously. 'I remember, because Edmund needed two witnesses. I had to promise my mate Eric a pint to persuade him to come to Braybrooke Farm.'

'How long ago was that?' I asked, in as low-key a manner as I could.

Jack looked uncertain. 'Must be dated, ain't it?' he replied.

'I've never seen it, Jack,' I responded truthfully. 'Roughly how long, do you reckon?'

Jack scratched the back of his head. 'Maybe four months. A little longer perhaps.'

'Did you know it was a will, Jack?' asked Lucy.

He nodded. 'Sure.'

'So Edmund told you?' I said.

'No, not Edmund,' said Jack scornfully, as if this was a patently ridiculous suggestion. 'It was a Tuesday, see, or maybe a Thursday, because Lesley was there. She told me.'

\*\*\*

Lucy and I looked at each other, astounded. Jack realised instantly that he'd said something revelatory, and worry crept over his face.

'What?' he asked cautiously.

Where to start? I took a deep breath. 'Did you see who this will was made out in favour of, Jack?' I asked.

He shrugged rather pathetically. 'No. Never even looked at it. Not sure I'd have understood it if I had.'

'And it was definitely Lesley who told you it was a will? You're sure she was there?' asked Lucy.

Jack had been looking embarrassed by his naivety, but now a question had come up to which he knew a definite answer.

'I'm sure because Eric was sat there dribbling at the sight of her,' he said firmly. 'It was a warm day for autumn; she wasn't wearing much. I teased him about it afterwards.' There was a pause, and I was just about to jump in when he began to add something. 'Also...'

'Go on,' I encouraged him.

'I don't think Edmund was pleased when she told us it was a will.'

'How do you know?' asked Lucy.

'Just an expression on his face,' replied Jack. 'He didn't say anything, but I'd worked for the man long enough to know when he was pissed off. And he was. She seemed eager to tell us.'

'Why do you think that was, Jack?' I asked.

He shrugged again. 'Maybe she was going to benefit from it?' he ventured cautiously.

'Would that have been likely, in your view?' asked Lucy.

Jack looked confused.

'What my wife means is, was Edmund sweet on Lesley?' I explained. 'Was there anything going on between them?'

Jack considered the question seriously. 'Well, he liked a giggle with her; I certainly saw that,' he said. 'And she played up to it, flirting and swishing her hair and all that, like women do. I saw a bit of that too. But as to whether there was anything more to it...' He raised his shoulders helplessly. 'Who knows?'

\*\*\*

After I had shown Jack out, I returned to the drawing room, where Lucy was deep in thought on the sofa.

'Well, that's a turn up for the books,' I said. 'What do you make of it?'

Lucy looked up sharply. 'I believe him. She was there.'

'I agree. But if there was such a will, and she was a beneficiary, she would surely be telling everyone by now of its existence. She hasn't.'

Lucy pouted thoughtfully. It's always highly distracting when she does that. 'Lesley would only be a beneficiary if there was indeed some sort of relationship with Edmund,' she said, after a pause for thought. She looked up at me for corroboration.

'Again, I agree.'

Lucy paused again and then came to a decision. 'I can see only two scenarios,' she said firmly, as if daring me to challenge her.

'Go on,' I replied evenly.

'Number one,' continued Lucy, 'she's not a beneficiary at all. I don't think that's likely if she was as eager as Jack says to tell him it was a will; it wouldn't have been of the slightest interest to her. And if she wasn't a beneficiary, surely Edmund could have asked her to be a witness, together with Jack. No need to call in lecherous Eric.'

'OK,' I said, accepting her argument, and waited whilst my wife gathered herself to continue.

'Number two: she is a beneficiary but dare not admit it.' She looked at me triumphantly. I didn't get it and stared back at her dumbly, until she jumped to her feet in frustration. 'Look, for God's sake, her husband is extremely jealous – we know that.'

'Yes,' I said cautiously, with the glimmerings of what she was driving at beginning to dawn upon me.

'What do you think Ned would conclude if he suddenly heard that Lesley was in line to receive a significant bequest from another man? One she worked for two days a week, so saw regularly, often alone?'

'Well, being the sort of chap he is, he'd certainly have his suspicions…'

'To put it mildly!' exclaimed Lucy. 'He'd have a fifty kitten fit! So assuming Lesley knows about the whereabouts of the will at all, she doesn't dare tell him.'

I collected my thoughts. 'All possible. But does it get us any nearer who killed Edmund?'

'I think so, Holmes,' replied Lucy, reverting to my Conan Doyle alter ego. 'I believe Ned found out something was going on between Lesley and Edmund, either through discovering the will or something else. And that's what led to the killing.'

\*\*\*

'Well, if that's the case, she must know it was him,' I said, after a momentary pause.

'Ah, but does she think he knows about the will? I reckon she's unsure, so she's uncertain what to do. She may not even be sure it's Ned,' replied Lucy. 'And it appears Andrew's got his hands on it anyway. So what's that all about? Where does he fit in?'

This stumped both of us for a few seconds.

'One thing's for sure,' continued Lucy. 'You've got to tell the police.'

I sighed in frustration. 'Look, they said they questioned Ned about his whereabouts around the time of the crime,' I replied. 'Lesley vouched for him.' But even as I said it, I had my doubts – the police had been so focused on that sheep rustling theory, they might just have gone through the motions with any alternative. Lucy's sceptical look tallied with this.

'OK, let's say for the sake of argument that there was a will,' I continued. 'Lesley knows she's a beneficiary. And now the man who made that will is dead. She's going to want to claim her inheritance. Except she doesn't know how, because she doesn't have a copy of the will, and she can't admit the existence of any sort of relationship with Edmund.'

'Hmm,' said Lucy, mulling this rather complex theory over. 'You make it sound almost as if she's got a motive for murder herself. You know, smitten admirer writes you into his will, but he's only in his fifties. Might have to wait decades.'

'But surely…' I began.

'What? The police must have questioned Lesley on her whereabouts too?' She raised her eyes cynically to the heavens. 'With Ned, according to her. But the time Edmund died is not very precise, is it?'

'Well, it's pretty simple then, isn't it?' I said.

'What?'

'Lesley's here tomorrow. Pin her down. Tell her what Jack told us: she told him that what he was signing was a will. Why did she do that? What had it got to do with her?'

Lucy looked unconvinced at this suggestion.

'Go on, Watson. Woman's intuition. You'll definitely know if she's lying.'

'It'll seem a bit nosy.'

'We're involved! I found the body! Jack spoke to us voluntarily! We're just trying to understand a few things as concerned citizens. If we don't, tell her we'll simply have to go to the police.'

'I bet she'll start talking soon enough then.'

# CHAPTER TWENTY

I felt guilty on the train to London the next morning, having left Lucy with the thorny task of questioning Lesley, but my wife had seemed impressively determined to confront the issue, so all I could do was wait. She also agreed to text me with any developments as soon as she practically could.

As the morning dragged on, I found myself impatiently conducting a time and space analysis to predict when I could expect any sort of update. I knew that Lucy would normally have a coffee with Lesley at around 11am on those mornings she was in, and that would clearly be the moment to broach the conversation. So I was on tenterhooks from around 11.30am.

But... nothing. Clare sensed that my mind was elsewhere and gave off a distinct air of hurt, since if it was anything work-related I would generally confide in her, but I ignored these disapproving vibes from my loyal PA. I'd make it up to her in due course, I decided.

By midday, I could stand the suspense no longer and texted a short, *Any news x?*

Still nothing. Then, after a few minutes, came an equally terse reply: *Can't talk x.*

This set my thoughts haring off in all sorts of other directions, since Lesley's mornings with us generally ended at midday, yet she was evidently still there. Why would that be?

I had to put my natural curiosity on hold for a while after that, since I had a lunch engagement, but no sooner was that over than I consulted my phone again, fully expecting a summary of developments. Still nothing.

Again I texted: *? x*

The reply came instantly: *Too complicated – wait till you get home xxx*

Infuriating. I thought about giving her a ring, but… not cool. I'd have to wait.

\*\*\*

Leaving the office unusually promptly that day, to Clare's ill-concealed disapproval, I was home before 7pm. Lucy began talking excitedly as soon as I came through the door, wide-eyed – she was clearly looking forward to imparting whatever news she had managed to elicit from Lesley.

I stayed her immediately with my hand; first things first. I poured myself a stiff whisky, offered her one too (she declined) and then we settled down together on opposite sides of the kitchen table: our normal ritual.

'So…?' I began.

'Well, all rather dramatic,' replied Lucy. 'There were several stages. I wasn't looking forward to the conversation, I can tell you.'

'Understandable.'

'I decided to raise it at our normal coffee break. I think Lesley realised something was up – she looked pretty uneasy when she sat down.'

'How did you go about it?' I asked.

'I started by saying that we'd had another conversation with the police recently, since it was you that discovered the body, and the question of a mystery will had come up. I didn't say who raised it,' responded Lucy.

'What was her reaction?'

'Non-committal. She just shrugged and looked at me. So then I said that we'd promised to relay any further information that came our way to the police and that yesterday we'd had a talk with Jack…'

'I bet that got her attention.'

'It did. She looked horrified, I thought at first. But then I could see that she was angry – really angry. She just looked at me, and then when I began talking again, she just said very quietly, "What business is this of yours?"'

'To which you replied…?'

'That Edmund was our neighbour; that we hadn't gone looking for this information but that we intended to tell the police, as we had promised, unless convinced that the whole thing was clearly irrelevant. She was still angry, I could see that, but she was getting on top of it and thinking hard. After a few seconds she asked me, "What has Jack told you?"'

I took a sip of my drink. 'So you told her, no doubt?'

'Exactly. I said that Edmund had asked Jack to witness a legal document and that it required two signatures, so Jack had asked his friend Eric to oblige. She didn't say anything at that point. Then I told her that, according to Jack, she had been present at the time, and it was her that had told them both the document was a will. They had no idea what it was up to that point.'

'How did she react?'

'She said nothing, for a long time – I'd guess nearly half a minute. Then she began to cry and to apologise for crying, and that almost made me cry in sympathy. I made her another cup of coffee. Then she looked at me long and hard, sizing me up.'

'What happened after that?' I said.

'I said, "Look, Lesley, you can trust me; we've known each other a long time. If you're in trouble, I'll try to help."'

'And is she? In trouble?'

'She sighed, seemed to pull herself together, dabbed away her tears and then told me she had an admission to make. She's been having an affair with Edmund for over two years.'

'Blimey!'

'Blimey indeed. I knew already that in effect she was married to Ned in name only; Edmund showed sympathy – she's an attractive woman; he had an eye for the ladies – and one thing led to another. But it became quite serious. Edmund wanted her to move in with him. That's why he rewrote his will, cutting out Amelia, to prove his intentions. She says that it was all his idea and that he wanted to marry her.'

'Does she have a copy of this will?'

'No. She says that once it was signed, Edmund was going to lodge it with his solicitor, who would send her a copy. But that never seems to have happened.'

I sat back to reflect. 'What if Amelia got wind of this?'

'She lives miles away. It's unlikely she could do much about it, even if she did.'

'Did you tell her Andrew had a copy?'

'I said that he appeared to have a copy,' replied Lucy, 'as he'd shown the signature page to Amelia. But not that he definitely had one: we don't know that.'

'I just don't get what Andrew's got to do with it,' I said. 'It doesn't seem that he has any claim on the farm at all. Either the original will is still valid, in which case it goes to Amelia, or the new one is, which leaves it to Lesley.'

Lucy contemplated this in silence for a few moments. 'On balance, I still say that Ned's the culprit,' she said. 'Whether he got wind of the will or not I don't know, but he probably cottoned on to the affair. And that was enough.'

'Did you run that theory past Lesley?'

'I suggested it as a possibility. She said it was too awful to contemplate, and she'd been with Ned that day. And then she just said, "Poor Edmund," and started crying again.'

\*\*\*

I sat back thoughtfully and came to a decision. 'I'm going to talk to Amelia again,' I announced and looked up to gauge the reaction.

Lucy hadn't been comfortable about my two tête-à-têtes with that fair lady so far, recognising feminine allure when she saw it, and I saw the reluctance in her expression.

'Shouldn't we just tell the police and let them follow up?' she replied.

'There's a fair case for that, I agree,' I responded. 'But for one thing.'

'What?'

'Well, consider. Lesley is a great help to you here, isn't she?'

Lucy nodded.

'I don't think she is going to take it well if we immediately reveal her affair with Edmund to the police, do you?'

'But surely, it's pertinent that she was having an affair with the murder victim? And as we agreed the other day, she needs the dosh; she's not going to throw her hand in here, is she?'

'Unless she suddenly comes into a lot of money, I suppose,' I said, musing aloud. 'What sort of mood was she in when she left?'

Lucy paused. 'Hard to tell. Still rather angry about the whole conversation or upset at least. But grateful for the sympathy I'd shown her. She didn't explicitly say that what she had told me was in confidence. I think she was more concerned with bracing herself to face Ned again. No harsh words were exchanged.'

We lapsed into a thoughtful silence.

'I agree we should tell the police,' I said eventually, 'but we can do better by them if we do just a little bit more research. That may entirely justify us going to them. It won't take long; I'll call Amelia now. If I can fix something up, come with me if you want.'

Lucy nodded. 'Alright,' she said unenthusiastically.

***

I called Amelia straightaway, on the Braybrooke Farm landline. She picked up immediately, thereby confirming she was still in residence, and seemed rather surprised to hear from me. I detected curiosity rather than anything else. I hadn't thought through what I was going to say and made rather a muck of it. Eventually, she cut through my lengthy preamble.

'Look, you and Lucy want to discuss something, and it has to do with Edmund's death, is that it?'

'That's about the size of it, I suppose.'

'Much easier if you'd simply said so, Robert,' she responded kindly, as if to an errant teenager. 'Do you mean now? And face to face?'

'Well, that would be ideal of course, because I have to be back at work in London tomorrow,' I responded. 'We can come over to you, or you can come here if you prefer…'

'Here,' Lucy was mouthing silently at me. 'Offer supper.'

'We can offer supper in the kitchen if you like?'

There was a pause on the end of the line. 'Well, I haven't eaten yet…' responded Amelia doubtfully. 'Alright. Give me fifteen minutes to get changed.'

I glanced at my watch – it was 8.35pm. 'No rush,' I said. 'Lucy needs to prepare something anyway. Let's say 9pm.'

'Fine. See you then. Do I need to worry?'

'No, I don't think so. But a few things have come to light lately, and we'd like to discuss them with you. I think there's quite a lot you may be able to clarify.'

'I'd be surprised, because there's quite a lot I don't understand.'

'Well, two heads are better than one.'

'Yes, see you shortly,' she said and rang off.

Lucy looked rather cold as I turned to her after replacing the receiver, and I was mystified as to why. 'Three heads,' she said tightly.

# CHAPTER TWENTY-ONE

Considering she had had only fifteen minutes to prepare, Amelia was rather a vision when she arrived, having walked the five hundred yards or so from Braybrooke Farm: jeans and a casual shirt, but somehow smart rather than scruffy. Some women can carry that off, and she was one of them; other women don't much like it, and I could instantly sense Lucy bristling. I don't think it was anything nearly as strong as jealousy, but all the same, it's always rather gratifying when your wife starts circling the wagons.

I offered Amelia a glass of plonk from the box on the sideboard (Lucy and I already had one), and the two of us sat at the kitchen table whilst Lucy finished preparing a cottage pie.

'So I'm all ears,' said Amelia, after taking her first sip. She wasn't at all defensive. 'What do you want to know?'

'It's about this wretched will you mentioned to me the other day,' I responded. 'The one Andrew showed you.'

'He didn't; he just showed me the signature page. I don't even know if it was a will. You'd have to ask Jack – he signed it.' She took another sip and awaited my response, looking slightly wary now.

'We have,' said Lucy quietly, provoking what I fancied were the first stirrings of unease from our guest, who looked at me questioningly.

'It's definitely a will,' I confirmed. 'Jack was told so at the time. Guess who by?'

Amelia shrugged with seeming nonchalance. 'Well, Edmund I suppose.'

'Lesley,' said Lucy, with understated triumph; she knew she'd scored a bullseye.

'What? What on earth has she got to do with it?' said Amelia, turning towards my wife with something like anger.

Lucy kept her calm, rose to her feet and took the peas off the boil.

'That's one of the things we thought you might be able to help us with,' I explained, trying to lower the temperature a bit. 'She did work there, I suppose. It might just be happenstance.'

Amelia looked vexed and was about to say something when Lucy invited her up to the sideboard to help herself. She got up to do so with a strained smile. I followed, then Lucy, and it was a couple of minutes before we were all seated at the table again. Amelia had used that time to think.

'If it was a will, who was it in favour of?' she said and took her first mouthful. Then she looked up. 'Well?'

'We don't know. Jack didn't see,' I replied.

'Bloody Jack,' Amelia replied sourly, spearing her next mouthful. 'Imagine signing what was obviously a legal document without even looking at it. Who does that?'

'Plenty of people, I'm afraid,' replied Lucy, calm as ever.

Amelia made to reply, then thought better of it.

'Do you talk to him – Jack?' I asked curiously. 'After all, he's back at the farm now.'

'No. He's completely monosyllabic. But I will now, you can bet on that.' Her eyes flashed defiantly, as if daring us to contradict her; she looked rather magnificent.

'So let's assume that this will exists,' said Lucy, bringing us back to the matter at hand. 'How did Andrew know about it, and why did he show it to you?'

Amelia looked genuinely puzzled.

'Bit of a mystery, I'm afraid – he's been saying ever since he got up here that he thought there was another will, and that it favoured him, which made life rather tiresome. He looked hard enough. Perhaps he simply found it?'

'In which case why not show you what it said?'

There was no logical answer to that, unless…

We all reached the same conclusion simultaneously. 'It wasn't in his favour,' the three of us said together.

\*\*\*

'Well, it can't have been in mine,' said Amelia confidently, 'because I was the sole beneficiary of the original will. I've still got that. What would be the point of producing a new will saying exactly the same thing?'

'And if it wasn't in Andrew's favour…' Lucy began.

'…And Lesley was there when it was signed, couldn't apparently be a signatory herself and made a big thing of it…' I continued.

'…Then I'd say she's hot favourite,' concluded Amelia. 'Wouldn't you?'

We all paused to reflect. Lucy shot me a triumphant glance – that was what we had concluded earlier, and now Amelia was saying the same thing. Holmes sensed that Watson was mulling over the wisdom of telling Amelia about Lesley's affair with Edmund and shot her a warning look. She nodded back to me briefly but then pressed on, addressing the issue tangentially.

'How long had Lesley worked for Edmund?' she began innocuously.

Amelia pursed her lips thoughtfully after taking her last mouthful and laying down her knife and fork tidily on her plate. She took another sip of wine. 'I'm not entirely sure. She started well after I left. At a guess I'd say she's been working there for five years at least.'

'So they got to know each other pretty well, then?' responded Lucy delicately.

I got her implication of course, and so did Amelia. She didn't seem in the least put out by it. 'I suppose it's possible Lesley was a beneficiary of the will if she and Edmund were having a thing,' she responded, after a pause of a few seconds to reflect. 'And knowing him, he would almost certainly have tried it on. Especially with someone like her.'

Lucy and I exchanged glances.

'They were having a thing,' I said firmly. 'Lesley told Lucy this morning.'

'Why on earth did she do that?' asked Amelia, wide-eyed. She seemed much more focused on this inexplicable revelation by Lesley than the fact of the affair itself; perhaps she already knew, I remember thinking at the time.

'Because Jack told us about the will, and I told Lesley we'd promised to tell the police anything pertinent to the case that we turned up,' I replied. 'Unless she convinced us the whole will thing was irrelevant, we were going to do that.'

'Of course it's bloody relevant,' Amelia replied decisively. 'If we're right, and Lesley benefited from this will, then the only reason she did so was because she was sleeping with the murder victim. I'd call that pretty damn relevant, wouldn't you?' She looked from me to Lucy, daring us to challenge her.

'Yes,' I replied defensively. 'I agree. But she's been a great help to us here, and still is. We didn't want to go straight to the police without hearing her side of the story. That's why Lucy sat her down this morning.'

'Well, now you've heard Lesley's story,' snorted Amelia, with ill-concealed contempt, 'I trust you are going to call the police first thing tomorrow morning? Because if you aren't, I most certainly am.'

This forceful reaction resulted in a slightly awkward pause, until Lucy said firmly, 'We are.'

\*\*\*

'Good.' Amelia nodded approvingly. She took a further sip of wine and looked up, waiting to see what came next.

'Can I ask you a question about something else which may or may not be relevant to all this?' I asked cautiously.

'Sure.' She looked at me defiantly, daring me to do my worst.

'Marlene Filler.'

Amelia looked surprised. 'What about Marlene Filler?'

'I heard the row in the road outside the other day,' I said, feeling rather shamefaced about it. 'I just happened to be sitting in my garden reading, with a glass of wine. It wasn't deliberate eavesdropping.'

Amelia grimaced. 'No, I know. You could hardly have been oblivious from there.' She paused for a moment, thinking. Then she continued, with a resigned sigh. 'What exactly did you hear?'

'Well, not a great deal from you,' I replied. 'It was all Marlene. She wasn't being very complimentary, was she?'

'No.' She braced herself and turned to focus directly on me. 'Look, I've told you about Edmund and women, haven't I?' she asked.

'You have.' I nodded.

'And I mentioned that one of those dalliances became serious, didn't I?'

'Yes.'

'That was with Marlene. And it was what convinced me to call time on Edmund,' she explained.

Lucy and I waited for her to continue whilst she gathered her thoughts.

'I confronted him. He was shocked, because I'd always shrugged my shoulders before. But it was once too often; it was too public; and it had gone on for too bloody long. It was humiliating.' She waved a hand across her face, with an expression of distaste. 'Enough.'

'Obviously though, things didn't work out afterwards between Edmund and Marlene,' ventured Lucy diffidently. 'She's still with her husband.'

Amelia grinned ironically. 'That's because Edmund immediately ditched her when he realised I was actually about to go. He did it in front of me, in desperation: called her on the phone; told her there and then it was all over. So then she realised she was just another of his bits on the side – it wasn't the great love affair she imagined. I didn't hear the full conversation, but she wasn't pleased. Especially with me.'

'What did she expect you to do – shuffle off quietly into the sunset?' I asked.

Amelia shrugged resignedly. 'That's pretty much what I was doing, what I actually did in fact. I was going to let them get on with it.'

'But Edmund didn't want that when push came to shove, did he?' I asked. 'Actually, he preferred you. Hence why she hates you, since presumably when you finally did go, their relationship never recovered.'

'Shouldn't think she was too fond of Edmund either, after being dumped like that,' said Lucy.

We all looked at each other, realisation dawning.

'But if so, and if it was her, why so many years later?' asked Amelia.

\*\*\*

Our deliberations on that score went on for sufficient time for me to open another bottle of wine. Eventually, they turned to what Lucy and I should actually tell the police the following day.

'Let's just tell them the truth, for God's sake, and forget all the amateur detective work,' said Lucy. She turned to a bemused Amelia to explain. 'We've been playing Holmes and Watson with this, and it's been fun, which I'm ashamed about, because it's a personal tragedy for you. But the time for all that nonsense is over. We've got reason to have genuine doubts and suspicions about people. It's not for us to follow up on those. Leave it to the professionals.'

'I agree in principle,' I replied. 'But what would you call "the truth"?'

Lucy looked tired and dispirited. Amelia saw this and stepped into the breach. 'How about this?' she began and sat back for a moment to consider. 'You have uncovered a few things which you think they should know, in view of your recent promise. These are, in no particular order: one – Edmund's original will leaves his entire estate to me, still his wife when he died; two – there is supposedly another will floating around, which Andrew has been hunting high and low for, it was originally witnessed by Jack and his friend, in the presence of Lesley, the beneficiaries are unclear, but she's the most likely one, because; three – Edmund had been having an affair with Lesley for some time, which she confirmed to you yesterday; and four – he previously had an affair with Marlene, which led to me leaving the village, but he broke up with her because of that. Consequently, Marlene has a grudge against me, which you witnessed, and possibly against Edmund too, for breaking things off with her.' She paused to reflect. 'Yes, I think that just about covers it, don't you?' She turned her gaze on each of us expectantly.

'Ninety-five per cent,' I replied.

'Go on,' said Amelia calmly.

'Ned. There's still the possibility that he's behind all this, having found out about Edmund's affair with his wife. All the rest may just be irrelevant background mush.'

Amelia nodded gracefully. 'Fair point. Another possibility for them to look into, certainly.' She didn't seem very convinced about it though. 'Tell you what,' she said after a pause, 'what if I meet the police with you? There'd surely be some value in that; they could corroborate much of what you tell them there and then.'

Lucy and I looked doubtfully at each other. I was wondering how to say 'no' politely when that concern became irrelevant.

'Good idea,' said my wife.

# CHAPTER TWENTY-TWO

The next day was the day before Good Friday. I called Fiona Challis from my office mid-morning and asked if it would be possible to meet the following day.

'Sorry to muck up your Easter weekend,' I ended apologetically. 'If it's possible at all, that is. Difficult for me at any other time because of work.'

'No uninterrupted weekends in this business, Mr Rowland,' replied the detective, with something approaching levity, a first from her. 'Where and when?'

'Well, I thought at Braybrooke Farm. Ten o'clock, maybe?'

'Braybrooke Farm? The Ayling place?' She sounded surprised, which in fairness I expected.

'Yes. Mrs Ayling's still about, as you probably know. She's happy to meet with us all there. We've been talking to her, my wife and I.'

'Have you indeed?'

'And we've decided there are a few things the police should know, if you don't already. Better if you see us all together.'

'All?'

'My wife Lucy too, of course.'

She paused. 'I see. Quite a formidable group. What sort of things are we talking about here, Mr Rowland?'

'Questions we don't know the answers to. Possibilities we believe merit investigation, if you're not already onto them, which indeed you may be. And that's a job for the police, not us.' There was no immediate reply, so I continued after a few seconds. 'After all, you did make us promise to tell you anything we came up with, didn't you?'

I could sense Fiona Challis thinking; it was another fifteen seconds before she replied.

'In confidence, we are still investigating Mrs Ayling. I have nothing adverse to say about her, save that those inquiries are not yet complete. So I am reluctant to talk openly in front of her. Do you understand?'

'I do. But actually, I don't think you need to be completely open in front of her. Just listen to what we have to say. You can then decide for yourself what is credible and worth investigating.'

There was another long pause.

'All right. Ten o'clock. See you there.'

'Thank you.'

'Not necessary; it's my job. Though please go easy on me; I'll be outnumbered.' She still sounded surprisingly playful.

'I promise,' I said.

\*\*\*

I had texted both Lucy and Amelia immediately after my call with Fiona Challis, confirming that the meeting was on and suggesting that the three of us convene at Braybrooke Farm at 9.30am so we had time to get our ducks in a row. Both had responded positively, so I assumed everything would be plain sailing when I got home that Thursday evening.

Just after lunch, Ginny called me.

'You know you were going to pick us up on Good Friday?' she asked plaintively.

'Yes,' I replied cautiously. 'Tomorrow. You were going to text me the train time.'

'That's it, Dad! Everyone's knocking off early for Easter. We're free now! Can we travel home with you tonight? I called Mum; she said it's fine.'

I couldn't see any problem with this; indeed, we'd enjoy having the children home for longer.

'Sure. See you at St Pancras. Five past six train,' I replied. I sensed a momentary hesitation on the line. 'Yes, I'll pay,' I said resignedly.

'Thanks, Dad, good of you to offer,' enthused Ginny. 'We'll see you tonight.'

I was still grinning ruefully to myself as she rang off, and Clare came in clutching a letter for signature. She saw.

'Good news?' she asked light-heartedly.

'Ginny,' I replied. 'She and Will are travelling home with me for Easter tonight.'

'And I bet she got you to pay,' replied Clare perceptively. 'Daughters always do. My father still pays for me. Whenever I visit my parents, he insists on sending me down to the local garage for a tank of petrol. I used to arrive running on fumes in my youth. Not now of course.'

Perish the thought. I raised a cynical eyebrow without making a reply and reached out silently for the letter. My non-answer was answer enough. Clare gave a little grin of triumph.

\*\*\*

Cynically, I was expecting a breathless, last-minute arrival, but Will and Ginny were already standing on the crowded St Pancras concourse when I arrived, both in jeans and sweaters, with backpacks at their feet. They had plenty of clothes at home and always travelled light whenever they visited. Ginny flung her arms around me with female abandon; Will gave a measured nod. Neither he nor I were great ones for male tactility. They both looked happy and well. I expected no less, but, well, one always worries.

The train journey to Market Harborough was conversation lite, both my offspring donning headphones as soon as they sat down. I turned with resignation to my customary *Evening Standard*. At least we had seats – not a given on the day before the Easter break.

Our arrival home after the three-mile trip in the car was a noisy flurry of maternal and canine greetings. The two children disappeared upstairs to unpack and leap into baths, and Lucy and I settled down to wait for them. She always loved having her chicks home, so I was surprised to detect a slight frown of concern on her brow. I asked her what was on her mind.

'Tomorrow: I think we may be making a mistake,' she said.

'Explain.'

Lucy's worried sighs are never a good sign in our household, and I was treated to a classic of the genre now.

'Sit down,' I commanded kindly, and she offered no resistance as I led her to the kitchen table. She sat there silently whilst I mixed her a gin and tonic and helped myself to a whisky and water, then sat down opposite her. We both took a long sip.

'Well?' I asked.

'I'm not sure we should be allying ourselves to Amelia: that's the long and short of it,' Lucy replied. She sat back guardedly to await my reaction. 'We hardly know her, after all.'

'I'm not sure we are allying ourselves to her, are we?' I replied doubtfully. 'We're just going to outline some things we've uncovered to the police, as we promised, and she's there to join up some of the dots and provide corroboration.'

Lucy looked unconvinced.

'That's not all, is it?' I asked. 'Come on, spit it out.'

'I'm not sure I like Amelia much,' said Lucy, apparently reluctantly.

'Well, fair enough. As it happens I do, rather,' I replied. 'But surely it's irrelevant whether or not we think she deserves a place on our Christmas card list. What else?'

Lucy looked rather helpless, a look that always made me feel protective. I thought I saw her bottom lip tremble so reached out across the table to take her hands in mine and nodded my silent encouragement.

Lucy's eyes rose to meet mine, and she braced herself with a determined set to her jaw. 'There is something that woman is not telling us,' she said firmly. 'I am certain of it, and it makes me nervous. Can you not sense it?'

I paused reflectively. 'I don't sense anything untoward or sinister about her, put it that way,' I replied. 'But I'm not claiming that we understand everything either. Let's tell the police everything we know, see what reaction that provokes and, meanwhile, stand by to revive Holmes and Watson if we need to. How does that sound?'

Before she could reply, we heard the rumble of feet on the stairs.

Lucy nodded seriously, and I saw her consciously transform herself into the happy mother she always was to her children.

\*\*\*

We got to Braybrooke Farm punctually the next morning, though it was plain from the atmosphere in the house before we left that Lucy was going under sufferance. I knew from experience that when she was in a mood like that, I just had to suck it up till the tide turned, as any attempt to jolly her along would simply result in an argument. The children were still asleep. My tentative suggestion that we stroll the five hundred yards in view of the fine weather provoked an eye roll, so a glum minute-long journey in Lucy's Mini it was.

Amelia opened the door immediately we knocked and seemed genuinely welcoming. Once all the pleasantries were over, she turned and led us cheerfully into the kitchen. Glancing to my left as we passed the drawing room, I could see that a tray had been laid out with four cups and saucers for later. Meanwhile, we were offered a preliminary mug of coffee in the kitchen, which we both accepted.

'I've got some news,' said Amelia conspiratorially as she sat down to join us at the table after making a cup for herself. We must have looked blank, because she gave a little sigh of frustration. 'Andrew wants to meet me. He emailed overnight. Next week, probably Wednesday. It looks as if he's taking it as read that he can stay the night, of course. Might even arrive earlier.'

I sensed her irritation at the presumption and thoughtlessness of her brother-in-law. 'Did he say what he wants to talk to you about?' I asked, though I was ninety per cent sure of the answer. It seemed the obvious thing to say.

'No, of course not,' replied Amelia scornfully. 'This is Andrew we're talking about.'

There was a pause. Lucy still hadn't said a word. Suddenly, she piped up. 'Anyway, this morning,' she said, with the faintest hint of impatience. 'How are we going to handle it?'

She looked from me to Amelia and back again. I was clearly expected to answer.

'Well, pretty much as Amelia suggested the other night,' I replied.

This did not seem to go down well with my wife. 'Remind me,' Lucy replied in an innocuous tone of which I had learnt to be wary.

I gave vent to my own grunt of frustration and ticked the items off on my fingers as I recited them irritably. 'The original will. The possibility of a second will. Edmund's affair with Lesley. The earlier affair with Marlene, which is why she doesn't like Amelia and indeed possibly disliked Edmund too. And the Ned angle. Clear enough for you?'

'Look, children, I don't know what you are squabbling about, possibly the fact that you are here at all,' said Amelia perceptively, 'but please put it behind you. Detective Sergeant Challis is here.'

\*\*\*

'Well, everyone,' said Detective Sergeant Challis primly, once we were all settled in the drawing room. 'What have you got to tell me this Easter weekend?'

She was dressed rather more casually than normal, and I fancied that this choice, plus her slight emphasis on 'Easter weekend' was intended to make us all feel a little guilty; I know I did. Amelia and Lucy both looked at me uncertainly, so I was apparently elected spokesman by default. I sighed and took a sip of my coffee.

'I'm sorry it's Easter weekend. But I work in London during the week, and you did say...'

Challis held up her hand. 'Please. No need to apologise. If you have things to say which are pertinent to this investigation, then I am keen to hear them. Genuinely.'

'Very well. You may well know some of this already, but we thought we should make sure.'

Challis said nothing but gave the briefest of nods. Her ballpoint hovered over her pad.

'Edmund Ayling and Mrs Ayling here never divorced, though they lived separately for over a decade,' I began.

'I am well aware of that,' responded Challis, with a hint of impatience.

'All right,' butted in Amelia. 'However, my husband never changed his will. As far as I am aware, I remain the main beneficiary. Were you aware of that, Detective Sergeant?'

I saw that Challis had begun writing. 'Yes, but continue,' she said quietly. 'Please explain what you mean by "as far as I am aware".'

'Just that,' replied Amelia. 'However, my brother-in-law,

Andrew, believes there is another will, and indeed claims to have found it.'

Challis looked frustrated. 'Have you seen it?' she asked.

'Possibly,' said Amelia. She was being deliberately mischievous, provoking a helpless shrug from Challis, and this sparked Lucy into action.

'Let's cut to the chase,' she interrupted impatiently. 'Andrew showed Amelia the final page of a document – where it's signed and witnessed. He didn't show her the full text. So we don't know for certain if it's a new will, or indeed who benefits if it is.'

'Except we don't think it's him,' I added. 'If it was, why hide that fact?'

Challis had stopped writing, and I could see that she was thinking hard. 'You say there were witnesses to this document,' she said, after a pause of a few seconds. 'Remind me who they were again.'

'Jack Diggle was one of them,' I said conversationally, enjoying her obvious surprise. 'And a mate of his. Eric.'

'Plus, there's more,' added Amelia. 'Those boys had no idea what they were signing. Someone else told them it was a will.'

I could see that the detective didn't want to ask the question, but she had no real option. 'Who?' she said after a few seconds, with obvious reluctance.

'Lesley Logan. She was there at the time.'

I had replied in deliberately neutral fashion, leaving the detective to draw her own conclusions. She didn't articulate them, but I could see that her writing had taken on a thoughtful bent. She finished and looked up. 'Anything else I should know about?' she asked, this time with something approaching humility.

# CHAPTER TWENTY-THREE

There was another twenty minutes of going around the conversational houses, but it was pure speculation on everyone's account, including Challis's. Once we started covering the same ground for a third time, she sensibly made her excuses and left, but she looked pensive as she did so, and I thought we had given her plenty to chew on. Lucy and I had also demonstrably kept our promise to the police.

We all looked at each other in some relief once Challis had departed, and Lucy and I were starting to make tracks towards the door when Amelia spoke up.

'Are you going to Dingley tomorrow?' she asked plaintively. 'I used to love Dingley.'

Lucy and I looked at each other, surprised. But of course Amelia knew about Dingley; she'd lived in the village for years. I shot Lucy a querying glance, not wishing to commit us. Despite her previously articulated reservations about Amelia, she rose swiftly to the occasion. 'Yes, we're going: the children are back for Easter and the weather's going to be fine. There's plenty of food and drink. Come and join us at home about midday tomorrow, and then we'll head over in convoy, Amelia. How about that?'

Amelia looked genuinely thrilled. 'That is so kind. I was thinking of going by myself, but I'd feel a bit conspicuous if I did. I've got some provisions here too. I'll get organised and bring everything along!'

With that, we said our goodbyes, citing the brevity of the children's weekend with us.

'You've changed your tune a bit,' I said to my wife as soon as we were safely ensconced in the Mini.

Lucy shrugged. 'She's not too bad. The more I think about Edmund's death the less I think she has anything to do with it. Anyway, I've always enjoyed Dingley; there'll be plenty of other people to talk to.'

\*\*\*

We got home slightly later than intended, but the children were still not up. *Plus ça change.*

It was a lazy family day, the highlight of which was a four-mile dog walk around the reservoir at nearby Sywell Park, something we'd done often, ever since I'd had to carry the children on my back. Lucy always made a picnic (or at least coffee and biscuits) which we all sat on a bench halfway round and ate, the dogs doing as well out of the biscuits as the rest of us. We all loved it.

Saturday was of course Dingley day, and for once we didn't have to dig Will and Ginny out of bed. After breakfast, they started packing up the Range Rover with all the paraphernalia we'd need: food, chairs, tables, drink. Having been going to Dingley since childhood, they were well aware of the need to arrive promptly, and the family was ready by 11.45am. I looked at my watch.

'What are we waiting for?' asked Will, standing by the car's open door. 'We don't want to be too far down the hill.'

'Or on the left-hand side,' added Ginny anxiously, standing by the other door.

Both knew the form. Too far down the hill after a late arrival and it was a long, steep hike up to the bookies and the parade ring, plus you missed the atmospheric oversight of the course which elevation gave you. It was further from the beer tent too, which, though unsaid, I fancied was now becoming a factor in Will's calculations, if not Ginny's. Everything happened to the right of the entrance track, which led down the hill; the left-hand side was a social desert.

'We're just waiting for someone,' said Lucy calmy. 'She won't be long.'

'Who?' exclaimed our impatient offspring in unison. Whoever she was, she was verging on being late, an unforgivable sin, at least where Dingley was concerned, if seldom anything else.

'Amelia Ayling, the woman we went to see yesterday,' Lucy replied.

'I thought you didn't like her?' pouted Ginny.

'Well, she's on her own, and we thought it would be a kindness,' I said, sensing my wife's slight discombobulation. 'You'll like her.'

'Not if she doesn't turn up soon I won't,' replied Will forcefully.

But even as he spoke, Amelia's white Audi nosed into the

little cul-de-sac beside our house, and she emerged elegantly from the car, tight jeans showing her long legs to advantage.

'Not yet midday,' she said pointedly. 'I'm not late, am I?'

She turned to the children. 'Hello, I'm Amelia,' she said simply, extending her hand to Will. He was at that age where a glamorous older woman would invariably leave him tongue-tied, which Amelia duly did. I suspect she well knew she would have that effect on a twenty-year-old and rather enjoyed it.

'Will. Hi.' He paused awkwardly.

Amelia turned smoothly to his sister and smiled. 'Hello. And who is this lovely young woman?'

Ginny's pleasure was obvious as she extended her hand. 'Ginny. Hello, Amelia, it's very nice to meet you.'

I broke up the mutual congratulation society before the whole thing got too sickly. 'Come on, everyone. We need to get going. Ginny, why don't you go with Amelia?'

I suggested this to head off Will's stumbling blushes if Amelia had asked him to accompany her, and his unmistakable relief was ill-concealed as he clambered into our car. Ginny nodded her acceptance calmly, smiled happily at Amelia and moved towards the passenger door of the Audi.

'Stick close to me, whatever the wretched marshals say,' I said to Amelia, as she climbed back into her car, and I opened the door of my own. 'We need the cars to be together if we're going to have a decent picnic.'

Amelia shut her door and opened the window. 'Coals to Newcastle,' she said cheerfully. 'I may not have been there for a few years, but I've been going to Dingley for a lot longer than you.'

***

Getting into Dingley was the usual semi-chaotic bunfight, but we managed to keep the two cars together and ended up pretty much directly in front of the little commentary box, about thirty yards down the slope: ideal. No sooner had we stopped than the children spotted some of their friends a few cars away and were off: that, after all, is what Dingley is all about, so we could have no complaints. Lucy sighed tolerantly and began laying out food on the two small tables we had brought for the purpose as I leant against my car and began wrestling the cork out of a bottle of something.

Amelia sidled up and reclined against the car beside me. 'Nice children,' she observed conversationally. 'Ginny never stopped chatting the whole way here.'

'What, all four miles of it?' I grinned, as the cork finally came free.

'It did me good,' said Amelia quietly. 'Genuinely. I forgot about everything else for a while except the perspective on life of a lovely young girl. Most refreshing.'

'Here's something that'll refresh you more,' I said. I found us a glass apiece, plus one for Lucy, and filled all three. My wife was still busy with the food and indicated with a glance and a nod that I should leave hers on the car roof. I did so and returned to my position beside the car, where Amelia accepted her glass gratefully. As we did so, a young girl passed by hawking programmes, so we bought one apiece.

Amelia clearly understood the arcane form guide and made a quick decision after a long pull at her drink. 'Number nine for me in the first race,' she declared confidently. 'Listen to this. *Promising hurdler coming back strongly from injury.*

*Second; second; first; pulled up. Then this season third; fourth; second; first.* Writer's Block – good name.'

'How do they rate it?' I asked. 'Assuming it's running.' It wasn't always a given that all the horses declared in the race card actually did so.

'Ninety-eight,' she declared.

Hmm, middling. I reviewed the form guide myself and came up with number twelve, Spearman: *half-brother of the proven Hard Hat; needs to temper his enthusiasm; sixth; first; fell; first; second.* There was nothing about the previous season. He came in at one hundred, though I've never understood the basis for those ratings. I indicated him in the programme to Amelia. 'That's the chap for me, if he's running. Still over an hour till the start. Let's get something to eat and then go and look at them in the parade ring.'

We moved round to the open tailgate of the car. Lucy was sitting there with a slightly older local couple, Dominic and Kate Mallory, by the time we rejoined her. I've always rather liked them, particularly Dom, who was happily quaffing my champagne and wearing a regimental tie of some description. Some twenty years before they'd been innocent parties involved in some dreadful murder;[1] I can never quite remember the details.

Dom got quickly to his feet as we approached; I was about to introduce him when Amelia leant in for a kiss. 'My dear Dom,' she said and kissed him again on his other cheek. Then she turned to Kate. 'Hello, stranger,' she said fondly. It was unmistakably the tone of a close friend.

Kate Mallory rose too, and there was a gentle peck on

---

1   See *Past Unbecoming*

the cheek for Amelia. She leant back and pursed her lips in sympathy, a beautiful woman still, though well over sixty.

'We were so sorry to hear about Edmund,' she said simply. 'I know you had your differences, but I can't imagine anyone wishing him any harm.'

'Well, you two of all people know that bad things can happen,' replied Amelia.

Dom shook his head. 'That was all a very long time ago,' he said sorrowfully. There was an awkward, reflective pause, and Lucy offered them a plate of salad. It jerked Dom back to reality. 'No, but thank you,' Dom replied, draining his drink. 'We're here with the Frobishers and the Laidlaws. We should get back.'

The Mallorys wandered off hand in hand, which is good to see when couples have been married for as long as they have. No sooner had they gone than I spotted the children returning, together with four contemporaries. This happened every year, which was why Lucy had packed a generous-sized picnic.

'The gannets are here,' I whispered.

\*\*\*

And so they were. Lucy and I loved it of course. It was amazing how quickly all the children's friends were growing up and genuinely fascinating to learn what they were all now up to. Even more amazing was the rate at which they consumed our food and drink. We were pretty much cleaned out after half an hour, whereupon they departed noisily in the direction of the bookies, with twenty minutes to go until the first race. Lucy looked fondly after them with that wistful smile I have always loved.

'Do you want to get a bet on too?' I asked her.

She waved me away, looking around at the debris of lunch. 'Let me do a bit of damage repair here. You two go off. Put a fiver on something for me: the second favourite.'

Five pounds was about as much as we ever risked on a horse at Dingley, so I nodded and turned to Amelia. 'Ready to risk your fortune?' I said.

She nodded cheerfully and downed her drink; we headed companionably up the slope together.

'So good to see Kate Mallory again,' she said. 'We were really close when I lived in Braybrooke. I knew her well at the time of their trouble. We've rather drifted apart since I moved away. Distance.'

'Inevitable, I suppose,' I replied. 'Do you want to see the horses first or head straight for the bookies?'

'Horses,' replied Amelia firmly, striding ahead.

There were only six runners, but as we got up to the rail of the parade ring, I could see that Amelia was looking at them closely. Not being an equestrian, I simply went by the form guide, so I stuck to my pick of Spearman, not least because he was being led round by an extremely pretty stable maid: as good a criterion as any in my book. Amelia took longer but, after a couple of minutes, nodded with evident satisfaction.

'Writer's Block – definitely. Let's go and get our money on.'

The bookies were only twenty yards away, but again I could see that Amelia was no amateur: she hung back for several minutes to check the different odds they were all offering, until eventually plunging into the throng, where she secured odds of 5/1 and ventured the princely sum of £10. I tagged along in her wake and put my fiver on, at 7/2, plus a similar amount on Wedding Cake for Lucy, at 4/1 – the second favourite, as she wanted.

We were heading back down the slope towards the cars when Amelia suddenly stopped dead – I was a pace ahead of her before I realised.

'What?' I asked, surprised, turning to face her.

She nodded downwards, over my shoulder. 'Andrew.'

I turned round: there indeed he was, a couple of rows of parked cars away down, below us, his Porsche parked alongside an identical one, albeit white. They seemed to be a group of four men, all seemingly very jolly.

'I thought he wanted to meet you on Wednesday?' I said, angling off to the left so that we would pass well away from them as we made our way back to our own cars.

'He does.'

'So what's he doing here now?'

'I don't know. He said he might arrive early.' Amelia didn't seem pleased at this prospect and hurried on down the slope, anxious to pass through the row of cars where Andrew was parked in case he looked down the line and spotted her, even though we were a good thirty yards away.

I followed on, unable to resist a glance in the group's direction. As I did so, a fifth figure emerged from the passenger seat of Andrew's Porsche. There was no mistaking that striking female figure: Lesley Logan.

I hurried off in pursuit of Amelia. I didn't tell her of my discovery, and even at the time, I didn't know why. Still don't, in fact.

# CHAPTER TWENTY-FOUR

Though I greatly enjoy Dingley, it's a pig of a place to get out of, with only one exit: an unpaved track up the slope in the field to the left of the cars as you face them, leading onto a main road. Accordingly, course veterans like us tend to skip the last of the six races in an attempt to beat the rush – not always a successful one, as plenty of people have the same idea. If you are going to do that you need to start gathering everyone together during the fifth race, if not earlier, and though we located Ginny swiftly enough, there was no sign of Will, nor did he answer his mobile.

'Bloody boy,' exclaimed my vexed wife. 'Where the hell is he? I've a good mind to leave him here. It's only a three-mile walk.'

I thought back to my own behaviour at Will's age, and one particular location immediately became highly likely, if not a certainty. 'Give me five minutes,' I said confidently. 'Everyone else wait here.'

I strode back up the slope. The beer tent was no more

than a hundred yards away, just beyond the parade ring which sat at the top of the incline.

The fumes hit me immediately as I stepped through the narrow, low entrance, together with the cheerful sound of laughter. It took me a matter of seconds to locate my errant son, who clutched a plastic mug which contained the final third of a pint of lager. He was in a group – four boys; three girls – most of them smoking or vaping. I observed the dynamics for a moment and was pleased to see that Will didn't seem to be the odd one out, though he and one of the girls were the only non-smokers. He looked cheerful. They were all talking and laughing, though the acoustics were such that I couldn't hear a word anyone said. I didn't know any of the others; they weren't the same individuals who'd cleaned us out at lunch.

I had no desire to make a fuss, so I manoeuvred myself into Will's eyeline and gave him the evil eye. He looked sheepish, downed his pint and gestured with his head in my direction. His companions turned around and eyed me up and down, making me feel old and conspicuous. I could see Will mouthing 'got to go' at the non-smoking girl, who pouted at him rather fetchingly.

'Sorry,' I shouted at him over the din as he reached me. 'We need to go. Fifth race.'

He nodded phlegmatically, then leant in towards me. 'Need a pee first.'

'For God's sake…' I began. 'Go on then. Be quick. Come straight back here – I'll meet you outside.'

Will strode off purposefully – a man on a mission. In rather slower time, I made my way towards the tent's narrow exit. As I ducked through it, I met someone coming the other way, who stepped back to let me through. I turned to thank him and saw an anxious face. Jack Diggle.

\*\*\*

Jack had two friends with him of about the same age, one of them perhaps his will co-signatory Eric, and as I emerged from the tent, he gestured for them to go in without him. With a shrug of the shoulders from one and a sour, insolent look from the other, they did so.

'Pint of lager, lads,' Jack called after them and then turned to face me.

'Hello, Jack,' I said casually. 'How are things?'

'Alright,' Jack replied awkwardly. He turned abruptly as if to follow his friends, then hesitated.

'All OK at the farm?' I said, leaping on the moment.

He came to a decision and swung back to face me. 'Not really.'

'Why?'

'Bloody Amelia.'

I put on my best curious expression and waited for him to continue.

He shrugged. 'Ever since it came out that I signed the will, she's had it in for me.'

'In what way?'

'Oh, just petty stuff. No coffee. Sarky comments. Rolling her eyes all the time. Tossing her hair. You know what women are…'

He trailed off rather helplessly. I couldn't help thinking that Andrew's kind words about Jack in the church might lie at the root of this.

'And Lesley? Is she still there?'

'Sure – a couple of days a week, as normal, though I don't think Amelia likes her much. Andrew's back shortly – Lesley seems very pleased about that. I don't really understand, because he made her redundant as soon as Edmund died.'

'You too. And not much sign of that for either of you now.'

Jack nodded. 'That's true.'

'And by the way,' I added. 'Andrew's back already. He's forty yards over there, three rows down.' I nodded towards the slope where the rows of cars began.

Jack looked in the direction I had indicated. He looked surprised but said nothing.

'He's got Lesley with him,' I added slyly, watching keenly for Jack's reaction. There wasn't one.

'They get on,' he said. 'Though not in that way… Andrew's not…'

'I know what you mean,' I said. 'No need to explain.' I spied Will coming into view, looking curious at whom I was talking to. 'Keep in touch Jack,' I murmured, as I turned to face my son. 'Any problems, or anything you want to talk about, you know where I am.'

***

Will said nothing as we wandered back towards our car, but I could sense the question anyway. He didn't need to.

'Just a guy who works at Braybrooke Farm,' I said eventually. 'You know, for Edmund. I've spoken to him a few times.'

'You and Mum are getting quite into all that, aren't you?' Will replied. I sensed a hint of disapproval.

'Well, it's not every day you discover a murder victim,' I replied, intending it to be humorous. 'Surely you can understand that I'm interested?'

Jacked sighed in that patronising way Gen Z reserve for their obsolete elders. 'Leave it to the professionals, Dad.'

I said nothing. We were twenty feet from the cars by then. Amelia and Ginny were already in the Audi, chatting away. Lucy was at the wheel of our Range Rover, radiating impatience. Knowing that expression, I braced myself.

'Will needed a pee,' I said apologetically, as I climbed in beside her and shut the door. Will clambered in clumsily behind me.

'Let me guess – because he was in the beer tent,' replied Lucy icily.

Neither Will nor I denied it. My wife took this as proof that her astute diagnosis was accurate, so she switched seamlessly from impatience to disapproval.

'For God's sake, he's twenty,' I said, in a patient tone, which I knew would probably needle her. 'That's what they do.'

'So? It was thoughtless.'

'You were twenty once, Mum,' ventured Will sullenly from the back seat.

'Indeed, I was. And I was never thoughtless.'

I knew better than to make a retort, though Lucy had left me a pretty open goal. Will didn't, however. 'Practically perfect in every way, then,' he replied tartly.

Predictably, silence then descended for about five minutes, by which time we were halfway up the slope in the far field, crawling towards the exit. I thought a change of topic might lighten the atmosphere somewhat.

'You'll never guess who I bumped into,' I said brightly.

Lucy looked across at me sharply. 'Who?'

'Jack Diggle.'

'In the beer tent, I suppose?'

'Well, he was going into it, yes.'

I got another disapproving glance from Lucy, implying that the whole beer tent saga was my fault, and at that point I decided to shut up.

In that happy state, the three of us arrived back at home ten minutes later. There was no sign of Amelia and Ginny.

\*\*\*

We unloaded the car in rather grumpy silence, and then Will headed upstairs to his lair on the top floor. I thought I had better mend my fences and went into the kitchen to kiss my disgruntled wife on the cheek. She leant forward to accept it awkwardly.

'Friends?' I said, hopefully radiating that quality myself.

'Friends,' replied Lucy quietly. 'And I'm sorry; I know it wasn't your fault Will was in the beer tent. But he does drive me mad sometimes. He knows when we leave Dingley.'

'He just lost track of time. Nothing malicious. That's what they do at that age. He knows he's annoyed you. I bet he says sorry once he's worked out how to do it.'

Lucy gave me an unconvinced smile. 'I wasn't too hard on him, was I?'

'Harder on me, if anything. But my shoulders are broad enough.'

Lucy smiled, more genuinely this time. 'Who was with him in the beer tent?'

'Nobody I knew.' I shrugged. 'Two boys, two girls; all about the same age too. I thought he seemed rather sweet on one of the girls. He didn't introduce us.'

'Really?' said Lucy coquettishly. I knew that she was rather worried about Will's diffidence around the fairer sex, but it was just a transient phase; most male adolescents go through it at some stage.

'Where are Ginny and Amelia?' I asked, changing the subject. 'They left before us.'

Lucy shrugged. 'Search me. They're getting on like a house on fire.'

Something about her tone made me uneasy in an undefinable way, but before I could articulate this reservation, my mobile rang. I could see from my screen that it was Amelia, and her voice was instantly identifiable anyway.

'It's me,' she said, needlessly. 'Ginny's with me. I wanted to show her something.'

'OK,' I replied cautiously, knowing that there was more to come. In response to Lucy's gestures, I put the phone on speaker so that she could hear too.

'The police have just arrived. They want to question me.'

'Not about the murder, surely?' I replied, shocked.

'Not directly.'

'What does that mean?'

'About Marlene Filler. They've taken her in for questioning. I said you might have something to add, so they've allowed me to call you to ask if you'd mind coming over here.'

'What – both of us?'

I sensed hesitation on the other end, presumably whilst Amelia looked for confirmation from whoever was with her.

'Yes, the inspector says ideally both of you,' she replied a few seconds later.

# CHAPTER TWENTY-FIVE

Lucy thought she'd better freshen up her make-up on, but when I jibbed at this she eventually settled for a brush through her hair. Whilst she was performing that complex ritual, I yelled up the stairs to Will from the landing.

'Got to go out. We'll be back in half an hour.'

No answer: he probably had his wretched headphones on, but my conscience was satisfied; he'd just have to call us if he was concerned.

So we were there in about ten minutes. I detected faint impatience from Yardley, presumably tired of making small talk till we arrived, but we were doing him a favour, so I wasn't going to rise to that. Challis sat meekly in the corner; Amelia had just made everyone a cup of tea, and Ginny was finishing handing them out. Another two were quickly rustled up for Lucy and I, after which our daughter hovered awkwardly. I indicated a chair in the corner with what I hoped was an unobtrusive gesture of my head, and she settled down gratefully, curious for the entertainment to begin. Yardley made no objection.

'Now, everyone,' he began. 'I am anxious to learn more

about Marlene Filler, because I am not satisfied that she can account for her movements on the day of the murder, and Mrs Ayling here believes she may have a motive. She also believes you may have information to add.'

I am sure Lucy and I looked nonplussed, and Yardley turned to Amelia, who spoke hesitantly, most unlike her. 'It's only a theory...' she began.

'Go on,' said Lucy encouragingly.

'Well, if Marlene was involved – and let's be clear, I'm not saying she was...' She looked around anxiously.

'Nobody is inferring that,' said Yardley patiently. 'Tell them what you told us earlier.'

Amelia sighed and braced herself. 'Very well then. Marlene dislikes me. Intensely so.'

We all waited for her to elaborate. I saw Ginny's eyes widen. Amelia recognised that nobody was going to come to her aid, and so she continued reluctantly.

'You see, I confronted Edmund about their affair. I'd previously ignored his little dalliances. But this one got out of hand. I decided to leave him. He begged me not to and broke up with her there and then on the phone, in front of me. I left anyway. But I think Marlene had pinned all her hopes on a future with Edmund. I ruined all that by bringing everything to a head, and ultimately, she could see that he preferred me over her.'

'Which must have been humiliating,' murmured Fiona Challis quietly.

Amelia turned to her gratefully. 'Yes, I imagine so. I don't think Edmund was flavour of the month with Marlene either after that, quite apart from any feelings she may have had about me.'

There was silence for a moment. Ginny looked around with the artlessness of youth to see which of the grown-ups would break it.

'But if she did anything about that – if – why now, so many years later?' asked Lucy.

Amelia looked hesitant again.

'Tell them your theory,' encouraged Yardley.

Another little sigh. 'I think she may have got wind of the possibility that Edmund and I were going to reconcile,' explained Amelia. 'We weren't quite at that point, but it was jolly close. Likely, in fact.'

'So you think she couldn't bear that?' I asked. 'Both of you being happy and her left out in the cold. So she killed Edmund to wreck it all.'

'It's a theory, Mr Rowland, nothing more,' said Challis coolly.

I nodded, accepting this. 'Why not kill you instead?' I asked bluntly.

Ginny looked shocked.

Amelia smiled wanly. 'I wasn't here. Otherwise, I suspect she might have done.'

We all paused again to reflect. Lucy broke the silence, focusing on Yardley. 'Well, you clearly think that Robert and I have information relevant to this theory; that's why you asked us over. What do you want to know?'

Yardley stirred himself from what appeared to be deep reflection. He turned to me. 'Mrs Ayling has explained that you can corroborate Mrs Filler's deep dislike of her. Can you?'

I must have looked confused, because Amelia continued encouragingly. 'Go on – the row in the street.'

'Yes,' I said after a moment or two. 'It happened just outside my garden, no more than twenty yards away. I was the other side of the fence. More of a tirade than a row. Amelia – Mrs Ayling – said almost nothing. It was all one-way traffic.'

'Along what sort of lines?' said Yardley, with deceptive casualness.

I struggled for a moment to paraphrase what I'd heard. 'Difficult to pick it all up; Marlene had completely lost her temper. Bitch, whore – that sort of thing. Female insults,' I said awkwardly and tailed off. 'Sorry, Amelia.'

She shook her head. 'That's fine. That's exactly how it was, except it went on for about thirty seconds.'

Everyone looked uncomfortable except Ginny, who sat there with eyes like saucers, looking around all of us in apparent astonishment.

'You haven't arrested Marlene, have you?' I asked eventually.

'No,' replied Challis. 'But we have questioned her, and we are not satisfied with the answers. We are still making inquiries.'

\*\*\*

When we got home, with Ginny, Will was still in his room; he probably hadn't even noticed we'd gone. Our daughter was up the stairs in a flash.

'How long do you reckon?' I said wearily to Lucy.

'Long enough for you to pour me a drink,' she replied, taking a seat at the kitchen table. 'A minute at least.'

I fixed us both a gin, and we sat back together expectantly.

Lucy's estimate was near enough: Ginny flounced in after a few moments with a sulky pout, announcing loudly that Will didn't believe her.

Her sibling slouched down the stairs reluctantly a few seconds later, attempting to exude a cool, sceptical demeanour. He failed.

'Tell him!' said Ginny.

'Tell him what?' I replied, deliberately obtuse. It's fun winding up the younger generation occasionally. I thought for a moment that Ginny was going to stamp her foot.

'That Marlene's the murderer, of course.'

Both the children knew of course that I'd found Edmund's body, but I don't think the reality of his death had hit home till then.

'The police did not say that Marlene was the murderer, Ginny,' said Lucy firmly.

'They're not satisfied with her story, and she's got no alibi,' declared Ginny indignantly. 'That's obviously what they think.'

'Why didn't you ask me along?' began Will plaintively. 'Sounds interesting. Nothing interesting ever happens in Braybrooke.'

'We did. Headphones,' I said, with some asperity.

Our son looked reflective. 'Who's Marlene anyway?' he said. We all looked at him open-mouthed. 'What?' Will responded defensively. 'I don't live here. How am I supposed to know who all these old folks are?'

'I do,' said Ginny, preening. Will sulked.

We ran through the whole saga from beginning to end over supper, answering all the questions the two of them had. By the end of the meal, everyone was friends again, and even Will showed some understanding of the interpersonal dynamics of the case. I'd also revealed the parental alter egos, Holmes and Watson.

'Cool,' said Will.

He may even have meant it; though he'd have been loath to admit it, I rather think the fact that his ageing parents were pursuing a murder case might rather have impressed him.

\*\*\*

The next day was Easter Sunday, which was one of the few days each year when our family ventured the fifty yards or so to church: a feeble performance, I admit.

It was also a rare occasion when the congregation reached a reasonable size – many families, like us, had children home for Easter, and there were others whose periodic attendance records were as slipshod as ours but did turn out then. Lucy and I sat in the second pew from the front, to the left of the aisle, with the children between us; we have done so ever since spontaneously settling down there the first time we ever attended a service in Braybrooke, and none of the locals seem minded to supplant us, despite our sporadic appearances.

Nobody ever sat in the front row, afraid no doubt of being thought presumptive. It was empty.

Despite the best efforts of Lucy and Ginny, we were there pretty promptly, and I looked around surreptitiously. The children did so rather more openly. After about a minute, Ginny gave an audible gasp of shock and nudged her brother hard enough for it to be obvious.

'That's Marlene,' she declared, in a stage whisper which could have been heard a hundred yards away. I saw Lucy grip her daughter firmly on the thigh whilst, to any casual onlooker, still looking serenely ahead.

'What?' Ginny declared in an indignant voice at undiminished volume as she turned to her mother. Lucy remained serene.

Marlene was several rows back the other side of the aisle, sitting at the end of her pew. She affected not to have heard Ginny's exclamations, but she must have done, especially as they were followed immediately by a direct stare of undisguised curiosity from Will.

Now it was my turn to do the nudging. With a reluctant sigh, Will dropped his gaze and shifted his focus to the vicar. You never know quite who you are going to get in Braybrooke these days, and this time it was a burly, middle-aged, smiling character with long hair carrying a guitar, known colloquially in our household as 'Hippy Jim'. We liked Jim – his sermons were invariably cheerful and amusing, and famously he had once left us all singing the last hymn and departed post-haste to run a service in the neighbouring parish, for which he was running late. There had been a general drift to The Swan afterwards to laugh about it, less a few tut-tutting killjoys.

The service was standard Easter fare, with plenty of Q&A for the children included by Jim; it took around forty-five minutes, because communion was thrown in. At the end, Jim entreated us all to stay for refreshments, generously provided and served by members of the Women's Institute. I knew that Lucy had a family meal roasting away gently at home, but you can't really just cut and run in those circumstances, so I braced myself for a cup of tea, a scone and a small Easter egg, coupled with some fairly bland small talk with people whose names I could never remember.

But there was a silver lining, which I hadn't anticipated. After our supper the night before, the children were now fully appraised of who everyone was in the Ayling murder case, and I could see them taking a lively interest in certain individuals. Holmes and Watson had acquired some apprentices.

\*\*\*

I got Lucy and I a coffee apiece, and then we split up in unspoken agreement. There were a number of people it would be useful to talk to, and that wouldn't happen without some concurrent activity between us.

Glancing around, I could see that Ginny was already in animated dialogue with her new best friend Amelia; what they had to talk about which had arisen since our meeting the previous evening I couldn't imagine, but I left them to it and sought out Andrew instead, who was standing rather self-consciously by himself.

'Back for Easter?' I said, in a statement of the blindingly obvious, but one has to open a conversation somehow.

'Yes. Drove up late yesterday.'

'In time for the point to point though.'

Andrew looked bemused.

'I saw you there,' I continued, by way of explanation. 'With some friends I think.'

'Well, I caught a bit of it,' Andrew responded lamely.

There was a strained pause.

'Have a very good Easter, Andrew,' I said eventually, breaking the logjam. 'I imagine you're staying at Braybrooke Farm with Amelia?'

Andrew's smile of affirmative response was more of a grimace; he moved deliberately past me. In his path was Lesley, with her back to him. He was disconcerted when he saw her and stopped dead; on seeing me watching, he pulled his mobile out of his pocket in a moment of indecision and gave it his full concentration. *There's a man ill at ease*, I thought.

After looking around to make sure that Ned wasn't about, I approached Lesley from behind myself, who was deep in rather serious-looking conversation with an elderly woman I didn't know. Her blue outfit showed off her curves to advantage, no doubt deliberately so. She turned towards me as she sensed my approach.

'Hello, Lesley, Happy Easter,' I began.

'Robert,' Lesley exclaimed, with every appearance of pleasure. 'Happy Easter!' She leant forward for a kiss, which I wasn't in a position to refuse, though I made it as perfunctory as possible in view of her husband's paranoia about my intentions: I didn't want any rumours getting back to him which were likely to reinforce it.

I turned towards the second woman, expecting Lesley to introduce us, but she was already making off, seemingly in something of a huff.

'Who was that?' I enquired. 'Sorry if I intruded on anything.'

'It was nothing,' said Lesley, shaking her head. 'Ned's aunt. She's with us for Easter. Spinster.'

'She didn't look very pleased,' I replied. Indeed, I could see that she was heading determinedly for the door. 'Ned not here?'

'She never does,' said Lesley and then continued as if

talking to a child, 'look pleased I mean. And no, as you can see, Ned's not here.'

I had indeed asked a fairly obvious question. Lesley regarded me gravely, looking rather a vision; clearly the conversational ball was now back in my court.

'I saw you at Dingley yesterday,' I replied, simply because I had to say something. Lesley stayed silent. 'You were with Andrew,' I added.

Never add to a perfectly adequate comment if the other party does not respond immediately; I had learnt that the hard way in business and kicked myself as soon as I said it. You invariably reveal more than you mean to. And so it was here.

'I was not with Andrew,' Lesley said, her mood changing in an instant.

'But I saw you in his car,' I replied defensively.

'I took a drink off him, and I may have sat in the front of his car for a moment,' Lesley said in a low, vexed tone, 'but I was most certainly not with Andrew. Is that clear?' And with that, she was gone, striding forcefully past me.

I sighed at this second rebuff within the same number of minutes and looked around. My eyes alighted on my hovering children. They were amused at my discomfort, but I could also see that they had something to say.

# CHAPTER TWENTY-SIX

One glance in their direction was enough to beckon them over.

'Ned's not around,' announced Will, as he joined me.

'I know. I just pointed that out to his wife. You may have seen her reaction.'

'I don't mean here in the church,' my son responded. 'He's not been seen for a couple of days. By anyone.'

'Who told you that?' I replied.

'Ivor,' said Ginny, quicker to reply than her brother. 'He works for Ned, so he should surely know. Amelia doesn't know where he is either.'

Will indicated Ivor with his head, who was in deep discussion with Jack at the back of the church. I hadn't even noticed that either of them was amongst those present. Not far from them, Marlene was talking volubly to Lucy, her hands waving expressively, coffee cup resting on a pew: that would no doubt be a conversation worth hearing about in due course.

I nodded my acknowledgement to Will and Ginny and wandered unhurriedly over to the two farmhands; I was surprised they had much to talk about, working as they did on different farms, but clearly they did. They fell silent as I approached and turned to face me, presenting a united front.

'Hello, Ivor,' I said casually. 'I'm surprised Ned's not here; he usually is at Easter.'

Ivor and Jack looked at each other theatrically.

'That's what we were talking about, Mr Rowland,' exclaimed Jack, after a pause. 'Ivor says he hasn't seen him for over two days.'

He let the statement hang, inviting my reaction. I kept it low key, inferring I had no prior knowledge of this information. 'Ivor?' I enquired, raising an eyebrow.

The big man shrugged and puffed out his cheeks. 'Like Jack says. I'm getting worried. Not answering his phone.' He looked at me rather pathetically, seeming to seek guidance.

'Lesley?' I asked. 'Surely she knows?'

Both Ivor and Jack smiled knowingly and exchanged glances; clearly this topic had already been aired between them.

'If she does, she ain't saying,' replied Ivor. 'I've mentioned it. She just told me Ned was away. No explanation.'

'A brush-off, that is indeed odd,' I replied. 'What do you think, Jack?'

Jack looked pensive. 'Don't trust her,' he said. 'I'm not saying she's done anything wrong, but I just don't.' He looked at me stubbornly, apparently expecting a rebuke. Ivor's silent stare was obviously supportive.

'I'm not sure I do either, Jack,' I replied, as Lucy joined us.

***

Once we got home, I shared the news about Ned with Lucy, with the children listening intently.

'We found out, Mum,' interjected Ginny eagerly. 'Will and me. Ivor told him, and Amelia told me.'

Lucy smiled indulgently but looked faintly sceptical.

'What?' said Will, picking up the vibes.

'Ned is rather odd, darling,' replied his mother.

'Odd? In what way odd?'

Lucy raised her eyebrows in a 'surely you know' expression. With her better-developed local knowledge, Will's sister butted in. 'He hit his head. Quad bike accident. Never been the same since,' explained Ginny.

Now it was my turn to raise my eyebrows; I wasn't aware that my daughter knew this.

'I just think he's gone off somewhere, and Lesley's rather embarrassed about having to explain it – that's all. Nothing to do with all this,' Lucy declared confidently.

'Unless he did it, of course, and feels the net closing in,' I declared. 'He might have done a runner.' This brought about a thoughtful silence, so I thought I'd better change the topic. 'Anyway – Marlene,' I began, turning to Lucy. 'She seemed rather agitated. What was she going on about?'

The two children turned expectantly to their mother.

'She was agitated,' replied Lucy. 'You can guess why.' We all stayed silent, until Lucy gave in with a helpless little shrug. 'Marlene thinks she's been hard done by. Just because she was alone at home on the day of the killing and can't account for her movements, the police are treating her as an easy mark.'

'Not least because she was once involved with Edmund – it's not just the lack of an alibi,' I reminded my wife. 'You can't blame them for questioning anyone on that basis.'

'I don't think Marlene's the type to go round shooting people,' replied Lucy. 'She's just worried about neighbourhood gossip. Do you see her as a likely gun assassin, Holmes?'

The children grinned at this sally.

'No,' I replied. 'But I don't think anyone is a likely suspect for that sort of crime until it turns out they did it.'

There was another thoughtful silence.

'Normal people can't imagine it, is that what you're saying, Dad?' asked Will, after a moment or so.

'It is,' I replied.

'And since the four of us are all normal – or at least I hope we are – I don't think she can be ruled out as a suspect until the police decide that.'

\*\*\*

Bank Holiday Monday. The children were both departing by train that evening, so I had booked a family lunch at 1pm in The Swan, both to mark the increasingly rare times we were all together and to ease the domestic burden upon Lucy. It's an efficiently run, traditional village pub – they know us well, and I was looking forward to it.

To the slight astonishment of all of us, Amelia was there when we arrived, eating discreetly with Andrew at a corner table. It didn't look like fun – they seemed serious. She caught my eye but quickly looked away, deadpan: it was obvious that any intrusion would be unwelcome. Fortunately, we were being shepherded to a table at the other end of the room when we saw them, so Amelia was not going to be embarrassed by our proximity, and furthermore we could converse without any awkwardness, provided we kept the volume down.

'What are they doing together?' hissed Will, sotto voce, once we were all settled at our table. 'I thought you said that they'd fallen out?'

'I thought they had,' I replied uncertainly. 'Amelia definitely didn't want to see Andrew at Dingley on Saturday.'

'I think they're just being civilised,' said sensible Lucy. 'They're probably going their separate ways after the Easter break, and they've got matters to discuss. Why not clear the air over a meal? That's what I'd do.'

Ginny looked unconvinced by this adult logic, her scepticism apparent in a little shrug.

'Is that what you think too, Dad?' asked Will.

'Possibly,' I said. Which was the truth; I had no alternative theory.

'Can't Holmes be a little more decisive?' asked Lucy, coolly.

'OK – what are these matters you think they need to resolve so urgently?' I replied, with slight asperity. I hoped I'd concealed it but probably didn't.

'Well, it must revolve around the wretched will, mustn't it?' said Lucy, rather less confidently now she'd been challenged.

Ginny and Will looked at each other.

'Look, you said Andrew wasn't the benefactor,' began Will uncertainly.

'Beneficiary,' I replied. Will looked at me in bemusement. 'I said he wasn't the beneficiary of the will,' I explained. 'Or at least I don't think he is. That's the word you meant to use.'

Will paused, mouth agape whilst he digested this information. 'Whatever,' he said after a few seconds. 'If he's not then surely she must be – otherwise, what are they discussing?'

'No,' said Lucy, with a shake of her long brown hair. 'Amelia was the principal beneficiary of the old will. Edmund wouldn't have needed to rewrite it if his intention was that she remained so: Holmes and Watson came to that conclusion several days ago.'

I nodded my agreement.

'Then there's got to be a third answer,' cried Ginny, at dangerously increased volume, drawing glances from nearby tables. She earned a 'shhh' from her mother and pouted sulkily.

But she was right, nonetheless. The trouble was, none of us could think of one.

\*\*\*

Fascinating though it undoubtedly was, I'm glad to say that we moved on from the heady topic of the local murder and its ramifications for the rest of the meal, which was a genuinely happy, cheerful occasion, with everyone on good form. Part way through, the Aylings left, and though I glanced in Amelia's direction as they did so, she very pointedly did not meet my gaze.

The rest of the afternoon was the sort of semi-controlled bedlam that reigned whenever the children were leaving: Ginny had lost her phone charger (Will had 'borrowed' it); Will's room was in Lucy's view 'a disgusting tip', and furthermore he hadn't given her his washing that morning;

neither of them had even begun to pack. All perfectly normal. I kept out of the way as best I could and buried myself in my newspaper until the time came for me to drive them both to the station. Then came the customary round of goodbyes, expressions of endearment and maternal urgings to keep in touch via the family WhatsApp group. It took me about fifteen minutes to coax the children into the car from that point, as I knew it would. I made my 'time to go' statement sufficiently early to allow for all this and to check that they had everything. I knew they had at least bought their tickets this time, but phones, wallets, laptops, flat keys, essays, books – they had all been left behind at some point in the past.

Market Harborough is only three miles from Braybrooke, so the trip to the station was a brief one. I got a hug from Ginny and a 'too cool for school' nod from Will as I dropped them off, then watched affectionately as they headed off through the station doors without a backward glance, chattering like monkeys. They were well adjusted and happy young adults – certainly Lucy and I had suffered none of the horrors endured by some of our contemporaries.

'Yet,' I told myself, as I started the car. But I was reasonably confident we never would, no doubt as much through luck as our parenting skills.

Lucy was slightly despondent when I got home, as I knew she would be; though they sometimes drive her to distraction, she loves her children and always hates it when they leave. I accepted a cup of tea, and no sooner had I sat down than my phone announced the arrival of a text.

I picked it up and looked at it quizzically, for sufficiently long for Lucy to ask me who it was from. 'Amelia,' I said. 'Look.' I held the screen out to my wife.

*Sorry about the pub. Wanted to keep you out of it. Andrew and I seeing solicitor Wednesday. A x*

'Interesting development, Holmes,' said Watson. 'Make sure you tell her to keep us in the loop.'

# CHAPTER TWENTY-SEVEN

The next day, Tuesday, I went back to the office: a normal workday.

Usually, a bank holiday refreshes me, but I was out of sorts from the start, to the obvious disapproval of Clare, which eventually spilled over into overt impatience, most unusual for her.

Much tutting and increasingly ill-concealed eye-rolling later, I found my loyal PA presenting me with a coffee I had not asked for and then settling down uninvited opposite me with one herself, crossing her legs and obviously not going anywhere. My office door, normally kept open, was firmly shut. I looked at her balefully, waiting for an explanation.

'We need to talk,' declared Clare. She was nervous but entirely self-possessed. I took a sip of my coffee, which was scalding. An old sales trick, designed to prolong an unwelcome conversation – I didn't know she had such wiliness in her.

'What about?' I replied cautiously, flinching from the sip.

Clare took a deep breath and plunged in. 'If you have domestic problems, it is not fair on the rest of us to bring them into the office,' she announced forcefully and sat back with her arms folded across her slender body to await my response.

I looked at her in astonishment and then gave a wry smile as the penny began to drop. I detected the first signs of apparent unease across the desk; my reaction had clearly been a surprise.

'Look, I am sorry if I have seemed a little distracted of late,' I began. 'But your theory is incorrect. I do have some issues going on at home, but they do not fall into the category of "domestic problems". Far from it.'

Confusion, relief, sympathy – I saw a wave of emotions cross my colleague's face.

'How long have you worked for me, Clare?' I asked quietly after a few moments.

'Ten years, just about,' she replied defensively.

'And would you say that we are friends as well as colleagues after all that time?' I asked.

Clare coloured a little and lowered her gaze, and I flattered myself momentarily that she might just be a little in love with me, or perhaps I just wanted to think that. Still don't know.

'I certainly hope so.'

'We are,' I confirmed. 'Definitely. I like you as a person, and I trust you as much as anyone I know.' Clare was rather lost for words, but I could see that I had entirely disarmed her. 'So I am going to share this issue with you: I would appreciate a sensible sounding board,' I said. 'And you are very sensible.'

'Lucy?' Clare ventured meekly. 'Isn't that what a wife is for?'

I laughed. 'Lucy and I are grappling with exactly the same issue, together. I'd like a fresh take on it. Your take.'

'Well, alright,' Clare replied cautiously and waited for me to continue.

'Not here,' I said firmly. 'Get your coat. We're going for lunch.'

\*\*\*

There's a Corney & Barrow wine bar not far from my office near Monument tube station at the bottom of Gracechurch Street – I quite often use it for discreet, informal meetings, and what was now in prospect definitely qualified as one of those. You descend into a basement; it's dimly lit; the tables aren't too close together and you can be reasonably inconspicuous, which is useful at times in the City. I'd never taken Clare there – indeed I could only remember sharing a meal with her once before 'à deux', to celebrate her first five years as my PA.

It was not long after noon, so the place hadn't filled up yet. We sat down at a corner table, and I ordered a bottle of Merlot even before we had started perusing the light menu on offer.

Clare raised her eyebrows. 'That sort of lunch, is it?'

Her tone was faintly disapproving, but there was a hint of playfulness there too. We'd both been around long enough to experience the end of the City's 'long lunch' era, and my firm now tacitly discouraged such indulgences, albeit without being too hair-shirted about it: senior people like me were still permitted to exercise a sensible element of discretion.

'Will I need it?' Clare continued, as I poured her a glass and then filled my own.

'You might,' I replied and paused whilst the waitress took our orders.

That done, Clare took a sip of her wine and sat back to look at me reflectively. 'I'm listening, Robert,' she said eventually, and I could sense her genuine curiosity.

I sighed, wondering how to start. Clare gave me no help, so I had to grasp the bull by the horns. I hadn't planned how to address the issue, and it all came out rather more clumsily than I had intended.

'It's about the murder, you see,' I began and halted as Clare raised a quizzical eyebrow. I fancied that someone at a neighbouring table shot me a surprised glance and lowered my voice.

'Well, you know that I found a body about three weeks ago; I did tell you that?' I asked.

Clare nodded calmly. 'You did. And that the man had been shot. What of it?'

'Well, ever since then, the police don't seem to have made much progress; there's been a lot of talk in the village, and unofficially...' I stopped, embarrassed.

'What?'

'Lucy and I have appointed ourselves as sort of detectives. Holmes and Watson, we call ourselves,' I admitted shamefacedly.

I wasn't sure how Clare would react to this but didn't expect her sharp burst of laughter. She stopped when she saw I was serious. 'Go on then – tell me what Holmes and Watson have discovered,' she said.

So it all came out: Lesley and the secret affair with

Edmund; the unwarranted jealousy towards me shown by her husband Ned, now apparently disappeared; Amelia's undissolved marriage and likely benefit from the existing will; the possibility of a second will existing, maybe in favour of Lesley, witnessed by Jack and Eric; the Marlene episode; and Andrew's mysterious role. It took me nearly half an hour to explain it all, by which time we'd finished our meal. I ordered us an extra glass of Merlot apiece.

'So what do you reckon?' Clare asked, once these glasses had arrived.

I shrugged my shoulders. 'Marlene's got no alibi, but I think she's a very long shot: where would she get a gun from? Lesley maybe, if she thought the apparent reconciliation of Amelia and Edmund would leave her out in the cold. Or Ned if he was jealous of Edmund.'

Clare sighed contentedly and took a sip of wine as she pondered the mystery, but then she could afford to: she wasn't involved. 'I'm going to play devil's advocate,' she announced eventually and waited for my reaction.

'Go on then.'

'You say it could be Lesley if she felt the reconciliation of Edmund and Amelia would leave her out in the cold?' she asked eventually.

I nodded. 'It's possible.'

'Look at it the other way round. Amelia knew that a new will had been written in favour of Lesley, and that Edmund was going to run off with her. She wanted to prevent that and to stop that second will emerging.'

'But Amelia was nowhere near Braybrooke when Edmund was shot,' I replied.

'So she'd need an accomplice. There seem to be some likely contenders about.'

***

'Who do you suggest?' I said, in a rather patronising tone.

'Well,' replied Clare, 'I know I haven't met all these people, but what about the brother – Andrew?'

'They don't like each other: him and Amelia.'

'So it appears. Maybe that's a ploy.'

I shook my head. 'They're very good actors then. I don't think that theory will do.'

'Hear me out,' said Clare, leaning forward conspiratorially. 'Let's agree there was a second will, and that it was witnessed by Jack and Eric. That fact was likely to emerge, either via them or via Lesley. So that will had to disappear if Amelia was not going to be disinherited.'

'Hence all that kerfuffle about Andrew searching for a will,' I replied. 'Is that what you're saying?'

'It's got to be a possibility, surely?' replied Clare. 'They needed to find it. All the stuff about Andrew believing that it would be in his favour was simply a smokescreen.'

'What's in it for him, then?' I asked pointedly. 'Why would he help Amelia?'

Clare leant back thoughtfully for a few seconds. 'She needed an ally to forestall the new will and make it vanish. Maybe she agreed with Andrew to gift him part of her inheritance once she received it?'

I waved this away. 'Pure speculation. And why murder Edmund anyway?'

'Obvious,' Clare snorted contemptuously. 'If the will simply disappeared, Edmund would realise. He had to be killed so that the existing will remained in effect.'

I thought for a moment. 'You are talking about Andrew

being involved in a conspiracy to kill his own brother,' I said. 'Possibly even doing the deed. Not an easy thing for Amelia to suggest to him, is it?'

'Well, how well did Edmund and Andrew get on?' retorted Clare. 'You said they were very different.'

It was a fair question, to which I did not know the answer. I shrugged helplessly.

'It would at least explain Andrew's role in all this,' continued Clare. 'If it's Lesley – or Ned – what's he playing at?'

I shrugged again and asked for the bill. 'I'll run your theory past Watson tonight,' I promised my PA as we got to our feet. 'Now let's go and do what we're paid for.'

\*\*\*

Once I arrived home that evening, I poured Lucy and myself our customary drinks, and we settled down on opposite sides of the kitchen island for our normal evening catch-up.

'I took Clare out to lunch today,' I began and paused to gauge the reaction.

'Oh yes,' my wife replied neutrally. She'd probably only met my PA a dozen times, but though they got on well enough, I was fully aware that she didn't much care for the fact that I had a longstanding, close relationship with another woman.

'She was giving me grief about bringing my personal problems into the office.'

'What problems?'

'Domestic, she thought.'

Lucy smiled. 'Whatever gave her that idea?'

'I suppose I must have seemed a bit distracted over all the Edmund business. She put two and two together and came up with five.'

'So you took her out to lunch – why exactly?' Lucy asked delicately.

'To tell her the truth. She knows about Holmes and Watson now. She laughed about it.'

'Well, I suppose it is quite funny when you think about it. A middle-aged couple playing detectives.'

'Yes, but she's got a theory.'

'How can she have a theory?' replied Lucy impatiently. 'She doesn't know anybody involved.'

'Not personally, no. But I told her everything. She knows all the facts.' I saw Lucy's questioning expression. 'I wanted to use her as a sounding board,' I explained. 'She's got a very analytical mind, Clare.'

'Has she indeed?' replied Lucy sceptically, then paused for a moment, thinking. 'OK – let's hear it. This theory of Clare's.'

'She admitted that she was playing devil's advocate but outlined a rationale that led back to Andrew and Amelia, possibly working together.'

'Unlikely, to put it mildly,' replied Lucy unenthusiastically. 'They don't like each other much.'

'A ploy, Clare reckons.'

'What else does Clare reckon?'

So I outlined my PA's reasoning: the need to make the second will disappear to preserve Amelia's inheritance and for Edmund to be killed so that he wouldn't reveal its existence.

Lucy sat back and took a thoughtful sip of her drink. 'I

don't buy it,' she declared after a moment or two. 'Want to know why?'

I nodded.

'First – Lesley knew of the will's existence. She could declare that at any time.'

'Not without revealing her affair with Edmund, knowing that she had an unstable and jealous husband in the background. And without a physical will, it would be her word against both of theirs.'

'Her word and Jack's. And Eric's.'

I shook my head. 'They had no idea what they were signing.'

'But they definitely signed a document that required two witnesses. Assuming Lesley went public, they'd back her account to the extent that they witnessed something.'

I ruminated on this. It did seem to leave a large flaw in Amelia and Andrew's supposed plan.

Lucy saw my hesitation and pressed her advantage. 'And another thing,' she said, with quiet confidence. I waited for the big reveal. 'Clare's theory rests on the assumption that Amelia knew about the second will.'

'Yes,' I admitted.

'How did she find out?'

We circled around this conundrum for a bit, but ultimately, we didn't know. By mutual agreement, eventually, we let it be and settled for a TV supper and an early night.

# CHAPTER TWENTY-EIGHT

On the train down to London on Wednesday morning, I noticed a diary entry in my phone: *Amelia and Andrew to solicitor*. That might nudge things along a bit, though in what direction I wasn't clear, and there was no guarantee Amelia would tell me anyway. I decided it couldn't hurt to improve the odds a little.

*Good luck at solicitors today*, I texted Amelia. *Thinking of you.*

The reply came within a minute: *Thanks.*

I sat back to think. Unless there was some factor of which I was unaware, I simply couldn't understand how Amelia could possibly have known about the second will: certainly she had given every indication that the first she knew of the possibility was when Andrew had shown her the signatory page.

When I reached the office, I beckoned Clare in and sat her down.

'Your theory,' I said, 'Lucy and I don't buy it.'

Clare's impatience that we were still on yesterday's distraction was apparent for only a second; she had clearly been expecting a work-related discussion, but she switched focus smoothly.

'Why not, pray?' She waited expectantly for an answer, with the same arms-crossed-over-the-chest stance she'd used the previous day.

'How did Amelia find out about the will?' I said. Checkmate.

'Easy,' Clare replied scornfully. 'Didn't you say Amelia and Edmund were thinking of reconciling? So they must have spoken. He told her about it.'

'But if they were going to reconcile, then even if Edmund admitted the existence of the will, he'd have promised to rip it up as part of that discussion.'

Clare looked mildly discomfited. 'It's only a theory,' she said primly.

'Can I get on with some real work now? I'm still putting that PowerPoint presentation together for you. You wanted it by lunchtime.'

I waved my hand dismissively, and my PA retreated to her desk outside my office.

\*\*\*

The text from Amelia summarising the outcome of her solicitor's meeting with Andrew came just after midday. The whole thing appeared to have been a damp squib: *Andrew could not produce alleged new will*, complete with a thumbs up emoji. I forwarded it to Lucy.

My afternoon was quite a busy one out and about the

floor of the Lloyds' market, plus I'd arranged some bilateral meetings with underwriters since I knew I'd have to stay late – we were holding a company drinks party for clients at the top of The Gherkin scheduled for 6.30pm, and as a client-facing director, I'd need to play a leading part in that; I didn't expect to be able to get away much before 9pm. Tedious, but occasionally necessary, and I knew of old that I generally enjoyed such gatherings anyway once I got into the swing of them.

So I didn't look at my phone again for quite some time – not till I was on the train home actually, as it pulled out of St Pancras at around 9.45pm.

There was a text from Lucy from just before 7pm which appeared to make no sense: it said, *Where are you? Don't be late. Amelia and Andrew coming round, self-invited. Apparently important.*

My wife had clearly forgotten my evening engagement and that I was going to be home later than usual. I called her on the landline (mobile reception is sporadic in Braybrooke), but it just rang until it eventually kicked through to voicemail. Odd, since I knew she was at home – or was supposed to be. But I didn't think much of it and contented myself with a brief text to her mobile reminding her that I was going to be late, with an ETA of about 11pm, and not to wait up. Then I allowed myself to snooze gently, having ascertained that my neighbour on the inside seat was also travelling to Market Harborough and would inevitably wake me as he prepared to leave the train.

We were there around 10.50pm, and then it's only a ten-minute drive home from the station. As I pulled out of the car park, I was thinking of nothing but my bed.

My text aside, as a rule Lucy did not stay up late anyway, so I confidently expected her to be asleep, and I remember thinking as I got out of my car outside our house that I'd need to be quiet if I was not to wake her.

***

Two things then struck me one after the other.

First, the dogs both rushed up. Theo and Rosie sleep in the house; I couldn't for the life of me think why they were still running free outside in the dark at 11pm. They didn't bark, which I remember even at that stage being relieved about, just jumped around excitedly. I shushed them and shepherded them into the kennel pen we sometimes left them in when we went out for a few hours whilst I went in search of an explanation.

Second, as I turned towards the house, I saw that the lights were still on in the drawing room and upstairs. Lucy was meticulous in turning them off if she went to bed before I returned, save for a light by the back door to guide me and a dim one on the landing. So that was odd.

I opened the back door quietly, increasingly concerned, though not yet actually alarmed. Immediately, a third thing struck me: there were voices from the drawing room, twenty feet away behind a closed door. I couldn't countenance that Amelia and Andrew would still be there if they'd come over just after 7pm, so who could it possibly be?

I thought about announcing myself loudly, but some sixth sense warned me against that. Instead, I tiptoed along the corridor as silently as I could, pausing outside the painted wooden drawing room door, intent on eavesdropping so that I could establish what was going on before I made my inevitable entrance.

It's a quality item, that door: thick and heavy, with one of those brush edgings along the bottom as soundproofing. However, as a result, one thing it is not is acoustically porous. Even with my head against the door, I couldn't make out anything intelligible, though I fancied I did identify Andrew's deep male voice, and its tone was one of entreaty. There was a murmur of apparent female support – I supposed from Lucy, but it could equally well have been Amelia. I heard no response. Possibly there was nobody else there, and Andrew was pleading with one of them, supported by the other.

After a couple of minutes of this frustration, I decided that I definitely didn't like the sound of what was going on. Accordingly, I retreated back outside, walked to the far end of the garden and used my mobile to dial 999 – only the second time in my life I had ever done so; the first being less than a month before when I had discovered Edmund's body. As before, the call was answered impressively promptly; again, a female voice. I was asked which emergency service I required and answered firmly, 'Police please.'

There was a delay of only a few seconds, and a male voice came on the line. 'Police. Please state your emergency,' the officer said calmly.

'My name is Robert Rowland,' I explained. 'I live in the village of Braybrooke. I arrived home late from an engagement in London a few minutes ago. To my surprise, a conversation is going on in the drawing room of my house – at least three people, possibly more. Almost certainly one of them is my wife.'

'What is suspicious about that, sir?' enquired the officer politely, although I fancied I detected a hint of scepticism.

'First – it's unexpected. Second – although I couldn't hear what was being said through the thickness of the door, I definitely sensed a tone of pleading from the man,' I replied. 'I think there is an intruder in the house.'

'Are you certain of that?'

'No. Far from it. But I believe it to be highly likely.'

I could sense the officer thinking on the other end of the line. 'Please repeat your name and give the address of the property concerned,' he said eventually.

I did so.

'Wait there – I am despatching a patrol car immediately. Please meet it outside the property and brief the officers. Ten minutes or so.'

'Agreed. I'll meet them at the entrance to our yard. And please…'

'What, sir?'

'No sirens or blue lights. If there is an intruder, we don't want to alert him, do we?'

'Never fear, sir,' replied the officer rather prissily. 'We have protocols for this sort of situation.'

I rang off and loitered uncertainly in the garden, wondering what to do.

In retrospect, it was bloody silly of course, but I decided to return to the drawing room door for a few minutes to see if I could glean any further information with which to brief the police officers once they arrived.

But no sooner had I placed my ear against the door than my phone rang.

\*\*\*

I was shocked. There was no time to silence it before the door flew open. I found myself staring at Lesley in astonishment. She was dressed in jeans and a green sweater. Momentarily she looked shocked too, but I didn't like or recognise the expression that appeared a second later.

'Well, look who it is,' she sneered. 'The master of the house. We were expecting you. Do come and join us. Shut the door behind you.'

I was about to confront her when I saw with a start what she was holding by her side. Some sort of pistol, apparently double-barrelled. She raised it and gestured angrily.

Hardly was I in the room before Lucy was by my side, tears beginning to flow. I stood in front of the door and left it just ajar – consciously so I like to think now, but in reality it was probably inadvertent.

'Robert, thank God. Lesley has gone mad.'

Seated next to each other on the sofa were Andrew and Amelia, pale but controlled. I noticed with a start that the former's left forearm was in an improvised sling, blood seeping through it.

'Sit down, you two,' snarled Lesley at Lucy and I, gesturing forcefully again with her pistol. 'Now. Do what I say. I won't ask again. Andrew found that out the hard way.'

There were two single chairs opposite the sofa. It seemed prudent for Lucy and me to sit in them.

There was a long pause.

'Would someone please tell me what is going on?' I asked as calmly as I could once it seemed safe to do so, though I could feel my heart beating loudly in my chest.

'Lesley shot Andrew, about two hours ago,' said Amelia dryly. 'She shot Edmund too. I am not confident about Ned's prospects, either.'

'Be quiet, you,' shouted Lesley angrily, waving her pistol again. 'I am thinking.'

'Is that true, Lesley?' I ventured cautiously after a few moments.

'That I shot Edmund? Of course it bloody is,' she snapped contemptuously.

There didn't seem to be much to say to that, other than the obvious. 'Why?'

'Why do you think?' she replied, sullen, aggressive and apparently irrational.

'Well,' I began as cautiously as I could, 'I think Edmund had drawn up a will in your favour – you were going to live together, and that was part of the deal. But then you learnt that he was going to get back together with Amelia.'

For the first time Lesley looked disconcerted and uncertain how to respond.

'You couldn't allow him to rescind the new will. If he did, you would get nothing. Am I getting warm?'

'There is rather more to it than that,' said Amelia calmly. 'Which is what Andrew and I asked to come over to see you and Lucy about this evening. We had just told Lucy when Lesley appeared. It was a surprise, as you might imagine.'

I looked at Lesley cautiously to gauge her reaction. She turned suddenly and pulled out the stool from the alcove in our Georgian writing desk; then she pivoted and sat down, facing back into the room. From there, she glowered at us all sulkily with her pistol held loosely across her lap but made no attempt to quieten us or to converse; she was still pondering what to do.

She was about fifteen feet away – was that too far to rush her? Perhaps that was what Andrew had tried.

I was, and am, no firearms expert, but the pistol on Lesley's lap looked unusual, and much would depend on its lethality. Eventually, I decided to try and elicit more information, both to establish the feasibility of overpowering her and as a delaying tactic to avoid bringing things to a head before the police arrived. I was well aware that they should be only minutes away, and though they might be mystified when I did not meet them outside, they would surely investigate.

A sudden thought hit me: perhaps it was them who had called me when they arrived, thus inadvertently giving me away. If that was so, then they must surely be very close.

'Interesting-looking gun, Lesley,' I said as loudly as I reasonably could, hoping thereby both to identify the intruder to anyone who overheard and to establish that she was armed.

Lesley's lip curled in contempt.

'It's the one she killed Edmund with,' said Amelia, again in an artificially raised tone. 'And shot Andrew with earlier. Double-barrelled four-ten shotgun pistol.'

No fool, that lady. She had cottoned on, clearly, and was trying to tell me and anyone else listening what she could. I had never heard of such a thing as a shotgun pistol, but now was not the time to worry about such an anomaly. The key point I had learnt was that Lesley could fire only twice before having to reload.

As if to reinforce the point, Lesley raised the pistol and thumbed back the twin external hammers, one behind each barrel. The gun was cocked. She moved it in a threatening arc around all of us, with a hard smile on her face. She seemed to be enjoying the power the gun gave her and the inadvertent flinch she provoked in us all.

'Don't, Robert,' said Andrew, anticipating my thoughts. He was clearly in some pain. 'I've already tried that. She won't hesitate to shoot. It probably won't kill you, that thing, but I assure you it will be bloody painful.'

I paused and nodded an acknowledgement to him. 'Small gauge shotgun, so not a bullet; just pellets, and not a huge number of those,' I intoned thoughtfully, but again as loudly as I dared. 'I'd have thought that Edmund didn't have a quick death. Is that right, Lesley?'

She shot me a venomous look. 'It was quick enough.'

'A couple of shots to knock him down from close range, the police reckoned, and then one to the head to finish him off whilst he was helpless. He'd have known it was coming. Nobody deserves that.'

There was a small, stifled sob from Amelia.

I knew that I'd overstepped the mark; that's what happens when anger and disgust get the better of you.

Lesley's expression darkened in fury – her eyes narrowed, and I sensed her decide: she began to raise the pistol in my direction. Lucy screamed and hurled herself in front of me.

It caused Lesley to hesitate for a moment, but it was enough. There was a sudden crash from outside the window.

# CHAPTER TWENTY-NINE

The curtains were drawn, and they were made of heavy green brocade; nonetheless, Lesley swung and fired once directly at them, though she must surely have known that the shotgun pellets had little chance of penetrating. Immediately she did so, the drawing room door burst open, and she began to swivel back in that direction, raising her pistol against this new threat.

I instinctively sensed that Lesley's distraction was my opportunity and rugby tackled her before she had the chance to fire. The burly police officer who charged through the door in his incongruous hi-vis jacket hit us both a second later, his baton slamming down hard on Lesley's right hand as she fell. She screamed and released the pistol. It skidded away across the parquet floor, and Amelia was moving towards it in a trice.

'Don't touch the bloody thing,' I yelled, as I struggled with the writhing Lesley. 'There's still one loaded barrel.'

A second police officer emerged from behind the curtains, having had to break our latched window to gain entry it later transpired. He eased me out of the way surprisingly politely. Lesley fought hard, screaming and biting, but it was hopeless: within a minute, the two of them had her handcuffed, hands behind her back and face down. They stood up breathlessly, admiring their handiwork.

'Evening all,' said the one who had come through the door, looking around.

Even then I could hardly believe it – in his late twenties, he was far too young to have seen *Dixon of Dock Green*, but I suppose every trade has its clichés.

'Indeed, good evening, officers,' I replied. 'Thank you for coming so promptly, though I could have done without the phone call, if that was you. But all's well that ends well, I suppose.'

'Not us, sir,' said the other policeman, even younger, shaking his head. He was moving towards Andrew, and after a cursory examination, he withdrew to the other side of the room and started murmuring into his lapel radio; I presumed he was calling for an ambulance.

'What has happened here?' asked the first policeman. 'We were due to meet a Mr Rowland, the owner, but he was nowhere to be seen—'

'That's me, I'm afraid, Officer,' I replied shamefacedly, interrupting him. 'A spot of freelance reconnaissance to find out what I could before you arrived. It went wrong. Very foolish.'

\*\*\*

The policeman made to reply, but then Lesley started struggling again, her oaths and curses drowning out any chance of normal conversation.

'I think everyone's heard enough from you, my girl,' said the policeman firmly, whilst restraining Lesley from getting to her feet with surprising gentleness. 'In the meantime, please be quiet.'

'I want a bloody lawyer!' she screeched.

'All in good time, once you're down the station. Transport's on its way, not long now.'

He sounded very matter of fact and consoling, as if tackling an armed hostage-taker was a routine occurrence. His attitude was indeed very reassuring; Lesley was reduced to sulky pouting. His younger colleague loitered by the door, looking rather more exercised by what had just transpired but still very controlled. Overall, I was impressed.

We all sat there rather uncertainly, wondering what happened next, but not for more than thirty seconds, for then came the unmistakable sound of a car arriving at speed in our yard. My assumption was that it was transport coming for Lesley, and that seemed to be the young policeman's impression too, for he sauntered off towards the outside door.

He was back in the room within seconds, chastened, a brief shake of the head disabusing his colleague of this notion. Immediately behind him came another figure: Fiona Challis.

Pale and worried, she paused in the doorway, looking anxiously around. Her glance settled briefly on Andrew as she noted his injuries, and then it moved to me. She smiled, a smile of relief it seemed. I could see that she was very tired.

'Hello, Mr Rowland,' she said quietly. 'I am glad to see you well.'

I nodded my acknowledgement. 'Likewise, Detective Sergeant. Did you have any reason to expect I might not be?'

'We did, sir,' Challis replied shortly, only now noting the incapacitated figure of Lesley on the floor. 'I rang to warn you.'

I smiled wanly. 'That call is why I am sitting here with the others,' I replied. 'I was listening at the door. My phone rang in my pocket, and…' I left the sentence hanging and ended with a shrug. Challis looked momentarily disconcerted. 'No harm done, though,' I added, in a conciliatory tone.

She nodded briefly and turned to the more senior of the two policemen.

'When's she being picked up?' she demanded, indicating the prone figure of Lesley with her head. 'And where's the blasted ambulance?'

'Both called for and on their way, Sergeant,' replied the policeman stoically. I noticed his number on his radio clip: 1912. If it was on his shoulder too, the hi-vis jacket hid it.

I thought that he and his colleague deserved at least a modicum of praise for their successful resolution of a dangerous situation, but it seemed that Challis didn't believe in bestowing compliments, though perhaps she simply felt that this was something for later.

Sirens were now faintly audible, the volume increasing in a crescendo; it was almost deafening once the two vehicles fitted with them had pulled up in our yard, until they were switched off, fading away with diminishing whines.

We all waited to see what would happen next. I saw Challis balefully eyeing the pistol, which had come to rest against a skirting board.

'One barrel of two fired,' Amelia said to her, seeing where the detective was looking.

'The other one is cocked,' I added, probably needlessly.

Challis pursed her lips tightly.

Seconds later, there were two paramedics in the room. They stopped briefly to take in the scene.

\*\*\*

'Over there,' exclaimed Challis, but the medics (a male and a much younger female) were already moving in the direction of the man with the bloodied sling. Andrew began struggling to rise from the sofa to meet them, but Amelia pulled him back down. As she did so, Lucy piped up.

'He's been shot,' she explained briefly. 'With a shotgun. That one over there.'

The medics glanced briefly in the direction of her pointed finger, the young girl looking shaken.

'It's not too bad,' said Andrew, through gritted teeth. 'Most of the pellets missed. She only hit me with a few.'

He sounded forlorn. Lesley swore her regret at the lightness of Andrew's injuries unintelligibly from the floor. For the first time, I noticed damage to the sofa on which he was sitting, presumably caused by those shotgun pellets that had missed him.

'We'll be the judge of how bad it is, sir,' said the male paramedic firmly. He crouched down next to Andrew and made a cursory examination of his injured arm for around twenty seconds. Nobody said a thing. He straightened up suddenly and turned to Challis. 'This gentleman will be coming to hospital with us. Straightaway,' he said decisively.

He seemed to be expecting an argument, but Challis wasn't minded to give him one. She turned quickly to the junior of the two original officers. 'Go in the ambulance with him. Report in once he's admitted to the hospital,' she said in a clipped tone. 'You'll be relieved there.'

The young officer turned briefly to his more senior colleague, 1912, who inclined his head imperceptibly. Andrew rose stiffly to his feet and was led away by the two paramedics, with the young policeman who was to accompany him in tow. Amelia reached for Andrew's uninjured hand and gave it a brief squeeze, together with a sympathetic smile, as he moved off. He grimaced back painfully.

No sooner had this little party departed than two more policemen entered the room, again in hi-vis jackets; they looked tough and serious. Challis stayed them with her hand. 'Get her up,' she ordered, turning to 1912.

He helped Lesley to her feet; she would have struggled otherwise with her hands restrained behind her. She stood morosely, staring down at her toes. The fight seemed to have gone out of her.

'Look at me,' barked Challis.

Lesley was not minded to, but a quick shake of her upper arm from 1912 made her think better of it. Suddenly, she raised her face defiantly.

'Lesley Logan,' intoned Challis, 'I am arresting you for the murder of Edmund Ayling and the attempted murder of Andrew Ayling. You do not have to say anything, but anything you do say may be taken down and given in evidence. Do you understand?'

We'd all heard these words before on TV of course, but they were no less dramatic for that. Even Lesley seemed taken aback. She nodded almost imperceptibly, disconcerted, and lowered her eyes.

'Take her away,' ordered Challis, turning to the two newly arrived policemen.

Lesley was gone in seconds, leaving us all on tenterhooks. Challis nodded briefly to 1912. 'You can go too. Take a picture of that damn gun in situ, unload it and take it with you. I'll finish up here.'

'Thank you, Officer,' I said to 1912 as he passed. He smiled briefly, and I sensed his gratitude. I looked reproachfully at Challis. Someone had to do it.

\*\*\*

Once Lesley had been taken away and Andrew removed to hospital, it wasn't long before all the emergency staff had left, leaving only Challis and our little group of former hostages: me, Lucy and Amelia. Being very English about the situation, we offered Challis a cup of tea, which she accepted.

'I can't stay long,' she said, perching on the stool so recently vacated by Lesley. 'Though no doubt you've got plenty of questions. So have I. Between us we might make sense of all this.'

We all waited whilst Challis paused for thought. She turned abruptly to Amelia. 'First – please explain what you were doing here, Mrs Ayling,' she said.

I turned to Amelia with interest. Beyond Lucy's text telling me that she and Andrew had invited themselves around, I was in the dark about their motives too.

Amelia sighed. 'Andrew got out of his depth trying to be clever,' she began hesitantly.

'Explain,' ordered Challis shortly.

'Well, he never got on with Edmund much,' she replied,

'as I know only too well. They were very different. And beyond that…' She hesitated.

'Go on,' I said, as encouragingly as I could. She gave me a brief smile.

'Well, he was broke – he's always been pretty extravagant, the Porsche and all – though it wasn't immediately apparent, certainly not to me, who hadn't seen him for a few years. I thought he was pretty prosperous these days and over that phase. But it was all an act. He told me so today.'

'So?' said Challis cautiously.

'So when he heard that Edmund had been shot, Andrew got himself up here pretty quickly, as he thought there might be something in it for him, only to be scuppered when I told him that I was the sole beneficiary of the original will, which to the best of my knowledge had never been rescinded. Lesley was working in the house at the time. She overheard that conversation. I saw no need for secrecy in front of her.'

Challis said nothing and simply waited for Amelia to continue. Lucy and I glanced at each other – we could see where this was going.

Amelia shrugged. 'I know it now, because he made it clear today. Lesley simply waited till she could get Andrew alone. And that's when she told him about the existence of the second will in her favour, saying that she couldn't find it.'

'But Andrew wouldn't buy that, surely?' I said. 'Why on earth would Edmund leave everything to Lesley?'

'Oh, she was apparently quite open to him about the affair,' replied Amelia airily. 'And she can be very persuasive, even if her feminine wiles were probably wasted on Andrew.'

'That story would give Lesley an obvious motive for the murder,' I declared firmly.

Amelia shook her head. 'Not if Andrew didn't know about the planned reconciliation between Edmund and me, which would have torpedoed the new will,' she countered, with a hint of triumph. 'So he didn't know she was the killer, or at least that's what he says. Apparently, she offered him a fifty per cent cut if he could help her find it.'

Challis gave a small grunt of disapproval. 'Then he must have a particularly naive nature,' she sniffed.

'And he did find it,' Lucy said to me. 'We went over all this before Lesley arrived. That's why there was such a change of tack about Jack.' I must have looked puzzled, because Lucy's impatience became obvious. 'You know, one moment he was sacking Jack, and the next paying him extravagant compliments in the church,' she explained forcibly. 'Because in between those events, he'd discovered the will and that Jack was a witness to it. So he needed Jack onside.'

I pondered this uncertainly. It seemed to make sense, but there were still a lot of loose ends. 'How did you find all this out?' I said.

Challis turned to her with interest.

Amelia exhaled loudly. 'He confided in me, earlier today. Even though they'd found the will, and even if it was validated, Lesley couldn't be seen to inherit by Ned.'

'So she got rid of Ned,' continued Lucy eagerly. 'He disappeared. That's when Andrew realised that he'd thrown his hand in with a psycho. And it was a pretty small step from there to concluding that Lesley had killed his brother too.'

'Andrew was scared,' said Amelia. 'She'd kill him too if she had to, he was sure of it. So he told me everything. We agreed that we'd come and talk to you two about it.'

'Why not the police?' said Challis flatly.

Amelia put her hands up defensively. 'I know. That's what we should have done. But we just wanted a third-party reality check before taking such a significant step. I know it was stupid of us.'

Challis looked at her disapprovingly; there was a difficult silence.

# CHAPTER THIRTY

Eventually, I broke the silence. 'You said you realised I was in danger,' I said to Challis. 'How so?'

Challis shrugged. 'Not you specifically, Mr Rowland. Everyone. I was ringing around.' We must have all looked bemused, because she continued with hardly a pause. 'Look, we found Ned Logan this afternoon, shot dead, or rather Ivor Chubb did, you know, the hired hand. He called 999.'

'Where was he?' I said. I remember no feeling of shock whatsoever at this horrifying news, perhaps not surprising after the sort of day I'd had.

'On the farm. In the boot of his own car in fact.'

'Hadn't that been searched? He went missing days ago.'

'Apparently not very thoroughly,' replied Challis, colouring a little. Then she continued. 'Lesley wasn't there, and Mr Chubb didn't accuse her of anything when he called us: he just told us he'd found the body.'

'But you were sure it was her who shot him? She must

have been pretty desperate; the body was bound to be found there before long.'

Challis paused. 'Temporary hiding place. She never got the chance to dispose of it.' We waited for her to continue. She took a few seconds before doing so. 'We've discovered some interesting background on Lesley Logan recently. We were about to haul her in for questioning when Mr Chubb called. And then we couldn't find her. Nor did she answer her phone. Her own car had gone. So of course you make deductions at that point.'

'Like Sherlock Holmes,' I ventured.

'And Watson,' Lucy added swiftly.

Challis looked at us both with resigned tolerance. 'I suppose so, yes.'

'But why were we in danger?' asked Amelia.

Challis paused again. 'I wasn't sure you were,' she replied. 'But you were all involved in this saga. Lesley seemed to be on the rampage. The first place I called was Braybrooke Farm – your landline, Mrs Ayling. No answer, so then I went there. Jack Diggle was in the yard. He told me that you and Andrew Ayling had headed off to see the Rowlands a couple of hours before, and that it seemed urgent. And apparently, he'd told Lesley Logan the same thing when she called him half an hour earlier on his mobile. That's when I rang you, Mr Rowland. I had your number stored in my mobile but not the landline here. So I called that. I wanted to warn you to steer clear of Lesley, that she might be on her way, and to report her if you happened to see her.'

'We'd seen her by then all right,' said Lucy. She sounded resigned and tired.

'When did she arrive?' I asked. As yet, I'd had no chance to discuss that aspect with anyone.

Lucy sat back. 'At 7.30pm, as arranged. Amelia and Andrew had been here about half an hour,' she said. 'And they'd told me everything. Or rather Amelia had – Andrew just sat there miserably. I was pretty shocked, as you can imagine. Then someone rang the bell.'

'And I suppose you answered it?' I said drily.

Lucy looked indignant. 'Why shouldn't I answer my own damn doorbell?' she demanded aggressively.

'Because on the doorstep was a murderess with a pistol, perhaps?' I replied sarcastically.

It wasn't clever, and Lucy coloured angrily. An apology was due. 'Sorry,' I said. 'You couldn't possibly have known.'

'Enough,' said Challis, raising her hand. 'This is no time for trivial domestic point scoring. What happened, Mrs Rowland?'

Lucy looked as uncomfortable as I felt. 'Well, having just heard what Andrew and Amelia had told me, I was scared of course.'

'She wasn't armed?'

'Not obviously so at that point.'

'When did that become apparent, may I ask?' said Challis.

Lucy looked flummoxed.

Amelia stepped into the breach. 'We heard Lucy saying "Lesley" in a fairly horrified voice and went to investigate,' she said stoutly.

'Not very wise,' said Challis reproachfully.

'Well, we didn't know she had a gun,' said Amelia, in a defensive tone. 'You wouldn't, would you? We didn't know what had happened to Ned at that point, remember.'

'Lesley produced the gun from her Barbour jacket when the other two appeared behind me,' said Lucy coolly. 'She ordered us back into the drawing room and told us to sit down. I did that, and I thought Amelia and Andrew were going to do so too, opposite me on the sofa. Indeed, Amelia did. But Andrew tried to rush her.'

'And got shot for his pains,' I said. 'Fortunately, it didn't look too serious.'

\*\*\*

Challis left soon after this, saying that she'd be in touch the following day. Immediately the door closed behind her, all three of us began talking loudly at once.

'Stop!' I ordered forcibly after a few seconds of this babble, raising a hand. Rather to my astonishment, Lucy and Amelia both did so, looking at me in surprise. 'First things first,' I said. 'I think we've all earned a drink.'

No dissenters to that proposal, so it was a couple of minutes before we settled down, Lucy and I with strong whiskies on the damaged sofa and Amelia opposite us in an armchair, clutching her equally generous gin and tonic.

There was a moment's silence – none of us knew where to begin. I kicked things off. 'Tell us about Andrew,' I said.

Amelia shrugged elegantly. 'Andrew's always had rather bigger appetites than his finances will support,' she said archly, as if being indiscreet. 'Or at least that was definitely the case when I was with Edmund. We bailed him out a few times.'

'Significant sums?' I asked.

Amelia paused. 'Pretty significant, I think. I didn't get involved in the detail; Edmund did all that. Thousands, certainly.'

We all digested this.

'But he seemed to be over that when I met him again after Edmund's death,' Amelia added. 'Years since I'd seen him of course.'

'So he fooled you,' stated Lucy, as if it was a proven fact.

Amelia shrugged again. 'He projected a certain image of prosperity; I'll give him that. And it took many people in. But not Lesley.'

'Clearly not,' I replied. 'I wonder how she saw through him? Sensed his financial vulnerability?'

None of us knew. Suddenly, Lucy leapt to her feet, her old smile breaking through the strained expression she'd been wearing ever since I'd made my dramatic, if unplanned, appearance an hour or so earlier. 'I'm going to put the cat amongst the pigeons,' she announced gleefully and pulled her mobile from her pocket. She tapped away for at least a minute, then handed the phone to me. 'What do you think?' she asked.

I digested the draft message, intended for our family WhatsApp group, '4for1'.

*Case solved by Holmes & Watson, after temporary incarceration as hostages with Amelia. Lesley arrested. Andrew shot (a bit). Having a drink. All's well that ends well!*

There were a couple of rather dubious emojis and a kiss. I smiled and reached over to give the phone to Amelia. She took it and looked down at the screen, seemingly serious. Then her eyes flashed upwards. 'Shall we have a sweepstake on how long it will be before one of them calls?' she said.

***

We hadn't even settled on our bets before Lucy's phone rang: Ginny. It must have been less than a minute.

I couldn't pick out what she was saying, but her tone of alarm was obvious, despite Lucy's frequent soothing noises. It all ended after a couple of minutes with a rather doubtful, 'Well, if you must, darling,' from Lucy. She turned to me, somewhat abashed. 'It's too late tonight. Ginny says the first train tomorrow gets to Market Harborough at 7.03am. She'll be on it, and she wants picking up. And she's going to try and get hold of Will, too.'

'Sorry,' she said in a meek tone.

I shook my head tiredly. 'It's no problem.'

Amelia sensed the change of atmosphere and downed the remainder of her gin swiftly. 'I'll be off,' she said decisively. 'We'll speak tomorrow.' She started gathering her things and only hesitated when she reached the door.

'How did you get here?' I asked gently. There had been no additional car in the drive when I'd arrived.

'We walked,' Amelia said briefly. 'Talking all the way. But it was daylight then—'

'I'll drive you,' I interrupted. 'Got to stay up anyway. It won't take five minutes.'

Amelia hesitated and then nodded gratefully. I turned to Lucy, who gave a brief smile of agreement. I stood up and ushered Amelia towards the door.

Once we were in the car, a sense of déjà vu overtook me. I turned to my passenger as we pulled out onto the main road. 'You know, aside from finding Edmund's body, my involvement in all this really started when I gave Lesley a five-minute lift home,' I said. 'Like I'm giving you now.'

Amelia smiled, and I suddenly sensed her exhaustion.

'Well, let's hope this little trip ends the whole saga.'

We stayed silent for the remainder of the short journey, and I pulled up outside Braybrooke Farm a couple of minutes later. 'You'll be OK here by yourself?' I asked anxiously as Amelia opened the car door.

'I'll be fine, Robert,' she replied, turning tiredly to face me. 'Once I've had another drink, anyway. Thank you for the lift.'

\*\*\*

Lucy and I started discussing everything once I got back but then decided that we'd need to repeat it all once the children (or at least Ginny) had arrived so parked it for the moment. My wife was grey with exhaustion, so I packed her off to bed and treated myself to a hot bath before joining her.

The train the next morning was punctual; you can see them arriving on the raised rail line from the small pickup area in Market Harborough – even smaller these days, now they've filled most of it with a huge, underused cycle shed. I knew it would take passengers a couple of minutes to reach the ticket office foyer from the platform so made my way the thirty yards there unhurriedly from my car.

There's a long descending pathway from platform level to where I intended to wait, and scarcely had I arrived than I saw Ginny running down it, at such a speed that she looked in danger of falling over.

'Careful,' I warned, reaching out to her, and seconds later, she was in my arms, weeping.

'Dad, Dad – thank God,' she began and burst into renewed floods. A few passengers on that early train began giving us concerned looks.

'It's alright,' I reassured one of them who caught my eye. 'Bit of a family drama. All over now.'

He passed on by with a nod, minding his own business. Behind him I saw Will, ambling down the pathway at a much more leisurely pace but still looking distinctly worried. He carried Ginny's bag as well as his own. 'You OK, Dad?' he said as he reached me.

'Judge for yourself. I'm fine.'

'What about Mum?'

'Mum's fine too, but she's very tired. Still in bed. Everyone's fine.'

'Even Andrew?' interjected Ginny, with a hint of sarcasm.

'Even Andrew. Lesley shot him in the arm with a very small shotgun,' I said, trying to underplay things. We had reached the car.

'The gun that killed Edmund, I suppose? So not exactly harmless, was it?' she replied, climbing into the back. So much for that tactic. 'What were you both thinking of?' she began crossly, as she did up her seat belt. 'Honestly, dabbling as detectives with an actual murderer on the loose in the village? Totally irresponsible.'

I had a sudden sense of generational role reversal – a father being disciplined by his twenty-year-old daughter. Hadn't expected that for another twenty years. Will grinned amusedly from the front seat. I couldn't think of a suitable retort so did what I'd learnt over many years to do in that circumstance: kept quiet. Because it was true.

When we got home, I told the children that everything would be explained when their mother was ready. There was mild resistance, but after brief greetings to the dogs, off they went up the stairs, and the murmur of conversation drifted down from the landing. I visualised them sticking their heads around our bedroom door to greet Lucy and see how she was getting on. They didn't seem to get much response, and their footsteps padded off down the corridor to their rooms; thankfully, they'd left her in peace.

I made myself a coffee and sat down, pulling out my mobile phone. After a moment's reflection, I began an email to our managing partner, Harry Tate, copying in Clare.

*Harry – not in today I'm afraid. Break-in at home and physical confrontation with culprit; now arrested. Will be tied up with police. Lucy and I both fine. Will call. Clare – please rearrange any diary commitments. Hopefully back in tomorrow. R*

I sat back to examine the email critically – best not to make it too dramatic. Then I pressed 'send' and it whooshed away.

The coffee went down in one gulp, and I placed the cup in the sink. Then I fed the dogs and had a bowl of cornflakes.

# CHAPTER THIRTY-ONE

We all had a bit of a lie-in and thus were caught on the hop when the phone rang just before 8.30am. I reached it after about twenty seconds.

'Mr Rowland,' began Challis, with what I fancied was a hint of amusement. 'Good morning. I trust this is not an inconvenient time to call?'

'Not at all, just having breakfast. What can I do for you, Detective Sergeant?'

'Well, it's more what we can do for you, sir,' she replied politely. 'In terms of explaining what happened, which you deserve to know. Plus, there are a couple of loose ends to tie up. Detective Inspector Yardley thought it might be mutually beneficial to meet.'

'When?'

'After lunch, if that's alright with you and Mrs Rowland?'

'We would welcome that,' I replied. 'Will you come here?'

'We will – both of us. Say 2.30pm?'

'Fine, er…'

'What is it, Mr Rowland?' asked Challis.

'Well, our two children are here. They're worried, came straight home this morning after they heard. Student age – you've met my daughter already. Is there any reason they cannot sit in on that meeting? They won't interfere, and it will save us a hell of a lot of explanation. They're very sensible.'

There was a momentary pause, and I could sense Challis cogitating. 'I wouldn't have thought that would be a problem,' she said eventually. 'I'll clear it with Chief Inspector Yardley, but assume no news is good news.'

'Thank you,' I replied. 'And what about Amelia? Mrs Ayling? Surely she should be here too?'

'She's apparently visiting her brother-in-law in hospital; I haven't managed to speak to her yet. But yes, if you manage to get hold of her, you can invite her. I'm tied up with other matters all morning, so I'd appreciate it if you would. Otherwise, we'll speak to her later.'

'Fine. By "other matters", I presume you mean to do with this case?' I ventured.

'No comment,' she said primly and then softened. 'Though that would be a reasonable assumption.'

'Understood. See you later then.'

'Bye.'

She rang off, and Lucy appeared at the top of the stairs. 'Police?'

\*\*\*

By about 11am, everyone had had breakfast (or more accurately brunch), and our two offspring were impatiently awaiting clarification of their parents' recent adventures.

'The police are coming this afternoon,' said Lucy, in an effort at reassurance. 'All will become clear then.'

Ginny literally stamped her foot.

'No, it won't! They'll tell us all the background I'm sure, and how jolly clever they've been in catching Lesley, but I don't want to know any of that half as much as what happened to you two last night.'

Her lip wobbled. Will moved closer to his sister and turned to face us. Solidarity.

I sighed heavily. 'Sit down,' I said.

And so, we explained it all, much as Amelia and Lucy had explained it to me the previous night, admitting that there were still a few holes in our understanding. Ginny's gently simmering indignation boiled over when she heard that it was the call from Challis that had snared me in Lesley's net.

'Utter incompetence!' she snorted, with all the intolerance of youth. 'And she's coming today? I'm going to give her a piece of my mind!'

'She wasn't to know I was sneaking around outside the drawing room,' I replied. 'If anyone's at fault it's me – it was silly to do that, but given that I did, I should at least have put my phone on silent. And if Challis hadn't rung and I'd run into Lesley anyway, you'd have criticised her for that too. Admit it.'

Ginny pouted sulkily and declined to answer – a sure sign of discombobulation. Will moved a couple of paces apart from her.

'But I love it that you care so much, Ginny,' I said, trying to soften my demolition of her logic and instantly regretted it. Fatal: torrents of tears, which any father of a teenage daughter will know is disconcerting to deal with at the best of times – which these weren't. I looked at Lucy helplessly.

'Look, everyone, let's settle down,' my wife declared sensibly. 'In retrospect, your father and I may not have acted terribly wisely, but we are unhurt; Lesley is behind bars; and we'll all have a story to dine out on for the rest of our days. That's not a bad outcome. So let's just wait until we hear what the police have to say, and then we can have a proper family discussion over supper. Speaking of which, what would you like to have to eat tonight?'

This was a sure-fire winner of a tactic, and even though they knew they were being bamboozled, Will and Ginny fell for it, debating the whole gamut of favourite family meals at length.

With the choice settled on pot roast, they retired to their rooms; Lucy started hunting out the ingredients she would need; and I took Theo and Rosie off for a walk, consciously revisiting the spot where I had found Edmund's body. Somehow, it seemed the right thing to do with the police about to close the book on the whole saga.

\*\*\*

There was soup for lunch given our late breakfast, and even that was interrupted by the unexpected arrival of Amelia, who had apparently been contacted by Challis and directed to come over to us before the 2.30pm meeting. I remember thinking that she might have called first, but she joined the table cheerfully enough, and I noted that Ginny's condescending view of her parents' naive foolishness was not extended to her new best friend.

'How was Andrew when you saw him this morning?' I asked once Amelia had a bowl of her own.

'He'll live.' She shrugged, as she prepared to take her first sip. 'He's worried what the police will make of his involvement in all this.'

Lucy paused to reflect. 'Unless they're keen on the idea Andrew and Lesley were in it together from the start, I wouldn't have thought he has much to worry about other than being thought a damned fool by everyone,' she said after a moment.

'And of course there's no proof he ever knew about the second will till after Edmund's death,' added Ginny, who had been following the discussion keenly.

We all nodded in agreement and returned to our soup. There didn't seem much else to say; we'd already been around the houses several times by then.

\*\*\*

Two-thirty came and went.

We were all peevish about it, trying not to exhibit undue keenness, but secretly everyone was eager to hear what the police had to say. They were only twenty-five minutes late but encountered a certain coolness when they arrived – primarily, I noticed, from the distaff side. Will and I were of course relaxed about it, or so I like to imagine.

'Legal complications,' mumbled Challis, as she passed me en route to the drawing room. 'Sorry.'

'Please don't concern yourself, Detective Sergeant,' answered Lucy brightly, overhearing. 'Coffee? Or tea? Biscuits?'

Once we had got the logistics out of the way and were all settled, which took about ten minutes, we sat back expectantly, looking at Yardley, who had been carrying a leather holdall which he placed carefully at his feet. 'Well,' he said, smiling around benignly. 'This looks very much like an inquisition. I hope my answers will prove satisfactory.'

# CHAPTER THIRTY-TWO

We all sat there transfixed. Eventually, Yardley began with a simple statement. 'They've both been talking,' he said quietly. 'Lesley and Andrew.'

We all looked at each other.

'And?' asked Lucy.

'Lesley has an interesting backstory,' continued Yardley. 'Born into a farming family in Dorset – not a happy one. The eldest of four children: girl, boy, girl, boy. Abusive father, now dead – whether he ever tried anything on with her we don't know. Aged seventeen she was convicted of grievous bodily harm for an attack on the elder of her two brothers with a hammer. Life-changing injuries. Lesley said he had been molesting the younger sister, Amy, who would not corroborate this but did not deny it either. She went to a young offenders' institution, where she was a model prisoner and was released on parole after a year.'

'Having of course demonstrated a prior capacity for extreme violence,' I pointed out sharply.

'The parole authorities did not consider Lesley a further threat to society,' said Challis smoothly, acknowledging my point with a nod. 'She was permitted – indeed encouraged – to apply to agricultural college and of course chose one a long way from Dorset. Moulton, in Northampton, in fact. As anyone would in the circumstances.'

'Where she met fellow student Ned, presumably,' I added.

'Indeed,' replied Yardley. 'They soon became an item, and married, moving here a couple of years later once Ned's father died. He was an only child. They were quite successful initially.'

'Yes,' said Amelia. 'I remember them well. We weren't really rivals. Edmund liked Ned, and I liked Lesley. That's why I offered her a job when they fell on hard times.'

'Which was after Ned fell off his quad bike, wasn't it?' interjected Will. Yardley smiled at him benignly.

'It was, young man,' he said. 'About ten years later. It took a bit of time for things to go downhill at Ritche's Lodge Farm after that, but once they did, the decline was quite rapid.'

'And she couldn't chuck it all in and go home to Dorset, could she?' murmured Lucy.

I didn't detect a huge amount of sympathy for Lesley's predicament from anyone.

'Do you know when the affair with Edmund began?' ventured Amelia, with apparent disinterest, though it didn't fool anyone.

'Not long after Lesley began working for him,' replied Challis. 'Very little time at all, in fact.'

'Predictable as ever,' muttered Amelia under her breath. I flashed her as sympathetic a smile as I could muster and saw Ginny do likewise.

'She was quite certain Edmund was going to marry her. The offer to change his will to prove his intentions came from him, apparently. She didn't pressurise him into it,' continued Challis.

'Well, she would say that, wouldn't she?' responded Amelia sarcastically.

I couldn't help thinking she was right, but Challis was quite firm in articulating her belief in Lesley's innocence, on this charge at least.

'So when a likely reconciliation between you and Edmund became apparent, Mrs Ayling,' began Yardley, 'we come across a very old criminal cliché—'

'Hell hath no fury like a woman scorned!' interrupted Ginny triumphantly.

Yardley gave her a little wink as he nodded. 'That's about the strength of it.'

\*\*\*

'Edmund and I hadn't actually decided upon a reconciliation, you know,' said Amelia crisply. 'We were getting on well, certainly, but nothing had been finalised.'

'Lesley sensed the way things were going, Mrs Ayling,' responded Yardley, in rather a patronising tone. 'She challenged Edmund on it.'

'On what?'

'Well, the catalyst was apparently the new will,' replied Yardley. 'He hadn't lodged it with his solicitor. Lesley wanted to know why. She says they had a row.'

'Did Edmund expressly tell her he was going to get back together with me?' demanded Amelia. 'If he did, he was getting ahead of himself. He never even asked me; it was nothing more than a vague inference.'

'We believe he was thinking of asking you, Mrs Ayling,' interjected Challis smoothly. 'That's why he put the new will on ice.'

'Lesley thought it might vanish altogether – be destroyed,' added Yardley. 'She was desperate. Her escape route to a new life was disappearing before her eyes. The man she thought was her knight in shining armour proved to have feet of clay, in her eyes at least. Love can turn to hate pretty suddenly in such circumstances. The one thing she could still salvage was what the will left her – provided it still existed.'

'And Edmund didn't, of course,' replied Amelia bitterly. I thought I saw her pucker up for a moment, but she has steel, that woman. She regained control in an instant; I don't think anyone else noticed.

'Was it a spur of the moment thing, or planned? The actual killing?' I asked, partially in an effort to deflect attention from Amelia whilst she recovered herself.

'Lesley says it was unplanned. But it's hard to argue that when you've got a gun in your back pocket, so her story is that it was Edmund who took the gun up to the field because he was worried about his sheep.'

'Being rustled?'

'So she says.'

'And Lesley just came along, got the gun off Edmund and then killed him in some sort of random act?' said Lucy scornfully. 'Hardly a believable story, is it?'

'No, Mrs Rowland – it's not. But she has to explain the presence of the gun somehow if she's to avoid a charge of premeditated murder,' replied Challis.

'What does she say happened?' asked Will, clearly interested. The obvious question, really. We all fell silent and waited for the police to answer it.

'Well,' began Yardley reluctantly, 'bear in mind that we take this with a pinch of salt, but her story is that she called Edmund that afternoon so they could have a meeting to clear the air.'

'Any proof of that?' I suggested hopefully. 'If she arranged a meeting specifically to confront him that surely suggests premeditation.'

'"If" being the operative word, Mr Rowland,' replied Yardley, again with a faint hint of patronisation. 'We've never found Mr Ayling's mobile phone, so we can't verify that.'

'Suspicious in itself, surely?' cried Amelia.

'Suspicious, yes. But not proof of anything. And I'm interested in proof.'

We all fell silent and waited for Yardley to continue. He sighed gloomily. 'Anyway,' he said. 'Lesley says that when she called, Edmund said he was up at Top Close and likely to be a while. She pressed him for a time she could visit him at home. He wouldn't give her one and eventually put the phone down on her. Not wise, as it turned out.'

'So then she thought, *bugger it* and decided to go up to Top Close,' exclaimed Ginny excitedly. Her mother suppressed a smile.

Yardley nodded. 'Two theories. The most likely is that she took that gun up there, checked to see if anyone was around and then killed Edmund once she was certain that the coast was clear. The alternative is that Edmund took the gun up there as Lesley said, in case his sheep were under threat. She arrived by her own account in a foul temper.

He wasn't expecting her; she says it was a warm day (which it was), and the gun was resting with a Thermos of tea on a Barbour jacket Edmund had laid on the ground. She sat down. Angry words were exchanged. She seized the gun and shot him.'

'Three times,' I said, with heavy emphasis. 'That's deliberate, surely?'

Yardley inclined his head to acknowledge the point.

'Tell me about the gun,' said Amelia coolly. 'I'd never seen it before. Whose was it?'

\*\*\*

Yardley's face broke into a wry grin, and he smiled at Amelia. 'Well done, Mrs Ayling,' he said. 'That's the crux of it.' He reached into his leather holdall. 'You mean this gun, I take it?'

We all goggled at the weapon he then produced, which most of us had last seen from the business end when being threatened with it by Lesley. It looked small and inoffensive now.

'Pretty rare,' Yardley stated portentously. 'Double-barrelled shotgun pistol. I've never seen one before. Anyone know why?'

None of us did. Yardley moved the top lever to the side and broke the pistol open so that both chambers were visible, and the twin barrels could be distinguished from the grip. 'How long do you think those barrels are?' he asked the room generally.

'About a foot, maybe,' ventured Will. 'Perhaps a little longer.'

'Not bad,' nodded Yardley approvingly. 'Fourteen inches. And what is the minimum legal length of shotgun barrels in this country?' Again, none of us had a clue. 'Twenty-four inches,' said Yardley in a self-satisfied tone. 'This gun is illegal. Has been since the Firearms Act of 1968. It should have been handed in for destruction then.'

'What is the point of that restriction?' asked Lucy, with genuine curiosity.

'You've heard the term "sawn-off shotgun"?' replied Yardley. 'In effect a gun with barrels this short amounts to the same thing, though this gun was constructed that way. Criminals were using shortened, easily concealed shotguns – very dangerous at close range. There was a glut of such crimes. The 1968 act tried to put a stop to that.'

'Ergo, that gun predates 1968,' I said.

'This gun was in fact made in 1932 and bought from Frank Gilbert's. There were no legal restrictions on owning such things then. They were known as rabbit guns. A lot more rabbits around in those days of course, before myxomatosis. They caused a lot of damage.'

Frank Gilbert's is a notably old-fashioned but popular ironmongers in Market Harborough. It probably hadn't changed greatly in the last ninety years, save for the little matter of selling firearms legally over the counter back in the day.

'So who bought it?' demanded Amelia, returning to her original question.

Challis preened, and I sensed we were about to hear a revelation. 'I have been back through the records,' she declared solemnly. 'That gun was bought new by Edward Logan on 12 July 1932. It cost £3/17/6, including a box of twenty-five cartridges.' Challis looked round expectantly, to be confronted by a sea of mystified faces. 'No – not Ned,' she added hastily, seeing the way our thoughts were drifting. 'His grandfather, Edward, after whom he was named.'

'So therefore...' I began hesitantly.

'So therefore,' said Amelia, jumping in ahead of me, 'that gun has been in the Logan family ever since. I was sure I'd never seen it before.' She smacked her knee in triumph.

'Got it in one, Mrs Ayling,' said Yardley admiringly. 'Although they should certainly have handed it in after 1968, the Logans were far from the only family that didn't comply with that legislation, and the police records of the day were far from comprehensive. And therefore, only Lesley could have taken that gun to Top Close; Edmund simply didn't have access to it. She could conceal it till she was close. Thus, it was a premeditated murder.'

\*\*\*

We all paused to reflect. As usual, Amelia was quicker off the mark than the rest of us. 'So what does Andrew say?' she demanded.

The policeman sighed. 'Forgive me for speaking ill of your brother-in-law, but Mr Andrew Ayling is a fool,' he said, after a moment's reflection. 'And like most fools, he is greedy. He is perennially short of money, as you well know. Lesley was certainly well aware of that – maybe Edmund had even told her. Having shot him, her plan then hit a bit of a problem: she couldn't find the will which she feared he was about to destroy.'

The policeman paused and took a sip of his tea before continuing. 'So she picked her moment, got Andrew alone and spun him a yarn about Edmund and her being about to go public about their relationship, inferring someone must have shot him to prevent that happening. She offered Andrew fifty per cent of whatever the will left her if he helped her find it.'

'Yes, that's what he told me. He must have been even dumber than you say to believe it,' snorted Amelia.

'I couldn't possibly comment, Mrs Ayling,' responded the policeman sardonically. 'In fact, I think Lesley had at least half-convinced him that you had something to do with the killing.'

'What?' replied Amelia, in a tone of astonished indignation. 'I was nowhere near Braybrooke when Edmund was killed – you have ample proof of that.'

'We know, Mrs Ayling,' said Challis patiently. 'But inference and innuendo can go a long way with gullible people. Andrew wanted to believe you had something to do with it so he could fool himself into believing that his motives in seeking out the will were noble.'

'Not simply greedy,' added Ginny. Out of the mouths of children. Challis gave her an approving nod.

'So they found it, and then…?' began Lucy.

'Yes, they found the will somewhere amongst Edmund's paperwork,' replied Yardley. 'And thus, we come to another criminal cliché…'

'Thieves falling out amongst themselves!' added Ginny enthusiastically.

Yardley looked her up and down, an appraisal. 'Very good, Miss Rowland,' he replied. 'Have you ever considered a career in the police?'

The remark was made with gentle good humour. Ginny said nothing and went red with embarrassment as she shook her head. But I knew she was pleased. Lucy caught my eye, and we exchanged a little smile of parental pride.

'Explain,' said Will, shortly. 'Why did they fall out?'

Yardley sighed again. Challis took up the running. 'Lesley had the will,' she explained. 'Now she had to produce it, thus revealing to Ned that she'd been carrying on with Edmund. Until that point, we don't believe she'd given serious thought to his reaction.'

'I can guess it,' I said drily, having personal experience of Ned's marital sensitivity.

'She didn't even try,' replied Challis. 'She knew. And therefore, Ned vanished.'

'Which is when Andrew finally began to get suspicious, I take it?' I said.

'He did,' confirmed Challis. 'He became worried by Lesley when she unexpectedly joined him at the point-to-point and behaved very oddly. When Ned disappeared, he told us he was pretty sure she had something to do with it and began to fear that he might be next – "unbalanced" was the word he used. Which is why he confided in Mrs Ayling.'

'And why we came over here that evening as soon as he'd told me,' added Amelia.

'Lesley must have been pretty desperate, getting rid of Ned like that, and hiding him in the car,' said Lucy. 'How could she think she would get away with it?'

Yardley shrugged. 'We don't yet know the exact circumstances,' he replied. 'It may have been a spur-of-the-moment thing, or it may have been more planned. I don't think she was thinking logically by then. Desperation.'

Lucy took stock for a few seconds, frowning, and then nodded her agreement. Watson concurred with the police.

# EPILOGUE

After that, it was pretty plain sailing.

Amelia was anxious about the possible penalties Andrew might face, but the police were reassuring on that front: none, they said. He wasn't guilty of anything more than greed and naivety, and after all, he'd got himself shot trying to take Lesley on, which was probably punishment enough.

Lucy was concerned about Jack. It wasn't a police matter, but Amelia assured her that there would always be a place for Jack at Braybrooke Farm for as long as she had anything to do with it; even if she sold up (which she was mulling over), she'd put in a strong word on Jack's behalf with the new owner.

Me – I was just pleased to get back to reality: Holmes and Watson were pensioned off.

Ginny had the last word. 'I don't know why all my friends at uni say that village life must be really boring,' she exclaimed indignantly.

'I'd hardly say so, would you?'